ALLSORTS

Leigh Leslie and others

Published by Nolan MacKenzie Books, 2025.

ALLSORTS

First edition. August 11, 2025.

ISBN: 978-0473754341

Written by Leigh Leslie and others.

Also by Leigh Leslie and others

ALLSORTS

Dedicated to fellow authors Norma Smyth and Lynia Antrum, and illustrator Janet Holden, dear friends who all left too soon.

A GREAT DAY FOR A RIDE

Jennifer Lilly

Desmond looked at himself in the mirror as he shrugged himself into his faux-leathers. He didn't look half-bad, he thought. Quite macho in fact. His eyes held just the right amount of indolence, yet still sparkled blue in anticipation. His lacklustre hair was truly beyond resurrection, a ghost of its former glory, yet, he kept it at a fashionable length, a final act of defiance against time. He ran his fingers through the ebony strands, despairing at their relentless thinness.He gave his reflection a wry smile and turned to the hall cupboard. Inside he reached up and took his full-face bike helmet from off the top shelf, blew away the dust, and closed the cupboard. One more brief glance of satisfaction in the mirror and he was ready.

He looked at his watch. Time to go. He picked his keys up from the bowl on the hallstand and whistled his way out the door.

It was a beautiful day.

A great day for a ride.

Still whistling, he strode around the side of the apartment and opened the garage. With meticulous care he walked his bike out onto the driveway.

His pride and joy.

Lovingly, he buffed the seat, wiping away the dust of neglect, before swinging himself onto the machine. His heart sang as he settled himself. It would just be the bike, the road, and himself for the next seven hours. His heart sank slightly, at the prospect of such a long ride, but it was necessary, and it would be worth it. He knew that at the end of the day he would find someone with whom he could share his love of the open road.

1

Well, he didn't actually *know*, it was more like a premonition, a feeling that he had.

His cousin Derek was always good for a bash, and Desmond felt sure that this engagement party would provide him with ample choice.

Desmond leant forward and turned the key of his 'nifty-fifty' and, without ceremony, rode out onto the road. He wondered if he was game enough to remove his helmet and let the wind blow through his hair. But he already knew that his law-abiding alter-ego would never allow him such freedom. The freedom that could only be dreamed about now that the police had become more vigilant. Still, he was on a bike, and he was going to a party.

By the time Desmond had ridden for an hour he was starting to feel uncomfortable. After two hours he was riding side-saddle in an attempt to alleviate the numbness that can only come from extended periods of time perched on a 50cc motorbike seat. Three hours was marked by a change of sides.

Wiiiir.

Desmond was riding at a steady 45 mph, the wind and sun were behind him and it was still a beautiful day, if numbing.

Desmond heard a deep throb creeping up from the rear. He glanced in his wing mirror and wished he hadn't.

Vroooom.

Seven deep throttled rumbling road bikes roared past him. Desmond kept his eyes fixed ahead as the bikies, genuine black leathers, studded and 'patched', raised gauntlets in offensive salutes. He could feel his face flush and his hands gripped hard on the handles. With a final burst of declutching and burning of rubber the bikies left Desmond to putter along in their wake.

He changed down a gear as the road started to climb and he looked at his watch. He was making good time. The mountain range that his bike was gradually conquering was past the halfway mark.

He smiled to himself for the first time in an hour. Damn the bikies and their more powerful machines. They probably had not had to save furiously for years to buy their motorbikes. No, they were probably quaking jelly every time they rode the roads, fearful that the police would stop them and discover their bikes where stolen. Or scared that the debt collector would call and reclaim their status symbols.

Desmond was happy again.

Down another gear and the screaming whine of the miniature motor under Desmond marked further progress up the incline. Desmond started to whistle to himself. It was a great day for a bike ride.

In the distance the wide sweep of the road ahead disappeared around a bend.

Wiiiir.

Desmond rode the 'nifty-fifty' around the bend and groaned. Slowly he eased himself back into a conventional seating arrangement before rolling to a stop.

Ahead of him was a line of cars. The last five cars that had passed him, and the seven road bikes. Gleaming black Harleys and Kawasakis dead in the queue. Seven black leathered bikies sitting astride their saddles, hands on hips creating an aura of defiance and magnitude.

Ahead of the congregation was a yellow bulldozer. But it was not the bulldozer obstructing the road. With deliberate precision the driver of the rig was slowly endeavouring to remove the debris from a raw scar on the side of the road. Desmond looked up at the slip. It appeared as though half the range had come down and landed on the road before tumbling into the ravine on the other side. The bulldozer driver had his work cut out for him for sure. Desmond thought. He looked at his watch. He really didn't have the time to wait for the way to be cleared.

With deliberation he rode slowly towards the face of the slip. He passed the car in front of him, smiling at those inside. They smiled back, unperturbed by his apparent queue jumping. But as he passed each car their occupants were increasingly anxious and impatient. Desmond reasoned that they resented his intrusion—especially since the bikies had preceded him in impudence. Finally it was only the bikies that separated him from the slip. He stopped, the 'nifty-fifty' idling.

Desmond gulped, but he was resolved. The engagement party, and its bevy of beauties, were waiting for his arrival. If he had to pass through a barrage of the bikies' jibes, then he would. He took a deep breath, revved his 'nifty-fifty' and slowly moved forward. The bikies looked around and laughed as Desmond putted past them. He didn't look at them. He didn't care.

When Desmond reached the face of the slip he stopped and cut the engine. He sat for a few moments, oblivious to the jeers from the bikies. He removed his helmet and shook his head. Gingerly he eased himself off the bike and waited for feeling to return to the lower half of his body. He looked at the scar, and the slip, and the bulldozer.

Carefully he walked towards the slip and bent down and picked up a clod of dirt. He absent-mindedly sifted the soil through his fingers as he gauged the distance to the clear road ahead. He brushed his hands off, then wiped them down the back of his faux-leather bike. Oh, that felt good, he thought, get the blood circulating again.

He walked back to his 'nifty-fifty', then looked at the queued cars and smiled before putting his helmet on again. He then flexed his hands and stretched his arms out in front of him. Theatricals were not part of his makeup, but he did need to psych himself up for the task ahead. He bent down, and with effortless ease and the amazement of the spectators, he picked up his bike. Deftly he turned his back on them and mounted the slip. Then, to the cheers of the crowd, Desmond picked his way across the slip. An accolade of horns followed him.

Once he had cleared the expanse of the slip he put the bike back on its two wheels, flexed his limbs again and looked at his watch. He had not lost much time. He looked back at the stopped traffic and gave the motorists a cheery wave before mounting his 'nifty-fifty' and turning the key.

Desmond was once more on his way to the engagement party which he was convinced would change his life.

Wiiiir.

Cheerfully Desmond whined along as only a 50cc bike can scream.

It was still a beautiful day, despite the slip, and uneventful till he was almost at his destination.

That was when Desmond heard a deep throb creeping up from the rear. Anxiously he looked in his wing mirror and groaned.

Carefully he resumed a forward sitting stance and steeled himself for the onslaught of abuse which he just knew was coming.

Vroooom.

Desmond kept his eyes fixed ahead. A chorus of horns accompanied the seven road bikes as they rumbled past. Genuine black leathers, studded and 'patched', gauntlets raised in a friendly triumphant salute. He could feel his face flush and he waved back. It was a beautiful day, and a great day for a bike ride.

A HOLIDAY AT THE BEACH

Lynia Antram

The car pulled up onto the sand beside the small Norfolk Pines at Mt Maunganui at the beach. The door opened and the children ran laughing and chattering to the water's edge. It was the 1940's when the world was at war and the trips away from the farm were few. Petrol was still scarce, and farmers had to work on their farms as workers were hard to find. Many of the young men were at war in Egypt.

"Can't afford the petrol to go far," father always said. Home for the family was a sheep and cattle farm up in the hills thirty miles from the sea. In the long summer holidays, the children went to the beach. It was always a wonderful holiday. Time was spent wandering the long ocean beach picking up shells or searching for starfish in the rock pools on the edge of the harbour.

The children by now were in the shallows of the harbour enjoying the warm still water and the hot summer sun.

"Hey look," said Meg, "what is the big hill?" The children raised their eyes to the slopes of the mountain.

"I know a story about that mountain," said Wiremu. "My Kuia told me one day on the ferry crossing the harbour after collecting paua. Come on, sit on the sand and I will tell you the story, I know all about it."

The children gathered in a circle on the sand and Wiremu began.

"My Kuia told me he was known as The Hill With No Name. He lived hundreds of years ago, and was a slave to Otanewainuku the highest peak in the Bay of Plenty. They were great friends and were happy to live together, however, they both fell in love with a wahine hill called Puwhenua who lived nearby. She chose to marry Otanewhanuku. The Hill With No Name was very sad, so he decided to drown himself in the sea. He asked his friends the forest people to help him. They made a huge belt of flax and put it around him and pulled him out of the mountain range across the harbour to where he stands today. When they arrived on the long sand spit beside the Tauranga harbour the night was almost over and the first shafts of light from the sun appeared over the sea.

"The forest people could only work during the hours of darkness and they needed to hurry away so they gave him a name, Mauao, which means lite by the first ray of light. See how he faces the East where the sun rises? So every day the sun's first light brightens his face. When the Māori people came to New Zealand, they named him Mt Maunganui after a sacred mountain in their Pacific homeland, so he has two names and is known by both."

"I think he looks stupid," said Ruth. "He sits at sea level and is so tall, his shadow falls along the beach."

"Did the forest people feel sad leaving him all alone and so far from the bush?" James asked.

"What's going on here?" a voice asked and there stood Dad with his trousers rolled to his knees.

"Look at your white Pakeha legs, Bill!" said Wiremu and rolled in the sand laughing.

Wiremu had joined the family when he was seven years old and was part of the happy bunch. He had been given to the family by his

Kuia who could not look after him any longer and wished that he be brought up with the Pakeha family. Father picked up Wiremu and headed for the water.

"How dare you laugh at me?" he teased, "I'll throw you in the tide!"

Wiremu called for help and the other family members went to his aid, pulling, pushing and tugging at their father to prevent him from reaching the water. Eventually, he stood Wiremu on the sand telling him how lucky he was not to have been thrown into the sea. The children laughed and danced, and all talked at once. They were so pleased to spend time together at the beach with their father.

"Dad! Dad!" shouted Meg, "Wiremu told us the story of Mauao. Can we climb to the top?"

"You are so noisy!" her father responded.

"Wiremu told us the story of how the forest people towed Mauao down from the mountain range, they must have been strong," said James flexing his muscles which sent them into more peals of laughter.

"You lot are trouble," laughed father. "Come on and we will climb the big hill. Go tell mother, Wiremu. And see if she wants to join us!"

"OK Bill!" Wiremu was off.

Eventually, he returned with an apple for each and a message that mother Win was happy to read her book.

"Come on gang!" invited father, "I will race you to the end of the beach." He re-rolled his trousers and began to run. Wiremu, who was the oldest of the group and very fit, raced past father at speed and challenged him to go faster.

"Don't go without me!" squawked Marianne who was well behind. Once father stopped and waited for her, and the rest of them reached the end of the beach, they climbed the embankment and were standing on the base of Mauao, looking down on the Mount

Wharf where they loved to fish for spotties. Behind a rickety fence grazed the donkeys who had spent the morning giving rides to visiting children on Ocean Beach. On seeing the children eating apples, they put their heads between the fence wires and were rewarded with bitten off pieces of apple. Father Bill patted them firmly and reminded the children how donkeys were on earth in biblical times.

"Gee! They are so old!" Wiremu responded, believing that the donkeys he was looking at were the donkeys from the Bible.

"Not these ones," father Bill smiled. "Their family tree goes back that far just as your family tree goes back to the Arawa Canoe. You call it your Whakapapa, we call it our family tree. Ask the donkey what he calls it!"

"He doesn't answer!" Wiremu shrugged and they all began to laugh.

"Let's go, kids, just follow the narrow track and keep in sight. I will have to bring Marianne, she's only little."

"I can help," Wiremu offered, he was very familiar with piggybacking Marianne when she moaned about sore legs.

"I will remember that," father Bill said, "it's a long walk to the top of Mauao."

The Pohutukawa along the harbour side of the track had dropped their red flowers on to the narrow walkway giving it a bright red edge. Already the children were looking down on the activity of the harbour. Pleasure boats fizzed about Pilot Bay joyriding in the tranquil waters of Tauranga Harbour. The ferry which transverses the harbour from Tauranga to Mt Maunganui chugged between the wharves loaded with holidaymakers. Tauranga was visible in the distance tucked above the sea. The family walked past the harbour entrance and looked across to Matakana Island and observed fishing vessels followed by gulls returning to the harbour after fishing in the open sea.

"There's a sacred rock at the entrance to the harbour," announced Wiremu. "You must give him kai when you go outside the harbour and more to thank him for protecting you when you come back."

"You are so right," said father Bill with amazement.

"Do you know his name? Did he come down with Mauao from the mountain range?" asked a younger member.

"Dunno!" shrugged Wiremu, "ask Bill!"

They were resting on the track side so Marianne could pick bunny tail grass, which fluttered in the sea breeze. The track was narrow and steep as it wound its way to the top of the peak. The mid-afternoon sun beat down on them, the ocean breeze helping to cool them.

Ruth stood looking from under her floppy sunhat at the Pacific. The scene below continually changed, from the tranquil harbour bordered between Matakana Island to the rolling surf of the blue Pacific Ocean.

"How many fish do you think live in there, Dad?" she asked.

"Too many to count," father replied.

"The biggest will be whales," someone else contributed. "They make a water fountain when they breathe."

"Come on! Keep walking," Father Bill reminded his chattering band. "We are nearly at the top."

"We are as high as an aeroplane!" Ruth announced. " I don't like being up high," she whined.

Tabby suddenly grasped her father's hand with some force.

"It's OK," father Bill reassured her. "You are very safe."

By now Wiremu and James had reached the summit. Wiremu was doing a dance holding out his shirt to form wings and pretending to fly when father Bill and the younger members of the family arrived.

"Man! It's high Bill, our heads are in the clouds!" Wiremu exclaimed.

"No clouds today Wiremu, but some days you would be in the clouds. Come over this side and see if you can spot the car." They moved to where they were looking at the curve of Pilot Bay.

"I can see Salisbury Wharf," Tabby said, pointing in the direction of the wharf.

"I can't see our car," James said, looking into the distance.

"I can see over the sand to Ocean Beach," Wiremu added. "And I can see mother reading her book!"

He stooped and guided James's vision to the area where the car was.

"Where is it?" James asked, still not able to pick it up.

"Gee Man! " Wiremu complained. "Your eyes are so bad, I can see everything even far, far away. I can see the tide is going out, I can see the ferry going back to Tauranga. Away up the harbour, I can see groups of people on the edge of the water. What are they doing Bill?"

"That's out from Matapihi Point and they will be collecting cockles for a hangi. Remember how Toi came to the farm to collect the mutton we had prepared for him and how he gave us a sugar bag with some cockles in it? Mother made some of them into fritters."

"I know! I know!" said Wiremu. "I ate some raw, but others wouldn't even try them. I took some to my Kuia when I visited her. She loves shellfish. I had to shell them for her because her eyes couldn't see what to do."

His Gran's poor eyesight was the reason he was living with the European farming family, as often when his Gran sent him to walk to school he hid in the fern on the roadside until late afternoon then he went back home. Father Bill was involved with education and he had to regularly visit Wiremu's Gran to report his absence from school. He knew her very well; her husband worked on the farm and went eeling. One night he had never returned, leaving her to cope with a very active grandchild.

Every Sunday morning a quiet farm hack was saddled up, Wiremu was given food, sometimes meat or maybe a pot of freshly made butter, to take to his Kuia.

He gathered enough wood to keep her fire going for a week and carried water from the creek to top up the tank at the house. Ruth and James enjoyed taking turns to go with him, riding on the pony behind Wiremu and holding tightly onto him. His Grandmother spoke fluent Maori, but her English was difficult for the European children. They loved her dearly and called her Granny Mau. A tall thin lady with a long plait of grey hair and a deep moko kauaeon her chin. She always wore a man's felt hat.

Wiremu understood her very well but she insisted his responses were in English as she rganized his needs had changed now that he was in a European environment. Money was not plentiful in the nineteen forties, so his Gran made do with clothes she was given. In winter she wore several dresses of different colours all of different lengths and buttoned to the neck. In summer she wore one dress, top buttoned to the neck and the rest hung at her waist with skirts at different levels. The children reported the number of skirts she was wearing to their mother on returning back to the farm.

She made fresh Maori bread which she cooked in a camp oven on the open fire in her one-roomed home. It was made of fermented potato and was topped with homemade butter or golden syrup. Much better, the children thought, than the bread that came twice a week with the mailman.

"Look down here!" Father Bill suggested. "That man fishing off the rocks is pulling in a fish. Watch carefully and you will see."

"Where's Marianne, Dad?" panicked Ruth, "I can't see her."

"She's behind us sitting under the trig station because she doesn't like looking over the edge. She won't even hold my hand and look, so she is just fine where she is." Father replied.

"There's the fish. It's a beauty, what will it be, Bill?" Wiremu asked.

"Probably a snapper, it's too distant to tell."

"Does that Island a long way away have a name?" Ruth inquired.

"It's Mayor Island," Father answered.

"You went catching hapuka to Mayor Island, didn't you, Bill?"

"Quite right Wiremu."

"Mummy Win made chowder from the heads and we had hapuka steaks and fresh bread for a feed. I took some home to Gran. We ate some for lunch when we came home from school," he related. Wiremu loved food, especially seafood, and cake.

"We really need to start back kids," said Father Bill. "Marianne is almost asleep under the trig. Now I will have to carry her."

"Bill, why are there so many pipi shells up so high? Look at them they are everywhere."

"Perhaps they walked up like us," Father Bill replied. What a tease he always was.

"No way!" said James, "Shellfish would die before they got here. They need seawater to survive."

"Quite right!" Father said, "I am pleased you think about what rubbish I sometimes tell you."

"I am nearly dying of thirst!" Ruth said, "It was so hot climbing up."

"Poor child!" Father Bill replied, "I'm pleased you didn't."

Wiremu made a weird choking noise and fell flat on his back whilst James remarked that he would be the eldest and in charge.

"Enough teasing," father Bill smiled. "Now to answer your questions. Seriously, boys, there have been two or three Pa's on the Mount and the seashells were bought to the summit for food, there are Pipis in areas of the harbour and tuatua's on the Ocean beach. The shells could be either."

"No waka could sneak past without being seen from here," Wiremu said.

"Come on, everyone!" said Father Bill as he picked up Marianne and put her over his shoulder.

"I will give her a ride," Wiremu offered, "on my back!"

"Not until we get down lower, thank you!" Father insisted. "It's too dangerous and she is too heavy, you are not very big."

"Can we see Otanewainuku from here, Bill?"

"Certainly can. Look at the range in the distance above Matapihi. See the highest peak. That's Otanewainuku. If you look to the top of the harbour beyond Matapihi you can see the road to the Mount at Welcome Bay just by the pear orchard."

"Gee whiz so you can."

"Show us! Show us!" Chanted the other children, "we need to see too."

In those times there were no bridges across the upper harbour so the route from Tauranga ran around the edge of the harbour through Welcome Bay to Papamoa and down the peninsular to Mount Maunganui.

"Look, Bill! Look! Look! Look something is on fire, I can see smoke!" an excited Wiremu yelled.

"It's a volcano, I think," said Ruth. "The smoke is going up into the air."

"The only volcano is Mauao," said Bill. "And he has been extinct for hundreds of years."

Eventually, he spotted what they were looking at.

"It's a steam train at Te Munga heading for Tauranga. Remember how we followed the railway line; it's coming down there. One day we will catch the ferry at Salisbury Wharf and cross to Tauranga and go by train to Te Puke then catch the ferry back to the Mount."

"Have you kids been on a train?" Wiremu asked.

"No!" chorused the others.

"I haven't been on a bus," James moaned.

"Your Dad is too rich," Wiremu announced. "He drives a flash car. My Grandma has no car, so we had to travel by bus, even to get food. Sometimes Bill brings home a food order for Grandma when he goes to the Judea sale."

Bill smiled and said nothing., amused that he should be thought rich when he owed so much to the bank. Indeed, he did own the only car in the district and used it to help the Maori community. Taking the sick to the hospital or bringing them back food or medicine after business trips to Tauranga.

The trip down the Mount was very slow but by now they had reached where the donkeys grazed. "Clamber down the embankment kids and walk along the beach."

Late in the afternoon and after such a long walk it was all too hard, and Bill needed to help all but Wiremu over the rocks. By the time they were all on the beach, Wiremu, with Marianne on his back, was heading for the car.

The tide was low, and the pleasure craft anchored in the harbour were sitting on the ocean floor. James asked what would happen to them now there was no water. His father, always a tease, told him that when the plug was put in the bath it would fill again.

"That's not right!" Ruth declared. "The tide goes in and out every six hours."

"Clever girl, you are quite right."

On arrival at the car, mother was pleased to see them. It had been quiet for such a long time. She produced a cold home-made lemon drink and a slice of homemade Christmas cake. They all sat on a blanket enjoying the afternoon tea. Father Bill complained that the sun had burned the tops of his feet and that they were quite sore. Wiremu giggled and remarked that maybe his Pakeha legs would be brown. Father Bill reached over smiling and gave the child's leg a quick pull. At this time farmers doing heavy work wore only long trousers, so their white legs were a joke.

"Come on, Bill!" Mother said, beginning to gather up numerous items of clothing strewn everywhere by the returning children.

"We need to arrive at the bach before dusk so we can get set up and be organised."

"We will fold the rug," said Ruth. James, Wiremu and Tabs all took a corner each.

"Give it a good shake kids," father Bill said, "get rid of the sand. Put it in the boot, thank you."

Soon the cleanup was completed, and the children clambered into the large 1938 Chevrolet car to continue to the holiday bach which would be home for two weeks.

The sand from their bodies rubbed onto the leather upholstery of the car seat and they protested loudly that it hurt.

"Alright," Mother Win soothed. "It isn't too far to the bach."

The bach belonged to a family member and stood all alone in the sandhills surrounded by tall lupins at the end of Tay Street. Very primitive it was. A kitchen, living room area and two bunk rooms each with four bunk beds. Out the back door at the end of the section was an outside toilet, known as a long drop. An outside tap and an old bath propped up with a timber frame was the bathroom. Each child carried in their bedding and personal belongings to their special place.

Father Bill put them all through the outside bath and put on their pyjamas while mother prepared cold meat and salad for dinner.

After the evening meal, Father Bill hugged each child, reminded them of the dangers of the sea and demanded they behaved and helped their mother. She then started the car and headed back to the farm to feed the animals before bed. The next day he was once more at work on the farm.

The holiday adventure for the children was about to start.

How they loved a holiday at the beach where there were no jobs to do and no animals to feed. They ate fish, shellfish and had fresh bread every day, and Wiremu walked every morning to the nearest farm for a billy of fresh milk.

A NEEDLE IN A HAYSTACK

Leigh Leslie

Dennis looked at the clock above the door. And quietly swore. He only had another ten minutes before the centre closed. Ten minutes. Anytime now the grumpy old woman at the desk would be hurrying up, demanding that he shut down the machine and leave.

He rubbed his eyes and looked once more at the screen, willing the microfiche to disgorge the answers he was after. Three hours he'd been here in the windowless room, scrolling through one film after another before moving on to the microfiche. All for nothing. Nada. Except maybe annoying the woman at the desk with his presence. He was the only one here and no doubt without him she would have gone home before now.

If she was annoyed with him, it was nothing compared to how he was feeling about his grandfather. After all, he was the reason he was here.

Dennis shook his head. That was not fair. All his grandfather had done was bequeath him a small, battered suitcase, the same one that he had enjoyed rifling through as a teenager. He had been thrilled, at the time. Humbled in fact to think that his grandfather thought him the member of the family qualified to receive Pandora's box of sepia history. Each photograph meticulously inscribed, on the back, in his grandfather's hand, with names, places and dates.

All but one. The one that had him here in the local Family History Centre searching for A. Needle. The writing was not that of his grandfather's and the woman had no familial features. The name on the back meant nothing to Dennis.

He looked up at the sound of footfalls headed his way, and he sighed. His time was up. What was this woman in the sepia photograph doing in among his family? And why couldn't he find her in the records for Haystack, England?

"Did you have a profitable time, dear? Find what you were after?"

Dennis removed the microfiche, slipped it back into the paper sleeve and turned the reader off. "Total waste of my time," he said, pushing his chair back.

"Nothing is ever a waste of time. If you did not find anything this time it means that you have narrowed where to look next time."

"Can't see why that would be of any worth. I've been through all the records over a 50 year period. She's simply not there and will have to remain a mystery. She can't be family so what's the use of chasing a dead end?"

He laughed quietly at the unintended pun. Dead end, yeah, right. That's what it was. But why did his grandfather have the photograph if there wasn't some connection?

He shuffled the loose papers, which he'd been making useless notes on, into the folder he had brought with him, before standing up. The photograph missed the cull and fell to the floor. The woman bent down and picked it up.

"Is this who you are trying to find? Handsome woman." She turned the sepia photograph over and read the inscription on the back. "Is she family?"

Dennis put his hand out to retrieve the photograph and laughed. "More likely a ghost as I can't find her anywhere to be able to determine how she fits in."

The woman looked back at the inscription, then at the discarded microfiche. "Young man, I think I agree with your statement that you have wasted your time here this afternoon. You have been looking for the wrong person in the wrong place."

"What do you mean? I've been looking for A. Needle, in Haystack."

"That might be, but this woman is A. Nudle, in Haystock."

Dennis sat back down with a thud. A. Nudle. He knew how she fitted in. His grandfather's great uncle had married a Nudle. He took back the photograph and looked again at the inscription on the back. How on earth had he misread what had been written there?

"Don't worry too much, easy enough to glance over and not decipher archaic writing." She looked down at Dennis and tutted. If you had shown me the photograph when you had first come in ..."

A NEW CAR FOR A NEW BABY

Jennifer Lilly

"I'm worried," Ben mused, eyebrows puckered. He squinted across the darkened cubby he and his younger brother Peter had made under their bunkbeds.

"What about?" Peter asked and reached into the bag of goodies that sat between them. He pulled out an apple and bit into it. Ben could be so boring at times. They were supposed to be playing quietly and it had been Ben's idea to make the cubby and play in it. But all they had done was eat apples. All Peter wanted to do was read his book, or, seeing he was too little to read, at least look at the pictures. But no, Ben wanted the cubby, and it was too dark in here to see the pictures in his book.

Ben twisted his hands like he had seen his mother do when she was worried. She had said that rubbing her hands together was meant to rub the worries away, but he didn't see how that worked. He was still worried. "Money," he said as he reached into the bag. But Peter had taken the last apple, there were only cores left.

"Money?"

"Uh-huh. Money."

"But why are you worried about money? I saw you put money into your piggy-box yesterday."

Ben was glad of the dark as he rolled his eyes. Little brothers could be so dense sometimes. It wasn't *his* money that was worrying him. He sighed. "I heard Dad tell Mummy last night that he didn't have enough money for a new car."

"So?" Peter took another bite of his apple, and wiped his hand across his chin, then licked the juice off before munching loudly.

Ben scowled. He would have liked another apple. "Well, we need a new car because the one we have now doesn't always start and we need a car that will always start when we want it to."

"Why?"

"Because we are getting a new baby and babies always arrive in the middle of the night and they are always in a hurry."

"Was I in a hurry to get here?"

"I guess so. I can't remember."

"Why don't you remember?"

"Because I was too little when you came."

"Will I be too little when this baby comes?"

"No."

"So we want a new baby?"

"Yes, I think so. But we need a new car more."

"Why?"

"Because we need to get Mummy to the hospital in time to get the baby before someone else takes it home."

Peter thought about that for a bit, nibbling at his apple the way a rabbit nibbles at a carrot.

"What about me?"

"What about what about you?"

"Don't you want me anymore?"

"'course I want you."

"What about when the baby comes? You won't want to play with me anymore. You'll want to play with the baby."

"What makes you say that?"

"Well, I'll want to play with the baby."

"No you won't."

"Why not?"

"Because babies are dumb."

"Was I dumb?"

"All babies are dumb. All they do is sleep and cry and scream and eat."

"Then why do we want one?"

"I don't know."

Peter looked at his apple core and sighed. "What are we going to do?"

Ben looked at Peter strangely. "Do about what?" All the talk of babies had made him forget the original discussion.

"About the car, about the money."

"Oh. I don't know. That's what I'm worried about."

"Maybe we could dig for buried treasure," exclaimed Peter who was always looking at pirate picture books. "I've got a real super map in my box." And before Ben could stop him, Peter had rolled out from under the bunk and dashed to the toy box. Books and toys were flung into the air as he rummaged for his old shoebox of treasures.

"Here it is," he said as he crawled back to Ben grinning as best he could with a piece of paper clenched between his teeth. Once back in the cubby he proudly handed the map to Ben.

Ben could not see a thing in the dark so he stuck his head out from behind the blankets that made the cubby and looked at the sheet of paper. The juvenile scrawls of crayon meant nothing to him and he wondered what he was meant to be seeing. "What is it?" he asked Peter.

"It's a treasure map. See?" Peter pulled the blanket aside and pointed to a black squiggle. "That's where the treasure is."

Ben couldn't see a thing, but, knowing how crest-fallen Peter would be if he didn't show interest, and how mad his mother would be if they disturbed her rest with Peter crying, he nodded his head.

"Well?" asked Peter.

"Well what?" replied Ben.

"Well, when do we start?"

Ben scratched his head. He'd seen his father do that when he was thinking.

"Can we start now?" Peter whispered, his eyes sparkling at the thought of uncovering buried treasure.

Ben looked at his brother. Bouncing in excitement, Peter was almost hitting his head on the bunk above and Ben mentally sighed before answering. "Alright. How would you like to be the leader?" At least that way it would not be his responsibility to read Peter's treasure map.

Peter couldn't believe his ears. Ben, his older brother, wanted him, Peter, to be the leader!

Together they crawled out from the cubby.

"First, we need to get dressed," Peter said importantly.

"What do we get dressed in?"

"Pirate clothes of course."

Peter strode across the room to the wardrobe. He threw open the door and stood, hands on hips, and looked at the neat array of colour-coordinated clothes.

Ben stood beside his brother, looked at their clothes and shook his head. "Come on," he grabbed his younger brother's hand. "These are too good for the likes of us. Pirates need the dress-up box."

The two boys stood side by side in front of the full-length mirror in the hall. They looked resplendent in their father's old shirts with belts criss-crossed over their chests; shorts with their toy swords stuck in the waistbands and toy guns poeking out of the pockets; miss-matched socks and old Sunday ties tied around their head with ends hanging loose. They had even found some of their mother's makeup in the bathroom cabinet and inexpertly applied moustaches and beards.

Ben had to admit that they did indeed look fearsome. He was a pirate of the South Seas and adventure bound. "Come on my hearty! Hi Ho Silver! To the treasure!"

Peter grinned from behind a Kohl-sticked beard and red lips. "Follow me Ben Gun."

Together they tramped out through the kitchen and into the back yard. Peter stopped just outside the back door and consulted his map. He raised his sword and pointed in the direction of the hose that their mother had left spraying the tomatoes. "Thar she blows!" he said and swaggered off toward the garden shed.

Once inside the shed Peter selected a variety of garden tools.

"Are you sure we need all these?" Ben asked, eyeing the secateurs, brooms, buckets and rakes along with what he considered to be the only real requirement – a couple of spades, that Peter was piling into the wheelbarrow.

"'course we do. You want to find buried treasure, don't you?"

Ben supposed he did, and quietly picked up a trowel. Treasure hunts weren't his usual occupation—he was into his Lego and dinosaurs, so he couldn't really argue with Peter, who spent all his days living pirates. Ben wheeled the barrow out of the shed and waited for instructions while Peter stacked hoes and garden stakes into a pile outside the shed door.

Peter dusted his hands on the back of his shorts then pulled the treasure map out of his back pocket. He turned it around several times, regarding the garden between each turn. After careful consideration he stuffed the treasure map back into his pocket, picked up the hoes and stakes and marched purposefully towards the back fence. "Come on then," he called back to Ben.

Ben followed, the wheelbarrow squeaking in time to his steps. When they reached a spot in the garden at the edge of the vegetable patch and near the compost heap Peter stopped and unceremoniously dropped his tools, then took out the map again. Ben put down the handles of the wheelbarrow and rubbed his hands together.

"This is it," Peter said triumphantly.

"Here?"

"Yep. You can start digging."

"Me?"

"Yep."

"Why me?"

"Because I'm the boss." Peter was enjoying himself. "You said I could lead, well, you can start digging. Or, or I'll have you walk the plank!"

Ben stood there, looking at the bare ground. He was worried about what his father would say if he dug up the garden.

"You do want to find the treasure, don't you?" asked Peter, his voice had a slight quaver to it.

Ben could see Peter's eyes glistening. He figured that his father would yell more if they disturbed their mother rather than the garden. "Of course I do."

"Then start digging. Besides, you're bigger than me so's you must be stronger too."

That was true, and it was nice to know that Peter knew it too. Ben started to dig. It was easier than he thought it would be. His Dad must have been digging here not so long ago.

"How far do I have to dig?"

Peter looked at his treasure map again, "Oh, about three kilometres."

"Three kilometres?"

"Well, maybe only 500 grams then."

"Give me a look at that map." Ben grabbed the map. He still couldn't understand it. It looked like any other piece of artwork which Peter brought home from Kindergarten, only now it looked a lot grubbier. But he couldn't let Peter know that it meant nothing to him. He handed it back to Peter. "Silly. It says to dig as deep as your knees. Here, you give it a go now."

Peter was shorter, so they wouldn't have to dig so far if he was in the hole. "I've made the ground soft for you. Besides, it's only fair that you get to discover the treasure."

Ben moved aside so that Peter could get into the crater that he had made. He then climbed out and sat down on the lawn and watched while Peter started to dig using the little trowel.

"Hey Ben! I think I've found it!"

"What have you found?" Ben looked up from a fist full of grass that he had been pulling up from the lawn beside him.

"The treasure dopey. There's something hard here."

"It's probably only a rock, or an old brick."

"No it's not. It's the treasure. Look!"

Ben let the blades of grass fall to the ground and leant forward to peer down at his brother's feet. Sure enough, there, near Peter's feet was the corner of a box. Or a tin. He jumped into the hole and pushed Peter aside.

"Hey! What are you doing?" Peter gave his brother a shove. "That's my treasure."

"Let me have a look at it."

Together they tore at the dirt with their hands.

"It *is* a tin!" For the first time since agreeing to go on a treasure hunt and dressing up, Ben was really excited. "And it's old too, and ..." Ben attempted to lift it up. "And it's big too. Let's wait till Dad gets home from work, he can lift it out for us."

"NO! It's *my* treasure and I am getting it out, *now*," Peter said as he continued to scrape the dirt away from around the tin.

The two boys stood back and looked at the tin lying at the bottom of the hole. It was bigger than either of them had thought. They tried to lift it out, but it was too heavy for them.

"Let's try and open it where it is," said Ben, once again caught up in the excitement of the treasure hunt.

"I've tried," said Peter, struggling not to cry. "But it's stuck."

Ben looked closer and saw that there was a padlock. "Here, let me try." He clambered out of the hole and grabbed a hammer from the wheelbarrow, marvelling that his younger brother would have had the foresight to add it to the pile when they were in the garden shed. He and Peter then swapped places.

After much thumping and banging and grunting, accompanied with much excited jumping up and down from Peter, Ben was able to knock the padlock off.

"Yeah! You've done it Ben. You've done it," Peter continued his excited dance. "Here Ben. I want to do it now. It's my treasure. I found it. I want to open it. You said it was mine."

Peter jumped back into the hole and grabbed at Ben, pulling him away from the tin at the bottom of the hole. As luck had it, he caught Ben off balance and Ben fell back. Peter leapt to the tin box and prized open the lid. Both boys looked inside.

"Where's the gold?" wailed Peter. "There's supposed to be gold. Where's my treasure?"

"Plastic! Nothing but plastic! You and your gold," Ben said as he got out of the hole and marched back to the house, leaving Peter crying over his buried treasure.

"Hello there son." Ben looked up. It was his father. Ben cringed. "What have you been up to this afternoon? Not disturbing your mother, I hope?"

"No Dad," Ben hoped that his father wouldn't notice the dirt on his clothes and the tattered remains of his improvised pirate costume.

"Isn't that one of my shirts you're wearing? What *have* you been up to?"

Ben looked at his feet.

His father looked around, "And where's Peter?"

With that Peter burst into the house. "Ben! There's a funny pow..." He stopped short as he saw his father. "Daddy! You'll never guess what we did today!"

Ben cringed further and hoped against hope that Peter wouldn't blab about their activities.

"Hello there Peter. No, I'll never guess. You'd better tell me."

"Ben and I went on a treasure hunt for buried treasure. Ben even let me be the boss."

Their father looked at Ben, then back at Peter and grinned. "And did you find any treasure?"

"We thought we did. Didn't we Ben? Only ..." Peter hesitated and looked to Ben who wouldn't look at him.

"Only what?" Their father looked from Peter bubbling over with delight to Ben with his downcast eyes and scuffling feet and wondered what mischief the two boys had been getting into.

"Only instead of the treasure tin being full of gold, it's full of plastic," Ben's tone was so belligerent that even Peter's enthusiasm was briefly quashed.

"Well then, how about you pirates show me where your buried treasure lies, and ..." Peter whooped with delight and jumped up onto his father. "Steady there young fellow. This pirate isn't as fit as you are. Let's all go and take a look at this treasure of yours which isn't gold. Lead the way Ben."

"But I'm the boss Daddy," Peter squirmed in his father's arms. "I should lead."

"Ah, but I have captured you and you are my prisoner," his father laughed, wrapping his arms more tightly around the squealing boy.

"What's all the noise and commotion about?"

They all turned to see the boys' mother standing in the doorway. Ben slowly walked over to her. "I'm sorry Mum, we didn't mean to wake you."

"That's alright," she ruffled his hair, choosing not the notice the smudged makeup and general dirt and dishevelment of her sons. "I've been awake for a while. I have been watching you dig up your father's vegetable garden. Whatever were you doing down there?"

"So, it's *my* garden you have been digging up is it?" He tickled Peter before setting him down on his feet. "I don't believe you were looking for treasure. I believe you were burying bags of potatoes instead. You rascals," he made to chase the boys, who squealed and ran to hide behind their mother.

"Oh Mummy," bubbled Peter, clinging to her skirt and looking up at her "We really were looking for treasure."

"Treasure? In our back garden?" She looked down at Peter then at Ben who had come out from behind her. "Oh Ben, you are nearly eight. I thought you would have had more sense than to think that there would be treasure buried in our garden."

Ben felt that he had disappointed her badly. He put his hand out to her, and she took it, smiling kindly down at him. "Playing in the cubby was boring and going on a treasure hunt was the only way I could keep Peter from waking you up." She bent down and gave the top of his head a kiss, then ruffled his hair again. "You're a good boy, Ben."

"Well then my hearties," their father said brightly, "let's all go and take a look at what you have done to my vegetable garden and see what we can salvage of the non-golden treasure shall we?"

Peter and Ben, along with their parents, stood around the hole in the ground and looked at the open tin.

"It certainly is not what I expected buried treasure to look like," said their mother. "Where's all the gold? Or jewels?"

"That's what I want to know," wailed Peter. "I wanted to find gold *so* much."

"Yeah, and all Peter had me digging for was plastic," Ben grumbled.

"Hang on a bit," said their father. "That's not just plastic, there's something else in there."

"Yes," said Peter, jumping in beside the tin. "That's what I was coming in to tell you Ben. There is powder inside the plastic."

"Powder?" asked their father, looking at his wife.

"Powder?" she echoed, and carefully stepped into the hole beside Peter. She looked in the tin, put her finger to her tongue and went to touch the powder.

"Don't!" shouted her husband, knowing that she was about to taste the powder. Three pairs of eyes looked at him. "Think of the baby," he mouthed, then looked at Peter, suddenly realising that he had spoken out aloud.

"It's okay Daddy. Ben told me all about the baby."

"I think we had better call the police," their mother said reaching up for her husband to help her out of the hole. "You pirates run inside and get tidied up."

"Well Sir, those boys of yours did a wonderful job there. We've been wondering where this lot of heroin could have got to. We've been able to trace all the other shipments made by these dealers, but this last consignment had us worried." The police sergeant looked at the two boys and smiled. "There should be a good reward for finding this lot. What do you think you boys would like?"

Before Ben could answer Peter jumped up. "A new car please, so we can go to the hospital and buy a baby."

Peter looked around the room and suddenly felt shy, and puzzled, as everyone, even Ben and the policeman, started to laugh.

A SOLITARY SOUL

Leigh Leslie

Tane could feel the weak winter sun massage his back through the layers of clothing. Its warmth went some way towards relieving his melancholy, but not entirely. There was only one thing, in his mind, that could eradicate the sadness that had taken up residence in his soul. And that one thing was beyond his reach, unless the roulette wheel of luck chose to once more shine on him. He took a deep breath and plunged his hands deep into his trackie pants and uttered a deep sigh of resignation. He knew that his luck was a very close relative to lightning—not likely to strike the same place twice.

He deviated from his course and, kicking the sand, made his way towards the rockpools that marked the end of the cove. It was low-tide and they might have something for him.

Slowly he lowered his well-proportioned, gym trained body into a crouch, and peered down. His ta moko [Facial tattoo reflecting the individual's ancestry] mirrored the meanderings of the small black periwinkle-like sea snail as it circled the contours at the bottom of the rockpool. Just like me, he thought, trapped in a closed world not of my making.

He thought of his whanau [Family] back home and wondered what they would be doing right now. No doubt they would all be happy, their lives running smoothly, all with a purpose. For him alone things were so different to what they could once have been. His whakapapa [Genealogy] went back more generations than those of his teachers when he was at school. But what was his whakapapa to them? Nothing. For his teachers there was only one culture. That of the Pakeha. New Zealand history only began with the advent of the European. For them nothing else mattered. He had fought to keep a remembrance of his heritage, but it had been a battle when he was the only warrior on his side. The rest of his extended family were only too happy to take the ride that the Pakeha offered. Now, in his present Pakeha world his whakapapa was only a dream.

Pushing the maudlin thoughts of home to the back of his mind he returned to the present. He shattered the surface of the water in the rockpool with his finger and poked at the small shellfish, its horny carapace a barrier to its environment. Maybe the snail wasn't so like him after all. His moko was not an impenetrable barrier behind which he could hide. He would always see the stares and discrimination; hear the jibes and ridicule. What, for centuries, had been a hallmark of distinction, and for him a much thought about act of rebellion, defiance and pride in the Maoritanga of his youth was now simply a misunderstood stigma of his birth.

He let his fingers caress the sun-warmed water as he gazed beyond the breakers and dreamt of distant shores, wondering, again, at the absurdity which had brought him so far from home.

Home. What a strange word. What did it mean? For people here, home meant the abode where they went to each night after a long day at the office, or wherever they worked. The place where they retired to sleep. The place of refuge from the rat-race of society. A sanctuary.

For him home was only a memory. A memory of his whanau—his parents, brothers, sisters, aunts, uncles, his grandparents and tupuna [ancestors]. His marae [meeting house] —his second home, where the kaumatua [elders] guided him. The call of the kai karanga [the person giving the welcome]. The rotten-egg smell of sulphur that only the tourists smelt—the locals accustomed to it from birth, oblivious to the uniqueness of the air. The hot pools—the bubbling grey mud, or water simmering under silent wafts of steam, where he and his mates used to lark around when they ought to have been attending school. The sweat, mud and body-odour drenched rugby rooms filled with the camaraderie which could only be found among like-minded people.

But here he was alone in an alien world. He wondered if Maui, too, with his adventurous spirit had ever felt as alone and lost as he now did. Repentant of mistakes made and the foolishness of youth.

With a sigh Tane withdrew his hand from the rockpool and flicked the water off. The droplets lay abandoned on the bare rock around him and he gently stood up, still looking towards the distant horizon for a distant shore. A shore further away than that other shore which he had looked at across the expanse of Lake Rotorua. He had grown up with the legend of Hinemoa and her warrior, Tutanekai, and as a young boy had marvelled that love for someone could be that strong.

As he thought of Aotearoa he conjured up images of home, and of his family. Of the hangi [earth oven to cook food with steam and heat from heated stones] and tangi [rites for the dead], and he felt the pull of his ancestors. There was always that pull. No matter how much he had tried to forget his Maoritanga [Maori culture], it was always there. He remembered at school, the feeling of being different. As a Māori he was considered a non-achiever, a no-hoper.

Yet he had wanted to learn. Deep down he knew that to succeed in the Pakeha world he had to learn. But his teachers, and the other students, Māori and Pakeha, had already labelled him, so it was easy to be a truant.

The sea beyond the breakers was a smooth, almost hypnotic undulation of forward movement, and there on the surface a black object was floating. Aotearoa vanished from his mind and was replaced with curiosity as to the beckoning object and he wondered if it would be worth his while to wait for the current to wash it ashore.

For years now, decades in fact, he had patrolled the shoreline, collecting what the tides would deliver and scavenging enough to survive. Some days the sea would be bountiful, and he would be able to treat himself. To buy a slap-up meal in some restaurant and pretend that he didn't notice the way the other patrons would silently move their chairs away from him. Or buy a new pair of trousers, and hope that in his smart attire the world would look more kindly on him, his dark skin and his moko. Or he would buy a ticket to a concert, or go to the cinema, and in the close confines of the darkened cocoon, pretend that he was accepted, and not alone.

Home, that lost long white cloud Aotearoa. He was reminded once again of Hinemoa, and wondered if his kuia [grandmother] ever imagined that she was prophetic in her recounting the legend of Himemoa and Tutanekai. Only in his case it had been he who had followed the music—his gourds for floatation, the wings of an aeroplane. He could no longer remember the name of the siren who had called him away, but a name was not necessary. Memories were enough.

Memories. That was all he had left now. They had to be enough. Enough to know that he had done the only thing he could do, at the time. Enough to regret his youth. He had wasted his school days because that had been what was expected of him. Then he had drifted. The only sense of belonging that he had ever felt had come from the marae, and the kaumatua. From them he had learnt the great heritage that was Māori. And he was proud of that heritage, and all it stood for.

He had embraced his Maoritanga with all the enthusiasm he should have given education. But the kaumatua had not been able to give him a sense of direction in the Pakeha world. The two cultures were too diametrically opposed, and the Pakeha world had no place for the Māori culture. Not then.

Then she had come along. The siren who had lured him from his safe haven. There was enough Pakeha in him to recognise that it was in her world that the power and prospects lay. And she had shown him that he was caught between. She had given him a sense of belonging in the Pakeha world, and had also nurtured his Maoritanga.

For the first time in his life he felt proud of who he was. To her, his culture and whakapapa meant something, and he could walk proud. It was with her encouragement that he had acquired his moko, and he had worn it proudly. He looked down at his reflection in the now still rockpool. The moko that he had once been proud of, silently mocked him.

It was strange that he could no longer conjure up an image of her, his Delilah. She had pandered to his ego and he had meekly followed her, willingly leaving, not only Rotorua, but also the land of his birth and his heritage. She had introduced him to the world.

He thought of the experiences, most of them unsavoury, that he had encountered in her world, and shuddered. On reflection all of them had been destined to alienate him from his own culture and self-esteem. Had the two of them been that naïve to think that he and his tattoo would be accepted by her friends and into her society? Big, brown, brawn and no brains. No more than a passing novelty. How they must have laughed at him. He had not realised the contempt with which he was held until it had been too late. Too late to return home.

Now he stood here on the beach. He had no job, no money, no home. His pride was gone, and he felt that he had disgraced his whanau. They all thought him a hero, made good in the land of opportunity. He could not return. Even though he was now ready to.

He walked over the shelf of smooth rock and jumped down onto the sand, still watching the object floating on the swell.

Over the years he had been collecting there had never been enough, at any one time, for him to return home. Mostly it was small change. His pickings had increased when the government had withdrawn most of the paper money and replaced it with coins. But then so too had the competition. But that had not lasted long—there were not many awake enough to face the sharp shreds of dawn—and he had been able to continue combing the beaches, alone.

Once, and he grinned at the memory, he had waited and watched as an angry sea disgorged a fat black wallet at his feet. Foolishly he had handed that find into the police. He hadn't wanted to, for there was easy enough there for him to manage to get home, but there was something about the photograph of the young waterlogged family that was in with the money that stopped him from keeping it. His honesty had been neither acknowledged, nor rewarded.

Now here came another black object, it had to be a wallet, and a fat one at that. It was quietly riding the waves, beckoning him. Tantalised, he rubbed his hands together in excited anticipation. Maybe this time ...

As he watched the object, the wallet—as he was now convinced, reached the breakers and was bobbing about, buffeted back and forth between waves as though it were a ping-pong ball enjoying a game of table-tennis. Never making any forward progress to the shore where he was waiting. Could he wait ...?

To be seen to be too eager could cause the wallet to change course and then all would be lost. Then again, all it needed was a little guidance through the breakers. He hopped, undecided, from one foot to the other, leaving craters in the wet sand which quickly filled with water, removing any record of his ever being there.

In his mind he could feel the money as he counted it out. Enough to take him home. That was all the impetus he needed. He waded, impervious to the cold that caught his breath, into the water, the waves hungry for his clothes.

Despite years living near, and daily walking beside the sea, he could not swim, so he dared not venture too far. But he was anxious to assist the wallet on its way to shore, and to him. Impatient, he quickened his pace and started to use his arms like oars to help propel him towards his goal. Suddenly he lost his footing as he fell, floundering into a hole.

In a trance Tane felt himself tugged by the tide and he saw his whanau reaching out to him and he smiled at their moko. Here were people unafraid to be themselves. It was with them that he belonged. He stretched out his arms to grasp them and he called out. The sharp tang of salt rushed in and suddenly he was struggling.

The faces faded and a kaleidoscope of his life raced out of the water to greet him. He didn't want to die. His fortune awaited him on the surface. If only he could reach it. He wrestled with the surging water.

Gasping and spluttering his head broke the surface. He gulped in the salty air and searched for the black object. The prize was just out of reach. He kicked out with his legs but struggling, he sank below the surface.

Reach the wallet! The thought pounded through his head, but the tide had other ideas and relentlessly drove him towards the shore, only to pull him back into its embrace.

Visions of his life were replaced with those of his hapu [clan] and his iwi [Tribe], greeting him home. The local made good in the land of fortune. He had been the one who had gone away and found the end of the rainbow. With his wealth he would repaint, no, rebuild, no, create, a new marae with him as the tekoteko [carved figure at the top of a meetinghouse] of the wharenui [meeting house]!

Tane felt warm and happy, enfolded in the sea. He let the waves, as they surged now white-capped towards the beach, take the weight of his body. And he drifted, with the racing bubbles and churning sand massaging his body. Then, with an unceremonial thud he was dumped on the shore, ki tona okiokinga [To his rest]. He lay there, face down, his feet washed by the froth of the tide, one arm under his chest, the other reaching out as though to grasp the sand and haul himself up and out of the clawing tide. His hair splayed halo-like around his head. He didn't move. Beside him, within reach of his outstretched hand lay, not a bulging wallet full of promise, but a fat slab of black foam. The remains of someone's discarded summer sandal.

A solitary sole on the sandy shore.

ATTACK

Leigh Leslie

The scrunch of the jogger on the gravel behind her was quickly replaced with the thought 'How does my son know I am here?' It was that single flash of a thought that saved him from being poleaxed.

As she slid out from the head lock and turned to spew venom over her thoughtless son for giving her a fright she was confronted by a total stranger.

"Urgh! You're old."

Well, what did he expect? She looked at him. She was old enough to be his mother, and then some.

He looked at her. She did not have a bag, and there were no bulges from her pockets to indicate a purse or cell phone. What was he going to do now?

She returned the gaze. Used to petulant pubescent boys she felt like telling him to grow up.

"What do you want?" She could hear the schoolmarm intonation creeping into her voice. Would it never leave her?

"I want sex," he rasped, grabbing her by the shoulders and ramming her into the denuded bank alongside the path.

Too shocked to think of anything she found herself numbed by the speed of the attack. It wasn't so much 'why me?', 'why here?' or even 'why now?' as 'what have I got that I can use as a weapon?'

She looked around. There seemed to be no weapon handy. 'Shoes?' she wondered, then dismissed the thought. Soft sandals would do nothing. 'What about large sticks? Or tree roots? This is a wooded area.' But each stick she grabbed hold of crumpled between her fingers. Her frantic, yet methodical, thoughts were rudely interrupted.

"Why aren't you screaming?"

Scream? Now why hadn't she thought of that? She looked around her. Why would she bother to scream when there was no one around to hear her?

"I don't want to scream."

"You should be screaming!" He grabbed her shoulders and violently shook her.

This was getting ridiculous. Maybe she should knee him, but he was holding her too far away for that, and if she tried to kick him where it hurt, she'd lose her sandal. But why that should concern her was incomprehensible, like this attack.

She glared at him, "Why should I?"

"Because that is what you should be doing. Every woman screams."

"Well I don't want to." And she realised that she didn't. Screaming wasn't in her nature. Never had been. Her friends had thought her weird when she'd stand by the sideline, or at the edge of the pool and not yell out encouragement to her competing children. Why bother, was her philosophy. The children could not distinguish her voice above the roar, so why make an idiot of herself? She did enough of that after the event, fawning over the children with praise and affection and probably totally embarrassing them into the bargain.

He took a step back and fumbled in his pocket. "I've got a knife."

She looked down at his hand. He held a plastic-handled vegetable knife as if he were about to spread butter.

"You've never seen *Crocodile Dundee* have you?" She asked, barely able to contain the laugh that was fighting for freedom.

"What?"

"Never mind, you're too young to remember it. Shame really, you could learn a lot from a movie like that."

He swung back his arm and his clenched fist connected with her chin.

She shook her head to clear it as he lunged at her again.

"Why don't you just go home?" There was that voice again. She'd been out of the classroom and retired for how many years?

"What?"

"Oh, just go away." This really was getting rather tiresome.

He swung at her again, and she ducked. He had, somehow, lost his shoe in the scuffle.

She bent down and grabbed it, not too sure what she was going to do with it. It was a solid enough running shoe, but still too flimsy to be useful as a weapon. She noticed that it looked new.

"Give me me shoe back."

She looked at him. Was he mad? Give his shoe back? Fat chance!

"I've got a knife!"

"Not that again?"

He lunged at her again. She swung her arm and they both watched as the shoe sailed serenely through the air, over his head, and plopped into the fast-flowing stream beyond.

"What'd you do that for?"

She shrugged.

"What'll me Mum say? They were me new shoes. Christmas present they were."

He scrambled down the bank after the shoe and she took off in the other direction, the noise of him frantically scrabbling in the undergrowth diminishing with distance.

The last she heard was a plaintive "Mum's gonna kill me if I lose me shoe."

BEER FOR BREAKFAST

Jennifer Lilly

The cool morning air teased David's toes as they peeped out from beneath the blanket. The night had been too hot for the sleeping bag so they had dossed down on top of their bags and pulled a blanket over them. Two magpies could be heard practising as, inside the tent, David stirred. His feet felt cold. He yawned and with balled fists he rubbed his eyes.

"'ere. Give us some blanket ya moron," he said yanking the blanket over his feet.

"Wha?"

"Never mind." David stuck his head out the tent flap and gazed around. It was a crisp morning with the sun making a valiant attempt to persuade the night to leave. Already he could see shafts of pale light threading through the leaves overhead.

"Hey! Get a load of this will ya!" he yelled back into the tent. "The lake looks great. Should be great for fishin'."

"Yeah."

"Nah, I mean it. Come on!" He was struggling into his socks and rummaging amongst the conglomeration of paraphernalia at the end of the tent for his jeans and tee-shirt.

"Have ya seen me jeans?"

"Wha?"

"Me jeans. Have ya seen 'em ya oaf?"

"Nope."

David clambered over his recumbent companion and seized his jeans from underneath him.

"Shit! That's me pillow."

"Pillow? Them's me jeans and I'm puttin' 'em on. Get up why don' ya? Ya can almost see the fish jumpin' it's so crowded in that lake."

David emerged from the tent and stepped into his jeans and pulled his tee-shirt over his head.

The lake looked beautiful. There was a soft mist rising from around the shore and gentle ripples shimmered where the rising sun touched the water.

"Come on will ya! There's already a boat out there."

"Huh?"

David looked around, picked up a pinecone and flung it into the tent.

"Hey! Whacha ya doin'? I'm tryin' to sleep."

"Sleep? Bloody hell, it was your idea to come fishin'."

"Yeah, but I didn't know then that you was such an early bird."

"Yeah well, I thought you was a fisherman and knew that the best bites are in the mornin'."

"Maybe they is, and maybe I am, but right now I wanna sleep."

The sleeping bag could be heard to rustle, accompanied by groans. David looked at the tent, shrugged his shoulders and wandered over to the remains of last night's fire, and relit it.

"Well, I'm getting us breakfast. Whadda ya want'? One egg or two?"

"Wha?"

"Breakfast. One egg or two. Whadda ya want?"

"Don't wan' breakfast, only wanna sleep."

David broke four eggs into the pan and started to whistle.

"Can ya shut that bird up Dave?"

David stopped and walked to the back of the van. He took out a can of beer out and pulled the tab. Suddenly the side of the tent heaved.

"Wha's that?"

"Beer."

"Pull one for me Dave, I'll be right there."

David smiled as Trevor sprang out of the tent. "Why dinnya say there was beer for breakfast?"

"You never asked."

BLUE

Jennifer Lilly

He gazed at the yellowing picture in the old newspaper that lined the floor of the wardrobe he had just bought from the second-hand dealer. Her face was full of happiness, and it was as though her eyes were laughing at him. She looked radiant as a bride. Her new husband stood beside her, his arm about her waist. He could feel his stomach muscles tighten, even now, after all these years, at the thought of someone else holding his girl. So easily could she have been his girl. He had wanted it to be. So had she. But fate had other ideas.

He picked the newspaper up out of the wardrobe, carried it to the kitchen table and sat heavily onto one of the wooden chairs that were pulled up at it. He sat there, his head cupped in his hands, his elbows on the tabletop and stared at the photograph. So many years ago, yet it seemed like just yesterday.

Their courtship had been festooned with separations. At first it had not mattered, they always came back to each other. The quiet weekend retreats in the cottage in the bush by the coast were their time to be together. They would arrive late and, closeted in each other's arms, snuggle on the veranda to watch the moon set, or rise. And there they would remain, until the songbirds heralded morning and they would wake to the grey dawn mist. He would pad through to the kitchen and stoke the fires, and she would prepare a pot of tea for them to share, and together they would watch the sun rise.

Then one day it did matter. From the beginning they had agreed to an open relationship, long before it had become popular. During the week, she was free to be with other friends, and so was he. Only his friends were to be found in the open spaces which abounded on the coastline. Her friends took in the bright city lights. And it was those lights ... and David, that he could not compete with.

Slowly, she had continued to drift away from him, and he had unconsciously encouraged it—his painting was a jealous muse, consuming him to the exclusion of all else. He always looked back on those years as the stormy period of his life—not so much for the turbulent seascapes that had brought him fame, but for the constant emotional turmoil, as he wrestled between two mistresses.

How his ego had been boosted when she had begged him to fight for her, not to let her go. But he had been unable to bring himself to swallow his pride and plead with her to stay. He loved her, but he loved his freedom more. Or so he had thought at the time. His success had done little to compensate for a lifetime of loneliness

He had never really thought she would leave. But she had. And she had married. He had not even answered the wedding invitation. And now, he continued to stare at the faded photograph in the newspaper, he hadn't missed it at all.

As a seascape artist he could capture all the moods of the great ocean as it pounded purposefully onto the coast. But he had captured only one face on canvas. A face he could never forget, and it was in front of him now; surrounded by pearls and filigree lace.

Avidly he read the diatribe of social discourse for which bridal columns are renowned. For a girl who had never voiced aspirations for a fairy-tale wedding, her parents had done her proud. Bridesmaids, flower-girls, and pageboys, all resplendent in satin and lace. Where was the girl who loved bare feet and flowers in her long loose hair?

He looked to where he kept the portrait, covered by sheets and half hidden by old clothes in the corner of the room. Could he bring himself to unveil it? It had not seen the light of day since she had sent him the invitation. Would she still be the same? Would he still feel the same? Dare he?

With slow deliberation he walked to the corner and reverently pulled the package towards him. He laid it on the kitchen table and wiped the dust from the sheet before carefully unwrapping it. She was as beautiful as he had remembered, if not more so. It was funny how age gave you a greater appreciation of youth, and beauty. His fingers traced the outline of her face and drifted out across the russet arc of her hair as it gossamered into a halo about her, sprinkled with jasmine flowers from the vine outside the cottage.

The vine still grew there. Would her hair still be russet? He smiled and she smiled back. He gently touched his fingertips to his mouth and softly placed them on hers. Sentimental damn fool that he was. Kissing a painting. But memories were sweet. He would find somewhere to hang the picture.

It would be nice to be able to see her from wherever he was in the cottage. Maybe against the wall next to the front door. He stood up and held the picture at arm's length in front of him to get an idea of what it would look like.

"I wonder what happened to you?" he mused. His eyes misted over. He did not see the front door open.

"I came back. Like I always used to."

He looked up to see a white-haired lady standing sadly in the doorway, jasmine flowers hidden in her hair.

"Why did we ever call you 'Blue'?" he asked.

"The same reason we called you 'Blue'," she said, moving forward and ruffling his white hair.

He caught her in an embrace which erased years of unacknowledged pain, and they were together, again.

CYBER MUM

Leigh Leslie

"Go on mum, you'll see, it'll be fun."

I looked around the room, it sure didn't look like fun to me. Still, thinking back, I had to admit that the previous six months had been fun, most of the time. It was just now, looking across at Jordan, I was no longer sure.

"Go on mum, you'll see, it'll be fun." My daughter had said to me again. "I'll show you. Here." She sat me down at the computer and her fingers flew across the keys.

Me? All I could manage to do was turn the thing on, and search for the keys that I wanted to tap to let me in.

Before I knew it there was a screen filled with smiling faces. Young faces.

"I'm not too sure," I said hesitantly, wondering how an old face like mine was supposed to grace this website.

She laughed. "What shall we call you?"

Call me? My name, surely? It must have shown on my face, as she rolled her eyes.

"Come on mum, help me here."

"What's wrong with Shirley?" I asked in my ignorance.

"That's your name. You can't use your name."

"Why not?"

"Because they would then know who you are."

"But isn't that the idea? To know me?"

"No mum. Well yes. But not like that."

It was my turn to roll my eyes. I pushed the chair back from the desk. "No, sorry. I don't think it is a good idea."

"Oh mum! Here, how about we call you RJ64?

"RJ64? What's that supposed to mean?"

"Rare Jewel, 1964. You know, you are a one-in-a-million gem and you were born in 1964." She tapped away at the keyboard again; pages of boxes scrolled before me, and were filled with information. MY information. "Now, what are you looking for?"

"I didn't know I was looking for anything."

"Mum! You're not helping. It's been years since dad died, and years since you went out on a date. What do you look for in a man?"

I laughed. Here was my daughter, talking to me about hunting for a man, on the internet of all places! I was quite happy the way I was. Single, and enjoying not being answerable to anyone. Not now that the children had grown.

But they had taken it into their heads that I needed a man in my life, and they had decided that this was the way to go.

I sighed and started to list characteristics and personalities that were a fantasy.

The deed was done. And I must admit, that there was a certain clandestine thrill about daily checking my profile, and taking a look at what was on offer. And, over the past six months I had met, online and off, a number of men who I could now call 'friends'. And there was one in particular that had grown on me.

There had been something about his picture and profile that had struck a chord. We had so much in common. But it had taken a while before either of us could build up the courage to actually, physically, meet. And I made sure that none of my children knew!

The usual platitudes were exchanged, how unflattering our photos were, how silly it was for people of our vintage to be resorting to the internet to find a compatible someone, especially when that someone turned out to be virtually 'the boy next door'. Through our cyber interchanges it had transpired that we had gone to the same school, albeit in different years, and with different circles of friends, but we had been there at the same time.

We agreed to meet again, and again. We had become 'an item'. And now, here we were, sitting, or rather squashed, in my miniscule living room, playing musical chairs each time the doorbell chimed and another body entered the space.

What had started out as an intimate dinner for the two of us had turned into a family circus, without the frivolity. The stares and unspoken accusations being exchanged were brittle shards thrown across and around the room like atoms let loose in a laboratory. No one spoke. No one dared. I was fuming. Jordan looked bemused. I felt sorry for him, and angry at my ... In fact, I wasn't too sure with whom I was the most angry. My daughter who had set me up on my cyber exploits, or my sons for their unbridled curiosity. Damn them all!

DARK CORRIDORS

Leigh Leslie

My name is Rachel. Rachel Boyd. Of course, I was meant to be Samantha and was so called for the first three days of life until my parents were able to live with the disappointment that my arrival had not provided them with their planned son Samuel. I fear that I have been a source of disappointment ever since. For all three of us.

And that is why I am sitting here about to commit to paper, for posterity, some more of the tortured ghosts that are marching resolutely down the dark corridors of my mind. Maybe, if I meticulously record them I might be rid of them forever.

I look at the pencil poised above the desk diary wondering, and not for the first time, why they are called 'lead pencils' when everyone knows that it is graphite that runs down the middle of the wooden tube.

Beside the diary is my calendar. From habit it is devoid of decoration. There are no artistic reproductions, garish pop art splashes of colour, sentimental pseudo-inspirational thoughts or landscapes beckoning from far-flung vistas.

Rather, as the year progresses, and I turn over the page of my calendar, I am presented with another virginal grid with large numbers placed in the left quadrant of each square denoting another day.

Such is my life that there are never any embellishments. No appointments. No meetings, with either friend or foe. The calendar's sole purpose is to provide regimental evidence of the passing of my life.

At the end of each day, like now, I take morbid delight in crossing out the date, deeply etching a line with the finality that not only draws a close to the day, but inevitably also snaps off the sharpened point of my lead pencil.

But before I can mark off today, I turn to the diary. What memory will I dredge up today? Not that I need to ransack my mind. The memories are there. Constantly. Feverishly they fill my head, tormenting me as they relentlessly push any vestige of rationality to the edge, ready to topple into oblivion before I can grasp the tendrils of the normality that I see others enjoying. At least I can but assume that what I see in others is the normality that I envy.

Tonight what tumbles out is the nightly ritual of my solitary childhood, with one or other of my parents supervising the perfunctory ablutions conducted in loveless silence. This was then followed by me being dragged to the back room where I was unceremoniously plonked into my bed and then left to sleep.

I would lie in the dark and listen as their retreating footsteps faded down the long, carpeted corridor to the warmth and comfort of the living room. The room that was forbidden to me.

They would often retire to this, their sanctuary, and leave me to amuse myself behind the glass sliding doors of the desultory dining room. The dark and heavy furnishings—table permanently set and gathering dust and cobwebs, waiting for the expected guests who never appeared; the chairs, their leather backs and tapestry seats begging for company; huge sideboard with the crystal decanter and sliver candlestick holders— offered neither company nor comfort to me.

I was under strict instructions to not touch anything, nor to even breathe on anything—except for the bottom drawer of the dresser that stood to the side of the fireplace that was never lit. Looking back, I can but wonder what weird psychology they were using, in which they expected my exposure to the accumulated pieces of

Meccano and Matchbox trucks and cars would somehow, through osmosis maybe, morph me into the boy they so desperately wanted. But I digress. This drawer and its contents can wait for another day's diary entry. If that day ever ~~deigns~~ to arrive.

But back to the nightly ritual of my childhood.

Lying there in my bed, rather than dream of the comforts from which I was excluded, I would close my eyes to the shadows that flickered across the bare windows of the room. Once my eyes were tightly closed, I would start deep breathing, and in my mind watch and count as the giant made his nightly journey to my bedroom.

His steps, the span the width of the household doors, would pace outside the length of my bedroom window. One – two – three. Then he would take one step to the end of the house. Once the giant was at the corner of the house he would turn and walk down the side of the house.

One – two – three – four – five – six – seven.

He was now at the back porch.

He was only two steps away from entering the house.

My eyes remained screwed shut, and I would try to calm my rasping breaths. I had to be asleep, or at least make the pretence of being asleep. The giant could not find me awake.

One – two.

He was at the back door.

The door opened silently and with two steps he was at the end of the cupboard-lined corridor that led to my room. My breaths would now be taken in time with his steps as he walked towards my room.

One.

He was next to the first cupboard. The door, like all those in the house, was solid wood, the smooth round handle was just the right size to fit comfortably in the palm of anyone's hand, and at a convenient height. This first cupboard was home to our coats and associated outside wear. In the back left corner, closeted behind an old army-coat and mostly forgotten, was a point-twenty-two. My mother's rifle. I wonder where it is now?

Two.

He was beside the linen cupboard. Shelves filled with sheets, pillowcases, towels, blankets, extra pillows. All carefully folded and ordered according to colour. The out-of-season pieces snuggled in regulation plastic bags. A single bag languished on the very top shelf, its blue contents visible—a mocking reminder of what I can never be. Was it some sort of punishment that the baby clothes were so lovingly, and visibly kept?

It was always a gamble what would assail one's nostrils when opening this cupboard. It could be lavender, Naphthalene, or a mixture of both depending on which decorated drawstring bag was in favour that season.

Three.

The third and final cupboard. The cupboard which always smelt ... different. This cupboard housed the cleaning apparatus. The carpet sweeper with its *wrack-wrack* noise as it was pushed back and forth quickly collecting smaller messes that could not wait for the 'proper' clean. The vacuum cleaner had an elephant's trunk that suctioned the weekly lint and dirt into a long metal tube on wheels that I longed to ride. A row of pegs along one side of the cupboard displayed a regimented collection of feather dusters made from grey and black real ostrich feathers that would break off if wielded with an excess of vigor. Tethered to a large nail at the back was the rag bag, a motley collection of single socks, ripped shirts and worn-out cotton singlets. And on the shelf above all these were the accoutrements of cleaning, various polishes and waxes that my mother vowed were 'the best'.

Four, then Five.

He was at the door to the bathroom. If the door was open and he thought to look in he would see his reflection in the mirror above the hand basin on the far wall. The cold and uninviting room housed its own cupboard hiding a clothes drier. Next to this cupboard was a vanity. Reminiscent of movie stars' dressing rooms there was a large mirror surrounded by lights. The 'throne' resided in its own alcove to the side. Along the opposite wall was the shower – a dark cubicle with three tiled ceiling-high walls and fronted with a plastic curtain. Then the bath.

Set into the polished concrete floor was a multicoloured and multipointed star. It was an essential, but not a friendly room, and one which I would frequent only when necessary. So I was never surprised that the giant did not dally.

He was nearly at my room. Just one more step and he would be at my door, ready to take that final step into my room and be beside my bed. I would try and calm my breathing and relax my eyes. I had to appear to be asleep so that the giant would leave me alone. But, as he would not be able to see beyond my face and the form of my body under the blankets, my anxiety would transfer to my hands, clenched tightly at my sides. And I would wait, hoping that I would once more fool him.

Six - Seven.

Now was the time to hold my breath, before resuming the steady deep breaths. The giant had reached my room. I would count slowly to 10 and the giant would be gone. Disappeared. Dissolved. And for one fleeting moment I could congratulate myself for having achieved something. Something positive. I could then relax and sleep.

I let out a sigh as the end of my pencil snaps off. I now feel the release of being able to draw a line across that particular dark corridor.

DEFENDANT

Jennifer Lilly

Rachael used the back of her hand to wipe the stray lock of hair out of her eyes, and she felt the sweat on her brow. How she hated hot days. Especially when school was out. She shifted her weight from one foot to the other as she stood at the kitchen bench and looked into the living room. Martha and Ben were reading. It was all right while they were quiet. She sighed, that state never lasted for long. Why was it, she wondered, that some families were able to live and play together without rancour? What had she ever done to deserve the two tyrants that called her Mum?

She looked at the clock, and in doing so caught sight of her reflection. Tired eyes and dank hair. No wonder Brian chose to work late. She gave her image a wan smile and noticed the lines running further than they ought. She was getting old. Thirty-two and already past it. Whatever 'it' was. She laughed quietly to herself. It rasped out as a shrill plea for help. Martha looked up. Then returned to the book she was reading.

Rachael knew it wouldn't last for long. Peace never did. She sighed and looked sadly down at the pastry under her hands. That was all she was good at these days. Housework. 'Oh, I'm just a housewife' she'd often said when asked what she did. Now people didn't need to ask her. Frumpy clothes and flat shoes told the whole story, coupled with no make-up, and she couldn't remember the last time that she had seen the inside of a hair salon. She shook her head sadly and reached for the rolling pin.

"M-u-m?" A strident whine came from Ben. Slowly she raised her head. What would it be this time? Martha was still reading so she wasn't the cause, this time, maybe it would be a simple question. Simple? Gone were the days when Ben's questions were simple. At eight he was already showing signs of brilliance, and his knowledge of things scientific far outstripped her own.

He lay sprawled on the 'really ought to be tossed' sofa, his gangly legs half on and half off. Rachael noticed with trepidation that the foot that was off was slowly swinging ever closer to where his older sister Martha was curled up in a beanbag. Rachael glared at him in warning. But his intellectual acumen did not extend to interpretation of maternal signals. His foot advanced closer. Rachael sighed and wiped away the wisp of hair from off her forehead again.

Martha sat up and glared at Ben's foot as it advanced in arcs towards her.

Rachael wondered why she had even entertained the idea that she would bake today. High temperatures, and the children home was not the recipe for success in the kitchen. At least, not when the children showed no inclination to help. Then again, their being in the kitchen would have just been another recipe – for disaster.

"What is it Ben?"

"What does 'defendant' mean?"

Rachael wondered what book he was reading. She couldn't keep up with them these days and had long since stopped monitoring them.

"That's the stuff Dad puts round the vegetables!" Martha said in what was her most authoritarian voice, a sweet smile on her face. Rachael knew that smile and sighed once more. Why wasn't Brian here? He was never here when she needed him. It was all very well for him to come home and criticize her for his perceived state of the house, and the ill temper of the children. But he was never here to see the build-up of hostilities. If he were, then maybe he'd be able to diffuse the situation before it became a conflict too great for her to handle.

"No it's not. That's 'Defender.'" He made to kick his sister, but he was too slow. Martha threw her book at him. Smiling triumphantly as it caught him on his upper arm.

"M-u-m!" he wailed, "Martha hit me." He glared at her with brotherly malice and rubbed his arm.

"No I didn't." The fire was kindling in the dragon as Martha sat up and faced her brother.

"Yes you did." Ben sat up and breathed flames at his sister, nostrils flaring.

Rachael put down the rolling pin and sighed as she drew her hand across her forehead yet again. She could feel the perspiration come away on her hand. She wondered how long the altercation would last before she would need to mediate.

"Didn't."

"Did."

The two siblings were now at a definite standoff. Ben glowering from the sofa, hands on knees and elbows bent out as he leaned forward. Martha kneeling in front of him, clenched fists forced into the sides of her waist.

"I didn't hit you. I only threw my book at you." Rachael could hear the unvoiced 'huh!' in the air as Martha threw all the superiority of two years into her pedantic response.

"Well, it hit me." Ben rubbed his arm. Rachael managed to smile as she noticed that it was the opposite arm to that which had taken the brunt of the assault.

"So?" The feminine sugar dripped off the one word, and Rachael winced, knowing where her daughter had learnt that technique.

"So it hurt." Ben pouted, just like his father. Rachael just managed to save herself from laughing out loud.

Martha thrust her face a few inches from Ben's. "So, you're stupid."

"I am not." Ben stood up. At least, while he was standing he was able to gain some height over his sister. But not for long. Martha stood up too.

"Yes you are!" she almost sang and gave him a push on the shoulders.

"Not!" He stamped his foot, and Rachael could see him blinking rapidly. She would have to step in now, even if Ben would never forgive her for betraying his youth. Slowly she scraped the pastry from off her fingers and wiped her hands down the sides of her apron.

"Are!" Martha gave him another push, which sent him stumbling back onto the sofa

"Oh, for goodness sake. Ben. Martha. What is going on here?" She tried to sound tough, but she knew that even in that she was a failure.

"M-u-m, Martha says I'm stupid." He stood with as much affront as he could.

"Well he is." Martha was all defiance.

"Why is he stupid Martha?" All over a stupid word. If she had been more aware of the children, quicker to respond to Ben's initial query, none of this would have happened. She would have finished making the pie and peace would have reigned in the house. Well. She guessed not. Not really. If it hadn't been this, it would have been something else.

"Because he says..." Martha blustered loudly, then her words died. She turned to her brother, "What was it you said Ben?"

Ben traced circles on the carpet with his foot, head bent, and hands clasped behind his back. Martha and Rachael looked at him. Martha with impatience, Rachael with a faint smile.

"I dunno." He raised his head and glared once more at his sister, "She's made me forget."

EMMANUEL

Jennifer Lilly

The old man sighed as the image on the television died, and the flash of the headlights of a passing vehicle bathed the darkened room with momentary light. Another power failure. There had been so many this evening, every time there was a news flash, or so it seemed.

"Go turn the set off boy," he rasped.

The youth started to protest but the old man cut him off. "Ar, just do it. Who wants to watch it anyway?"

"I thought you did grandpa, you knew him. I thought you wanted to watch ..."

The old man fumbled with some matches and lit the stunted candle, trapped in a mound of wax at the bottom of an old jam jar. In the soft glow the youth looked across at his grandfather, wrinkled and grey. The flicker of light from the candle softened the pain in the rheumy eyes and hid the nicotine-stained hair.

"Tell me about him."

"Why?"

"Why not? We can't do much else with the power off."

"Fetch me a drink then."

"Can't. The grog's all gone till Mum gets back. Besides ..."

"Ah, skip it."

The old man lent towards the candle and lit a cigarette.

"Way back when your Mum was a nipper and we was livin' up the road a bit, there was this real big hullabaloo down the end of Nelson Street. Near the wharf there. A real humdinger of a fight. Some of the locals had been sportin' for fight for a while, all they needed was an excuse. Well, anyway, this night Charlie Brand came waltzin' into the pub all dolled up in his army gear. Back from Vietnam he was. He 'spected a hero's welcome and old man Supp's daughter pantin' for him. But she'd gone and done a bunk with Shirl Large's brother the week after Charlie had left. And there they were, the two of them, with two nippers in tow, one the spit of Charlie."

The old man wheezed a laugh and after coughing a bit lit another cigarette and continued.

"That's when the punchin' started, and it didn't take long to spread. Moved outside and down the street. The women runnin' everywhere screamin' and the bottles started flyin'. Can't say that the tourists took too kindly to it all, still, for them it was probably all part of the local colour. It was one of them balmy nights. An' I knew that there'd be trouble so I'd sent your Mum off up the street to tell her sister to come home, and her brother to stay clear. Only she never made it."

The old man's eyes clouded as he remembered that night. And the nights, and years, of anguish that followed. The visits and the tears. As tears welled in the old man's eyes the young man busied himself and rolled, and lit, his grandfather another cigarette. He knew the story. Could remember his uncle vegetating in the loony wing of the prison hospital, and his aunt, disfigured and now totally dependent on government handouts for her next fix. The old man drew back on the cigarette, coughed, and continued.

"She never made it. I should never have sent her, but I figured she'd know where to find them better than me. When the noise could be heard plainly from the house and they still weren't back I started to get worried. I started off up the street towards the noise and met your Mum, bawlin' like only she could. Only she weren't alone. There was a young woman with her. She looked pretty distraught too. And well in the family way.

"Anyways I hurried them inside. Gave your Mum a talkin' to and sent her packin'. Then I fixed the young miss up with a strong cuppa an' put in a tot of me own, figurin' like that she'd need it. Sprayed it all over the kitchen she did. That's gratitude for you. Anyhow, she reckoned that her man'd be along looking for her soon, so she wanted to go back out front and watch for him. He'd gone off some place to see if he could find an address where he'd been told they could stay. Didn't like his chances meself. Turned out I was right.

"'Bout five minutes later, with the brawlin' still goin' strong there's this horrible rattlin' and bangin' and backfirin' accompanied with some bloke bellowing "Mary!". The young woman dashed to the door. Actually she waddled, barefooted and holdin' her back with one hand and her belly with the other. Next minute she's back, grinnin' fit to split with a young man sheepishly followin' her. He was one of them hippie types, Jesus sandals and long hair, called me 'man' and smoked the darndest shaped roll-yer-owns I'd ever seen.

"The fightin' was riot scaled now and movin' ever closer. The young man hadn't found a place to stay and Mary was obviously in some discomfort. I fixed her into your gran's chair and wished to hell that she was with us. I sent your Mum next door to fetch Mrs. O'Reilly. Joe, the young man, was anxiously watchin' as the rioters came maulin' down the street towards his car. They was brandishin' fire torches now and smashin' and burnin' on a drunken rampage. We all knew better than to call the cops. Best not get involved.

"Joe gasped, the car exploded, the crowd roared, Mary screamed and a baby cried. Then the darndest thing happened. Everythin' suddenly went quiet. You couldn't even hear the crackle of the burning car. Someone musta thrown a handful of skyrockets and fireworks into the flames 'cos the sky became a silent fairyland. Then everyone melted home.

"When I turned 'round there was Mrs. O'Reilly beaming over loving parents and their new child. Your Mum sat wide-eyed at their feet stroking Rastus our cat. It didn't even occur to me to wonder about the other two. There was just this sense of serenity. It lasted some days - while the young couple was there. I couldn't turn them out, so I fixed up the Lilo for Joe, the camp bed for Mary and threw some pillows into the clothes basket for the youngster. Called him Emmanuel they did. Funny, they didn't look Spanish or Latin to me.

"The oddest people came visitin' our house that week. Don't know how they knew Joe and Mary was here, but they did. By the time Joe and Mary left they had enough money to buy another car, and gifts to set them right. Then they was gone. Never saw 'em again after that, but used to get a postcard from them every now and then. And the odd photo of the boy as he grew up.

"Then about three years ago there's a knock on the door and a man's standin' there. Sez he knows me, and how grateful he was to me. Don't know how he knew me. But I knew him alright. From his photos, and more recently from all the publicity he'd bin receivin' in the popular press like. Reckoned he knew how to set the world aright. Had some cock and bull yarn about the end of the world, and that he could save mankind. I invited him in and we yarned for about an hour.

"Quite a well-presented young man he was. Wouldn't ever guess that he was a fruitcake. I mean, he was really off beam. Even said he could make your aunt and uncle well again! I could tell even then that the public would make mincemeat out of him. I mean, who would believe that garbage these days? Love and Peace were tried when his parents were young, and no one listened. Who's goin' to listen now? 'specially to some upstart who goes around dressed like Mr Respectable and sayin' they can put on the brakes of destruction. No wonder they certified him.

"He got a fair few mindless people to believe him and follow his lifestyle. Don't know what'll happen to them after today. Still, he was a nice man when he called on me. I liked him. I didn't agree with what he had to say, but when he left I didn't need a drink for a while and I really felt lovely and warm. Hadn't felt like that since before your gran passed on."

The old man sat there quietly staring into the flame of the candle as it sputtered and died. His grandson struck a match to look for another candle. They both jumped as the television sprang into life and the naked bulb in the ceiling above flooded them with light.

"I thought I told you to turn ..." The old man stopped as the television screen displayed a man strapped into the chair. The camera zoomed in to show Emmanuel's face, full of anguish. His mouth opened.

"Forgive them Father, for they know not ..."

The body jerked and the image on the screen faded.

The old man and his grandson looked out the window and watched as the annual firework display lit the sky over the water. Police sirens could be heard not so far away. The old man hoped that his daughter was not on the street.

Emmanuel had been forgotten.

FELICITY - PROPER NOUN – HAPPINESS

Jacklyn Harris

She walked slowly down the Spanish Steps. With each step she took on those well-worn famous stairs she felt a pang of ... well, she didn't quite know what. She was in a peculiar mood. Her heart wasn't heavy, and yet it was. She wasn't happy yet she was. Was she really where she was? What was it that Byron had once said?

"Oh Rome! my country! city of the soul!
The orphans of the heart must turn to thee,
Lone mother of dead empires! and control
In their shut breasts their petty misery.
What are our woes and sufferance? Come and see
The cypress, hear the owl, and plod your way ..."

Plod your way. That was what she was doing now – plodding her way through life.

She stopped at the top of the last tier. In the distance in front of her, over the tops of the houses, she could see St Peter's Basilica. From below, in the piazza, rose the hubbub of traffic, Italians and tourists. At that moment she felt pity for the humble tourist, lost, as she was, in a strange world. Only her world, she thought, was not of her own free will. But more a consequence of growing up. Growing up in a foreign country in the late 1960s with late, no, pre-dawn parents. She tossed her head and roused herself from her dreaminess. Above, the much romanticized Italian blue skies threatened to drop a deluge.

She watched in fascination the tourists milling about the hippies whom her father described as "littering The Steps". Maybe they had something. Maybe they knew what life was about.

Felicity felt drawn to the Bohemian lifestyle, imagining herself to be a hippie. But then again, she did not fancy all that they offered. The idea of communal living, not having her own space did not appeal to her. Nor did the notion of shooting heroin. Still, she could see no harm in adopting their fashions. Her friends at school all wore their hair long, and loose, and went about in tie-dyed shirts, blue jeans and sandals. Why couldn't she? It always came back to the same thing. Her parents.

Her parents. They were at fault, and it was because of them that she was now suffering in her floating existence.

This current bout of unsettled uneasiness had begun a week ago when her over-conservative, over-protective parents—though to be fair it was mainly her father—had 'kindly informed her' that she was not allowed to see Hair when it came to the Sistine Theatre. There had been no reason given for the ban, except for the usual "Hippies are society's trash, and I don't want it said that my daughter is one of them." That was the speech her father always threw at her when she mentioned hippies, or broached on any subject which her father considered had some connection with the current wave of bohemianism.

What Felicity always wondered, and wanted to ask her father, was whether he was more concerned about what may happen to her if she followed the trend, or in saving face in front of his colleagues. She wanted to believe that it was the latter, but she knew, in her inner-most self, that it was the paternal concern which stood at the root of the statement. So she never asked. But that did not stop her from feeling sad. Sad that she was unable to get on the same wave-length as her parents. Why, if that were possible then she could probably have as much fun with them as she had with the few friends she had here in Rome. For that matter, her parents might even be able to get on with her friends. That way they could be one ~~happy~~ family, like the hippies sitting on the Spanish Steps, sharing each other's food, and ...

At that point Felicity was brutally awakened from her daydream by what she considered an obvious Italian 'wanna-be' hippie. She found the majority of Italian males obnoxious. For starters she had it on good authority that all Italian males thought that every foreign female only came to Italy to be swooned by them. The only Italian males she had seen were short, dark, not particularly good looking and, for goodness sake, they didn't even speak English.

Why her parents ever brought her to this cat-infested crumbling marble monument to antiquity she could never understand. She had been quite happy back home where the men were tall, blond and well built. And she had likeminded friends who accepted her for what she was and did not ostracise her because she wasn't one of the 'trendies'. She doubted that she could ever be happy here.

The Italian 'wanna-be' hippies she found even more objectionable. No bonafide hippie would buy their clothes from designer stores. The Italians only played at being bohemians, thinking it would be another way to win the hearts of the foreign women. She shook her head in despair, and realised that it had started to rain.

Down in the piazza a magnificent array of colour was blooming as the tourists busily put up their newly purchased souvenir umbrellas. Those Italians who had not come prepared with their black umbrellas scurried for cover under the virtually non-existent eaves. The hippies were huddling together along the sides of The Steps, covering themselves and their displays of handmade jewellery that they had for sale, under sheets of plastic.

Very soon Felicity was the only person remaining unprotected from the rain, standing on The Steps. She shivered, not because she was cold, but more because she felt alone; if she had to live here, then she wanted to belong, to have someone with whom she could hold hands and share life with.

Felicity came from a family who did not believe in seeing a place as a tourist, especially if they were going to be there for some time. So when her father's work had brought him here she had not been dragged around the tourist sites. She did not get to visit The Spanish Steps until quite some time after arriving in Rome. It had been one day, several weeks after school had resumed after the summer vacation, that she and her closest friend decided to skip school and go downtown. The Spanish Steps, with their multi-sensory vibrancy became a kind of personal retreat for her, a place to go to when she felt down and out. Like she did today.

Once more Felicity was roused from her daydreaming. Someone was standing beside her, offering her the protection of an umbrella. She was about to refuse, thinking it to be another pestering Italian. But instead, on turning around, she found herself confronted by a smiling, blue eyed ... hippie.

She accepted the proffered umbrella, thankful for its protection, but she remained where she was. She half smiled to herself, speculating on what her parents would say if they saw her.

Her Sir Walter Raleigh broke the spell. He was saying something to her in heavily accented Italian, and poor Italian at that. He was definitely American. With an accent like that, there was no doubt about it. Again, the half smile flickered across her face and Felicity had a momentary feeling of pity for him. But it was only fleeting as amusement and mischievousness jostled for a place in her mind.

He thinks I'm Italian, she thought to herself, and wondered if she should reply in Italian and let him continue to think that she was? What a game that would be. Already she was feeling better. Or would she just pretend that she didn't understand?

Felicity did neither. Instead, in her worst Italian she told her protector that she did not really understand his Italian, and that maybe it would be best for them to continue their conversation in English as that was a mutually understood language as she too was from the States.

She was glad to have chosen the avenue that she had, and not given in to her childish whims as she watched the relief spread across his face and the tension in his shoulders ease out of his posture.

"I didn't think that you were Italian, but I thought I'd better play it safe. At least for the first time. You come here often, don't you?"

Felicity felt her head reel, and her stomach heave. Her mouth felt dry. That voice. It was beautiful. Let him say more. At length Felicity was able to stammer out a reply.

"Yes, well... yes and no, I mean..., that is... you see," This was ridiculous, her young years were showing, if she didn't find the words she wanted soon she would miss out. She did so want her father to meet this man, then maybe he would think differently. She took a deep breath

"I guess what I'm really trying to say is that yes, I do come here often, but in bouts. Like now. I've come here fairly regularly for several days now, but before that I haven't been here for a few weeks." She shivered again.

Her protector put his arm around her shoulders and then, feeling Felicity tense up under his touch, removed it.

Idiot girl, Felicity thought savagely to herself.

"Let's get out of this rain. Shall we go to Babbington's?"

Babbington's didn't exactly fit her picture of a typical hippie hang out. She'd been once with her parents and found it, though pleasant, definitely only to be patronised by homesick expatriate English people of her parents' vintage.

"Why not a regular Italian bar?" she asked.

"Because, my Angel of the Rain, it is quiet there, and one can sit comfortably by the window, and watch the rain run down the panes, the tourists walk by and the horses wait patiently for work. Besides. Besides in Babbington's one can talk sanely, and in a civilised manner, without having to yell to be heard."

By this time they were at the foot of The Steps, and it was raining heavily. Quickly they turned right and entered the English tea rooms where Keats and Shelley were meant to have sat. They ordered tea and cakes, just to keep tradition alive.

"I suppose, before our conversation advances any further, we had better introduce ourselves."

Felicity pulled herself back into the present as he spoke.

"I'm Sean, and you're ...?

"Felicity."

"Felicity. Felicity – happiness. My Angel of the Rain is called Felicity."

"Why 'Angel of the Rain'?

"Because, my sweet, you appeared before me, today, as if God had sent you an answer to my prayers. A gift from the Almighty. A sacred blessing from heaven. You entered my life on this rainy, forlorn day, as the rain came from the clouds and entered the sky."

Felicity laughed. She felt as though she had known Sean all her life, and she wanted to continue her life with him by her side. She lost all her old anxieties and fears. Once more she was happy, she felt carefree ... and happy.

For a week Felicity was with Sean—school vacations were great. For a week she was happy, and for a week Sean was gentle and kind. But not once had he allowed her to meet his friends, nor would he agree to meet her parents. But most frustrating of all, he would not allow her to change her manner, appearance or speech. It was as though he did not want to share even one part of her with anything belonging to his world. The world that Felicity so much wanted to be a part of. The only dark times of that week were when his lifestyle came into the conversation.

It's not for you. This life. My Angel of the rain. You were promised to better things, he would say to her whenever she broached upon the subject of hippies. For that first week Felicity was content to leave it like that. Content just to be with him, and not to jeopardise their friendship. Time would tell. With a fair proportion of assistance from Felicity time did tell, and Sean finally agreed to take her to meet his friends.

Felicity was like a child waiting for Christmas and Santa Claus. For the next week she was full of expectation and could hardly wait for Friday night. Finally it arrived, and luckily her parents were going out. She met Sean, as arranged, at the OSRAM sign in front of the main railway station. From there they walked a little way and caught the bus to Trastevere.

She had been to Trastevere several times, either to eat out at one of the many restaurants with her parents, or to go with friends, to the English language cinema.

Although she found Trastevere fascinating, Felicity had never really liked place, nor felt comfortable there. As for living there, in one of the dingy apartments—what Felicity imagined to be entered through darkened, slightly smelly passages—had always caused a knot to form in her stomach and a prayer of thanks to rise in her mind that she lived in the newer, cleaner, more open area known as E.U.R. Now Sean was leading her down such a passage, and there was the smell, just as she imagined—was it urine, or what?

Sean reached back for her hand and lead her up a narrow flight of stairs. There was no light, nor was there a handrail. A scorpion skittled past her feet and into a hole on the landing. Felicity screamed. The door beside her opened, and she swung around to be confronted by a wall of smoke and music. A young girl was holding the door open, smiling benignly past Felicity, at Sean.

Felicity looked at Sean. He motioned for her to enter. Inside wasn't Felicity's particular idea of cleanliness and heaven. It was, in fact, what she had always been told a hippie pad was like, but, up until now she had innocently disbelieved it.

She turned, coughing, trying to rid her lungs of the sweet smelling smoke, and stumbled down the stairs, the music throbbing up through her feet, and the humiliating laughter of Sean's friends surging in her ears.

Once out in the fresh air and fast fading sunlight Felicity leant against the wall, crying, trying to compose herself, and her thoughts.

A handkerchief was waving in front of her. A white one. Felicity laughed, and looking up, met Sean's blue eyes, now filled with remorse and pain.

"Shall we go to Babbington's? I know it's a long way from here, but we can make it, together. This life is not for you. I think you realise that now."

Yes, now she realised it. She took Sean's handkerchief, squeezed his hand, and shaking her head Felicity turned her back on Trastevere, the cruel world of hippies, and Sean.

Slowly she walked away. Felicity turned around once. Sean was still there. He blew her a kiss and waved.

Dear Sean, you have taught me more than you will ever know.

He cupped his mouth with his hands and shouted after her. "See you one day on the Spanish Steps my Angel of the Rain. One day, my Angel, one day, we shall meet again and walk together for always."

She nodded and waved. She was happy. She was Felicity – Happiness. Yes, one day, and soon, they would meet again on the steps, changed people, and they would remain together. Together for always.

FLIGHT 48

Leigh Leslie

Terry Kepler stood at the base of the steps ready to welcome the passengers before they entered the small 19-seater turboprop that was to be their 'home' for the short flight. Not one of the passengers made eye contact, or responded to his cheery greeting.

Perplexed by the unfriendly passengers he followed the last one up the steps, pulled the door closed and latched it before turning around to see that everyone was seated. They were. Shaking his head he entered the cockpit.

"Sombre lot back there," he said to Greg Pitts the pilot as he clambered into the co-pilot's seat. "Even Captain Phillips didn't say hello."

"Phillips is on board?" Greg looked up from what he was doing. "Deadheading is he?"

"Guess so, he's in uniform," Terry reached for his harness and strapped himself in.

"Not like him to be unsociable, wonder what's up?"

Captain Bob Phillips was sitting towards the back of the plane on the starboard side. His captain's hat resting upside down on his lap, his right index finger tracing around the sweatband as he stared unseeing out the window. Had he made the right decision? In many respects he felt that the decision had been made for him. Now all that was left was for him to execute it. He patted the container in the inside pocket of his jacket and gave a slight nod of his head. All he had left to do was determine the best time. Before or after this, his final flight? He smiled, if he took them before then he would have already had his final flight. That flight was the one that had tipped the balance to the predicament he was now in. Why did all the women that he loved have to have been on that flight? His wife and daughter, and Wanda the flight attendant. Not that it would have made all that much of a difference. Not after his last medical. He patted his pocket again. Was he being a coward, he wondered?

Lucinda Hayward, sitting across the aisle from Captain Phillips tugged again at the long blonde wig that she was wearing. It had been a last-minute decision to anonymously accompany Craig on this flight. It was her way of hanging on, yet saying goodbye. Such an idiot. Both of them. Her for keeping quiet, he for feeling obliged to his mother and recently dead father. What about her and … The wig was starting to itch her scalp and she scowled. It was too late now. She bent down, pulled her handbag onto her lap and opened it. There, nestled at the bottom was her purse and inside that was the business card. She didn't know why she needed to look at it. She knew the address, and the time of her appointment. But she needed the reassurance of holding it in her hand. She looked up the aisle to where Craig sat, hunched over and seemingly hugging the window. Was she making the right choice? Should she have told him? Would it have made any difference? His mind was made up, and his mother was bubbling with righteousness. She looked at the card again, then out her window. Could she really go through with it and sever all ties with the man she loved?

Craig O'Conner fingered the photograph that he had carefully, almost reverently, slipped into his jeans' pocket. He knew that it would be bent and even creased by the time he left the plane, and hoped with it being so defaced it would be easier for him to discard it in the first rubbish bin he came across. He sighed. His life was not turning out how he had wanted it to. But he knew that the path he was taking would please his mother, and make her proud. She had put so much energy into grooming each of his three older brothers in turn to enter the priesthood and they had each disappointed her. He himself, being the youngest of the family had never been so groomed, but, once his father had died he felt it was his duty. He sighed, and fingered the photograph again. He prayed that Lucinda could forgive him.

Dee McKinnon did not know if there was room in her body for the mixed emotions that consumed her. She thought that she had liked her brother-in-law, but now she was simply fuming mad with him. And justifiably too. If it was not for him, she would not now be cooped up in planes for ... she didn't want to contemplate how long. Why did Cilla have to live in the nether reaches of Britain for pity's sake? She squirmed in her seat. Damn her sister. No, damn the man that her sister had married. She clenched her fingers and stuffed them between her knees. Never had she envisioned her reunion with her sister would be in a morgue. She cursed herself for not visiting before. Her sister had extended almost annual invitations, and had even offered to pay for the flights those years when she had used lack of finance as the excuse. What had happened that it should all end like this? How had she come from being a happy and accomplished businesswoman to a single parent of an instant family? Oh, those poor children. Her rage subsided when she thought of her sister's three children. How would they feel about leaving everything they had ever known and being transported back to New Zealand with an unfamiliar aunt just because there was no one else?

Mitch Brown was the picture of misery. He had thought that his future was not only mapped out for him, but secure. All he had ever dreamed of being, like all true kiwi boys, was an All Black, or at least to play professionally. And he could have made it. So easily could he have made it. He let his head hit the edge of the window, and winced. Wrong move, wrong side. Stupid. Stupid. Stupid. He ought to know better than to aggravate his broken collarbone. That's why he was wearing a sling. He should have asked for a seat on the other side of the plane, that way he could have leant against the side and looked out the window. He should not even be here in the plane. The provincial team that he was part of were playing right now and he ought to have been there on the field with them. Not here on his way home, in disgrace. If only he had not been out partying with the boys. If only he had not thought himself a hero and gone to the aid of the attractive drunk blonde. How was he to know that it was all a set-up? He shrugged his shoulders and 'ouched', it could have been worse. At least he'd avoided the king-hit.

Nikki Bly was glad of the thrumming of the engines filling the interior of the plane, it went some way to masking the sobs that kept threatening to burst out of her chest. Why oh why had they chosen America for a holiday? She had wondered that from when they had first announced their plans. And had been thinking it with a vengeance since first receiving the call. And now here she was. On her way to him. Or was it to her? They say that twins have an empathy that goes beyond the norm. But in their case the empathy had been transplanted with enmity. She and Janie had always been competitive but until their teens it had always been friendly. That changed when she had started dating Tim Chapman. That was when the competition became vicious, underhand and dirty. Janie had taken Tim from her. She had never forgiven her sister, or Tim. So now, when Janie had called to say that Tim was in hospital, who was she travelling halfway across the world for? Would she be in time to be reunited with the only man she had ever truly loved? Or would she be comforting her sister? She looked at her watch and gulped a giggle – looking at her watch would not make time go any faster.

Up in the cockpit Gregory received clearance from the control tower to take off.

"Guess everyone has their reason for not being enthusiastic about this flight," Terry grinned as the plane accelerated down the runway.

GETTING A ROUND TUET

Jennifer Lilly

"Whatever is your obsession with shopping?" he asked as they entered yet another junk-crammed shop. He looked around, scared to move, and holding his breath in fear of disturbing something. The shelves bulged with dust collectors, half the items he could not put a label to, the other half were of no useful consequence.

"Really Harold! What's wrong with having an interest in what is around you?"

He smiled at Beryl and marvelled at how little she had changed since he had first met her. She still had the same petite figure as when they were married, and her smile was as disarming as ever. Her eyes sparkled in anticipation of what she might find within the bowels of the shop and she gave him a quick wave before disappearing behind a rack of patchwork gargoyles. He sighed.

Long ago he had resigned himself to this periodic pilgrimage into any quaint or off-beat shop which presented itself to his wife. Once inside he knew that there would be no release until every artefact had been meticulously examined. He turned his head slightly and saw a defeated man smiling sympathetically at him. Balding head and tired grey eyes. Pity the woman who has to wake up to that face each morning, he thought. I wonder what she's like. Harold grinned at the man.

"Nice day," he said, and the other man nodded his head.

"These women, you have to sit tight on your wallet when they go shopping" the other man said, and Harold nodded in agreement.

"Don't know what they see in these kinds of shops."

"I know," agreed Harold, "give me a bookshop any day."

"Or a sports store."

"Yes, a store with a good range of Golfing paraphernalia." Harold was warming up to the other shopping widower. "Now there's a store for you! Funny though how the good woman never wants to spend time there though. They drag us around to all these odd-ball shops..."

The other man nodded his head sympathetically. "Not to mention the Op-Shops, and second-hand dealers."

"And what about the antique shops?" added Harold.

"Oh, I don't like it when she goes into them."

"No, they're expensive." Harold remembered the last time he'd followed Beryl into an antique shop. They'd come out again some hours later with a considerably depleted bank balance, and all because she'd been looking for the blessed tuet she was always after. She hadn't found one, but he'd bought several golf clubs, and a collection of golfing memorabilia dating from last century. Yes, it had been quite a find, but Beryl had come away unimpressed.

The other man looked pensive. Harold didn't want to intrude on his thoughts, so he looked around for his wife. He could hear voices drifting back to him from somewhere deep inside the shop. He decided that he didn't really want to know. He turned back to the other man.

"Whenever we go out my wife is on the lookout for a shop that she hasn't been in before, or not for a while, and we have to stop and waste time while she browses. I always thought that was what cows did when they were feeding. Then I got married. Now I know differently."

The other man nodded sagely. "My wife spends all her spare time looking for some fangled thing called a tuet," he said with an apologetic look in his eyes. Harold was momentarily surprised, but he knew exactly how the other man felt. He nodded his head.

"And it has to be a round tuet. Not a square tuet, or a small tuet, or a brown one. Always a round one," Harold said and looked at the other man expectantly.

The other man slowly shook his head. "She hasn't found one yet so we still stop at all the shops," He looked down at his watch. Harold noticed that Beryl had been gone a good thirty minutes and he sighed. He was glad that this trip had no time limit on it. But then, experience had taught him that he could not put time constraints on Beryl when they went anywhere. Or, if they were needed, then he had to take a familiar route where there was no possibility of ambush.

Harold looked around again. There she was, coming into view. "Are you nearly ready love?" he called out. The other man followed his gaze.

"I just getting around to it," Beryl answered.

Harold looked at the other man who simply shrugged his shoulders. "See what I mean?" Harold said helplessly.

"Who's that you are talking to dear?" Beryl asked as she came up to Harold and slipped an arm around his waist.

Harold turned to introduce his wife to the other man, but just then Beryl let out a triumphant squeal. The two men stared at each other in quiet embarrassment.

"That's it!" Beryl said delightedly, pointing to a large, ornately framed, round mirror.

"*That* is a round tuet?" asked the other man.

Beryl looked at her husband strangely. "Not exactly," she answered, "but it is just the mirror I've been looking for.

Harold and his reflection shrugged their shoulders and followed Beryl to the counter and quietly paid for the mirror.

HEART'S DESIRE

Leigh Leslie

The two men were sitting in a quiet corner of the pub, well away from prying eyes. One smart and professional looking, the other appeared to be in his mid-twenties, casually dressed, wedding band still shiny.

Not his usual punter, Tom thought, head to one side. Yet here he was. A number of photographs splayed across the tabletop between them, tacky from all the residue of stale beer that was calling the surface home. Tom could almost see the other man salivating as he looked over the photographs, and he wondered what had motivated Chris to seek him out.

"Well? Wha'dya reckon?"

Chris looked up from photographs. "I, I don't know," he said before looking back to the array. He reached out and nervously ran his fingers over one of the photographs. He imagined the feel of flesh under his fingers and felt a thrill course through him, unlike anything he had felt since his first experience. "Just wish I could afford all of them, they would definitely be an asset."

Chris looked briefly at Tom then at the photographs again and sighed. Could he really do this? With a flush of guilt he pulled his hand and eyes away from the images in front of him. What was he thinking? He ran his fingers through his hair and felt his sweat glands spring into action. What would his wife say if she found out? He would have to make sure that she never did.

Tom nodded at the photograph which had captured the attention of the young man opposite him. "She's a beauty, that one."

Chris looked down at the photograph again, and smiled. She had good features, and legs to die for.

"She's young, and she's clean. Never been under anyone. If you get my meaning," Tom smirked, and glanced around the nearly empty room. "I guess that would make her a work-virgin." His chuckle, at what he thought to be good joke, came out like a strangled goose.

Startled by both the sound and this revelation, Chris looked aghast at Tom.

"What I mean," Tom gave an embarrassed cough. "She is ripe for you to train her however you want," his laugh this time was a controlled giggle.

By now Chris was wondering if he was doing the right thing, but as the saying goes, the die had been cast, no matter what happened after this, he was committed now. Had been from the moment he saw her photograph. He knew that he was looking at a tidy piece of action and with good management—he unconsciously rubbed his hands together at this prospect—his investment would be profitable. He slowly nodded his head. He didn't want to appear too enthusiastic, after all Tom might put the price up if he knew how much he desired her.

But Tom wasn't fooled. He knew that he had made a sale. The one in the photograph that Chris was once more caressing was the best he had on offer, and would nett him a handy sum, even in years to come, if Chris trained her well. Which he hoped he would, seeing as how he had not effected a background check on the man opposite. He had ridden with his gut on this on. But habit dictated that he stick to the drill and use his usual spiel.

"You sure about this then are you? Don' wan' ya to feel pressured. Once you pay, she's yours. All care and all responsibility. No coming back."

Chris' heart was pounding as he contemplated what he was about to do. He had never been one to keep a secret, and certainly not from those close to him and who knew him, but if he followed through with this ... It was a big step, and one that he found himself immune to refusing. He looked at Tom and, not trusting his voice, nodded once more.

Tom beamed, half stood up and leaned across the table arm out ready to shake on the deal. "Good on ya. You won't be sorry."

Chris gulped as he shook the other man's congratulatory hand, and smiled. He had done it. He couldn't believe that he had accomplished his long-held dream.

"I think this calls for something better than beer. 'ere!" Tom called out to a passing barmaid, "Get us a bottle of champagne will ya love?"

She glanced at the photos between the two men and shook her head. "Men. You're all the same. Champagne coming up. And less of the 'love' thank you 'mate.'"

Tom settled back in his chair, relaxed now that the deal had been settled. He beamed at Chris. "Now, tell me, what's a man like you doing getting into this game then?"

Chris, not sure if it was euphoria or remorse that he was feeling, wondered where to start, it had been such a long time coming. He stretched his arms out and grabbed the edge of the table. He made a face as his fingers encountered the sticky surface. He lowered his head and shook it in embarrassment.

"It's just something that I have wanted to do. Ever since I first knew about it. I've fantasised about having one of my own. And the money that I could get from her."

Tom smiled. He had seen and heard it all before. Possession became an addiction. An addiction that was very hard to break. No AA meeting for the likes of these victims. A very sad business. But hey, it kept the wolf from his door, so he wasn't about to complain.

"What are you going to call her then?" He put both hands up and out in a stopping wave. "Not her name-name. I mean, what's her *professional* name going to be? I like to keep track of things like that, if you know what I mean."

"Well, as I told you earlier, this is something that I have wanted for a long time, so I want her name to reflect that," Chris pulled some forms towards him and scanned through them till he found what he was looking for, then tapping his finger on one entry. "It says here that she is a Heartbeater; her sister is Lady's Heart and her dam is Sapphire." He looked at Tom. "Any sibling to Lady's Heart has got to be a winner. So I am going to call her," he sat up straight, took a deep breath, looked the businessman in the eye and beamed triumphantly. "My Heart's Desire."

HOME FOR CHRISTMAS

Norma Smyth

Estelle King sipped her cappuccino slowly, enjoying the busy scene around her. Basically, Hamilton was still much as she remembered it. The Pavement Cafe was one of the changes that had been made over the last five years. The trees in Garden Place were lovely, fresh and heavy with leaf. People were still enjoying the respite offered from work and heat, workers eating sandwiches out of paper bags, reading books or languidly watching the world go by. Children wading and splashing in the shallow pools brought a nostalgic smile to her still beautiful lips. It was a clear sunny day. "Please hold over for Christmas," she whispered. "Just one more day."

"Estelle! Is it really you?" A gravelly voice jerked her back to reality. She raised startled eyes and looked straight into piercing blue eyes, set beneath craggy brows in a pleasant sun-tanned face.

"Richard!" Estelle couldn't speak for sheer amazement. She was stunned. Her breath came in gasps as she gazed at him. The man she had been totally in love with, who she had not seen for over five years, but with whom, she knew instantly, she was still deeply in love.

"May I sit down?"

"Of course." Estelle waved her hand vaguely in the direction of a chair. "Do you want coffee?"

"Yes, but I'll get it. I carry money these days."

They smiled in memory of the times he had felt in his pocket for his wallet only to find it was still in his briefcase in his car.

"It's been a long time." Estelle was pleased that she actually found her voice.

Richard leaned forward and studied her intently.

"Hey, not so close." Estelle laughed and moved back into her chair. "It's been ages, and time has moved on. Wrinkles have moved in."

"You're still very beautiful," He said quietly. "Just as I remember."

Estelle found herself blushing. He had always had this ability to make her blush; to feel young and beautiful.

"That was a very long time ago, Richard. We've both moved on."

"I know." Richard's voice was so low she had to strain to hear what he said. "It was necessary, but it wasn't easy. One's sense of commitment makes life difficult at times, but I've never forgotten your smile, how special you made me feel, and how it felt, holding you. You are still so beautiful. The years have been kind to you."

"Kind? Richard, stop! It wasn't long after we came to our senses that David died. Was that kind? I was devastated. Apart from my falling in love with you, David and I had a good marriage. We've all missed him dreadfully but we've coped, and got on with our lives."

"I'm sorry. I had no idea that David had died. Do you still live in the same place? Do you still live in Hamilton?"

"No, I sold up years ago. I've been out of the country for some time."

"And you're living back here now?"

"No, I've come home for Christmas. Oh, good heavens, I've just realised the time. I told Joanne I would not be long, and I've been here hours absorbing the atmosphere. I must go. It's been good seeing you." Estelle pushed her chair back and stood up.

"Estelle, don't run off. Can I see you again?" Richard rose to his feet.

"Is there any point?" she asked gently. "Haven't we both moved on? Look I really must go."

"Please."

"Well," she said, thinking quickly. "I'll be here at noon a week today."

"I'll look forward to that." Richard leaned over and brushed her cheek with his lips.

Estelle drew a sharp breath at his familiar touch and the scent of his skin, then smiled briefly and quickly disappeared into the throng of shoppers.

It was Richard's turned to sit back and gaze and unseeingly at the view. It seemed so long ago that he and Estelle had met. The attraction had been instant but only the odd smile and polite good morning had been shared until they met in the street that unforgettable day.

"Hello!" Estelle had exclaimed spontaneously. "I haven't seen you for ages."

"I've been away, in the States. Just arrived back and trying to make a few decisions."

"Decisions?"

"Yes, whether to stay here or go back to the UK, pros and cons, that sort of thing. Say, are you free for coffee?"

"Yes, I'd love one. Thank you."

That had been the start. His heart had done a flip. Why? He was in a reasonable marriage. She was gorgeous, blonde, smooth hair, good skin, lovely smile, a cup of coffee could do no harm. Famous last words. They had a brief, passionate, tempestuous affair, the intensity of which overwhelmed them both until, reluctantly, they faced up to family commitments which were receding into the distance. They had agreed they could not meet again. It was then that Richard decided to once more leave New Zealand. Life had been full, good times and bad, but he had never forgotten Estelle. He could not believe his good fortune in meeting her today. Trim figure still, perhaps slightly more rounded, same lovely smile and personality. I'm still in love with her. I've never stopped loving her. She doesn't know Kate was killed in a car accident. I must see her again, must get in touch with her. I don't want to wait till next week.

Estelle parked in the driveway of her daughter and son-in-law's home and sat quietly, still in a daze. 'I don't believe this. People my age don't have the feelings I've got. Do they? Richard looks great. I love him, I've never stopped. How juvenile. Grow up!' Estelle became aware of a face at the car window. "Oh, Joanne, you startled me."

"You startled me, mum. You've been sitting out here for ages – on another planet I would say. How about coming back to earth?"

Estelle smiled at her daughter's zany type of humour. "Sorry, love. Just ran into an old friend and it brought back memories."

"Anyone I know?"

"No, no-one you know. Anyway, what about a coffee?" Regardless of the fact that she had already drunk gallons. "Do you think you could manage one?"

"Of course. Gordon will be home soon and we'll have a gin and tonic then, but coffee now will be great."

Estelle leaned back against the kitchen bench and watched Joanne bustle around the kitchen preparing coffee. She was quite drained from her encounter with Richard but knew she had to put all thoughts of it behind her. She was here to see her family, she owed it to them to give them her entire attention. "Now that I've got going into the city out of my system what can I do to help with Christmas preparations?"

"Not a thing, dear Mother. The children have decorated the Christmas tree beautifully, the presents are all wrapped, Christmas dinner is organised, and it's Christmas Day tomorrow. Just enjoy being in the bosom of your beloved family. So there! But now down to something serious."

Estelle raised her eyebrows. What was coming? What could be so serious?

"Now, Mother." Joanne's favourite way of addressing Estelle when she wanted to make a point. "Are you home to stay, or are you once again going away? Sorry, that's being flippant. Seriously, are you going back to Australia? This is the first time you've been home since Dad died. No, don't say anything. We all know you stayed and helped us get through our grief, as well as your own, but you have been away for a long time and we'd love to have you here on a permanent basis."

Estelle looked steadily at her daughter. "Jo, I know I've been away for a long time but I needed that time. Things had been difficult between your father and me but I was so pleased our last few months together were so good. I've taken leave from my job. It's there for me if I want to go back, but now, as you suggest, let's enjoy being a family."

Christmas Eve was a great time to enjoy the family. The excitement of the children was delightful. Six-year old Lisa and eight-year old Jason bustled around preparing a plate of Christmas cake and a glass of lemonade for Santa Claus, before singing a Christmas carol and heading off to bed. They had been told that Santa Claus enjoyed coming to little people who go to bed early and by the time they listened to a bedtime story their eyes were closed and their breathing even.

Christmas morning was a very, very, early morning. Estelle groaned as she heard excited squeaks coming from the children. 'What was the time? 4:30 a.m.' Next moment there was a scrabble at her door and Lisa looked in. "Gran, do you want to see what Santa brought me?"

'Do I have to?' thought Estelle, then checked herself. "Of course, darling. I'd love to see what you've got. Come and get into bed with me. Where's Jason?"

"He's talking to mum and dad but I wanted to see you first." Lisa snuggled up close and started pulling things out of her Christmas stocking.

By 7:30 the entire family was assembled in the family room.

"Fruit juice, scrambled eggs and toast for everyone," said Joanne firmly. "There'll be plenty of party food during the day, and as soon as Auntie Val and Uncle Mike and the family arrive we'll have morning snacks and open our presents. So breakfast, showers, then get dressed.

"Mum," cried Val, Estelle's elder daughter, as she and her family arrived for the day. "Great to see you. I've missed you. I've wanted to be here but things have been frantic. We will have to make time just for us after the festivities."

"Indeed we will," Estelle said as they hugged closely. "Telephones and emails are great, but they don't replace the human contact."

Estelle revelled in the presence of her family. It was interesting to note the changes in them all. The children had developed their own personalities, and she was intrigued with their knowledge and ability. Her daughters had matured. It was good to see them secure in their own environment, with their husbands so different, their different ways of coping with life, but overall there was a good strong family feeling. It was wonderful to be home for Christmas. Perhaps she had been selfish being away so long.

"Oh boy." Joanne sank into a chair and stretched hugely. "Gordon, I'd love a glass of wine – to enjoy in peace and quiet after the wild zoo atmosphere we've had here today. It's been a wonderful day but it's good to have the kids in bed and the house to ourselves. Oh blast. Who's phoning at this hour?" She reached lazily for the telephone. "Hello, Joanne speaking." She sat up quickly. "Yes, yes, she's here. Who is this? Oh, one moment. For you mum. Richard Barton."

Estelle raised her eyebrows although her heart leapt. "Richard, hello, this is a surprise. I didn't know you knew where to contact me? Of course, I'd forgotten I'd shown you years ago where Jo worked. Very enterprising of you. Yes thanks, we've had a great day. It's been good being with the family."

Estelle hoped she sounded calmer than she felt. Richard's voice still had the power to make her go weak at the knees and want him fiercely. Totally ridiculous, and he had a wife anyway. "Have you had a good day? How are Kate and the family? What? Oh I'm sorry. How awful. Yes I'd like that. Give me your number and I'll call you tomorrow when I know what's happening here." She wrote the number down and repeated it. "Thanks Richard. Bye." She replaced the receiver and sat looking slightly stunned.

"Alright, Mother, spill the beans. Obviously someone out of your lurid past."

"Never a truer word," said Estelle bemusedly. "Richard Barton. We met through business years ago. He just told me his wife was killed in a car accident two years ago. How awful. I didn't know."

"You said 'Never a truer word' when I said someone out of your lurid past. You were good friends? Do you want to tell us about it?" asked Joanne gazing searchingly at her mother. There was more to this than just a simple friendship.

"Yes, I will tell you about it, and yes, we were very good friends, I met him very unexpectedly in the city yesterday and he asked to see me again. We were going to meet for coffee next week but I'll call him tomorrow. He remembered where you used to work and tracked me down through that, Jo."

"Great initiative shown. Why don't you phone him and ask him for a drink tonight, Mum? Why wait till tomorrow? Better still, I'll phone him. What's his name? Richard Barton? Now, where's that number? You wrote it down." Joanne picked up the scrap of paper with Richard's phone number on it and started to dial.

"Joanne, you're incorrigible. Gordon, make her put the phone down."

Gordon laughed. "Estelle, you know Joanne. When she makes her mind that's it. You should know, you produced her, you brought her up."

"Tried to," muttered Estelle.

"Richard Barton? Oh good. Joanne Byford here, Estelle King's daughter. Would you like to join us for a drink tonight? Wonderful, come as soon as you can. You know where to come? See you soon. Goodbye." She replaced the receiver. "He's coming, he was surprised, but he'll be here shortly."

"Oh Jo, what would one do with you? What a thing to do. I would have phoned him tomorrow," said Estelle crossly.

"Mum, we don't know how long you'll be here, you don't know seem to know either. Why waste time? I think there is something special and very mysterious about Mr. Richard Barton."

"Oh, you would, wouldn't you Madam? Well, I'll tell you the whole sordid story. We were lovers briefly until we came to our senses and realised we had too much to lose so we said goodbye. It wasn't an easy time. I went on holiday and Richard moved to the UK. As I said before, your father and I had been having a pretty difficult time, but after Richard left we got back on a comfortable basis and had a good marriage right up until David died. I grieved for your father, and I was grieving for Richard too, so I was bereft after your father's death. I needed to get away."

At that moment a car pulled into the drive. "Must be him." said Gordon. "Not expecting anyone else." He moved out to the front door. "Hi, I'm Gordon, Estelle's son-in-law. You must be Richard. Come on through."

Richard moved into the lounge. "Estelle, I didn't dream of seeing you again quite so soon but this is wonderful." He kissed her gently on the cheek.

Joanne looked critically at the man she now knew had been her mother's lover. She liked what she saw. He looked a real man, tanned, trim, craggy, nice face.

"You must be Joanne." He turned smilingly towards her. "Thanks for calling me. Your mother and I were friends years ago and it's been great catching up with her. A lot has happened since we last met and I'd like to make up for lost time."

"You live in the UK?" queried Joanne. "You are going back soon?"

"No, I'm back in New Zealand for good. I went over some years ago but my family couldn't settle and came back to New Zealand after only a few months. I stayed on but my wife was killed in a car accident so I came home to be with the family. After a while I realised I was happy here and didn't want to go back."

"We're just waiting for Mum to decide whether she's staying or going. We hope she's staying but it is her decision. You love it in Australia, don't you Mum?" queried Joanne.

"Yes I do. Australia has been good for me. It was exactly what I needed at the time."

"At the time," said Richard looking at Estelle very closely. "You've come home for Christmas. Maybe I could make you decide to stay so that you are already home for Christmas next year."

Joanne and Gordon looked at the two older people, obviously totally absorbed in each other, then exchanged knowing smiles. Estelle would not be going very far away at all.

"Gordon, Richard hasn't got a drink and I want to make a toast." Gordon poured a glass of Chardonnay and Joanne continued "My toast is to us all, we've all had a wonderful Christmas. It's obvious that you two know each other very well and I'm sure, Richard, that Gordon joins me in saying we look forward to getting to know you, and that you and mother will both be home for Christmas with us next year."

HORATIO

Jennifer Lilly

Captain Horatio Greenway RAN (retired) yawned and stretched. He fumbled for the curtain and looked out the port-hole window. He sat bolt upright.

"What the...?" he asked. But no one answered and so he leapt out of bed. He rummaged under the bed for his slippers and shuffled across to the door. There he pulled his dressing gown off the hook and, wrapping it around his rotund waist, made for the stairs.

Never before had he seen such a sight in the small fishing harbour. He wondered what had brought it here. He carefully walked down the stairs, one step at a time, and cursed the feebleness of his age.

For a few minutes he forgot about his errand and concentrated on the carpet, trying to follow its intricate pattern of flowers and leaves as they meandered down the stairs. It had been on the stairs when they had bought the house. He had wanted to tear it up straight away, but Milly had said no. Milly had loved their home just the way it was, and that was all that mattered to him. Then, when he had come back from the sea for the last time, and Milly was no longer there, he had not had the heart to change it, or anything else. Her ghost still walked the rooms, and she had loved everything about the place.

Still, Milly or no Milly, he really must do something about the carpet; it was nearly thread bare, and it would never do to catch his foot in a tear and end up arse over apex to the bottom. He wasn't ready to meet his Milly. Not yet.

He reached the bottom of the stairs and stood, his chest wheezing. It was still there; he could see it through the French doors in the dining room on his left. He ran his trembling hands through his thatch of thick white hair and waited impatiently. There should be no need to hurry, it would wait until the pain in his chest subsided and his breathing had stabilized. It had to.

The pain in his chest eased and he walked out the door into the wind. Funny, when he had looked out the window it had not appeared to be windy, but now there was a fierce breeze racing in from the sea. He stood still, straightened as much as his old bones would allow, and breathed in the fresh salty smell of the Southern Ocean. There was no other smell quite like it. Beautiful.

He set off at as brisk a pace as he felt permissible in the direction of the harbour. He wondered why no one else appeared to be interested in it. There were people about, but it was as though they could not see it. It was bloody big enough that a bloody blue whale would trip over it. But no one appeared to notice it. Hey! Look over there! He wanted to yell, but felt that no one would take any notice of him either. So he kept quiet and quickened his pace. The Blue Peter was flying. He had to get there before she sailed. He had to.

He stopped to catch his breath again. She was a beautiful ship. Her fluid lines and full sails made his heart ache, and his throat swell with emotion. He remembered long ago, in his youth, boyhood actually, seeing such ships as this and being inspired to go to sea. He had spent his waking hours reading about the new clipper ships, and dreaming of far off places. The shipwrecks didn't faze him. They were part of the glamour, along with Robinson Crusoe. But until he had been old enough to leave school he had had to be content with dreams and a little dinghy.

A wiff of smoke issued from her bow, and a boom brought Horatio Greenway RAN (retired) out of his reminiscing. He straightened again, puffed out his chest, and pulled his dressing gown closer to him. Stiffly he saluted the magnificent sailing boat then majestically walked towards her. Duty called.

As an apparition King Neptune appeared on the gangway. Horatio beamed in recognition as Milly, in all her fancy finery slowly walked towards him. Or flopped rather. Milly had always had an unfortunate walk. Age and weight had done little to improve it. She was oversized to say the least, and she would waddle, feet splayed apart under her body, toes pointing at ten to two. But here she was, King Neptune. Green and gold cellophane ringlets cascading to her waist. Goggles and snorkel obscuring her face and a creation of god only knew what camouflaging her figure. And, protruding from beneath all this, the reason for the 'flop-flop' which accompanied her, were the largest sized pair of flippers he had ever set eyes on.

He remembered the occasion well. His retirement farewell. The officers and crew on his last command had decided to have a fancy-dress party before his last sailing. Naturally it had a nautical theme. Milly had kept her costume a surprise from him until they had been ready to attend. He had been flabbergasted, to say the least.

There she had stood, at the top of the stairs with their carpeted flowers flowing down to meet him. A comical figure looming above him. His heart had swelled at the sight of her and he had been unable to laugh at her. Not that she would have minded. She knew that she was obese, and it didn't worry her. She had looked truly majestic, like she did now sailing towards him in Neptune's full finery. It was the flippers that undid it. Fl-op, fl-op, as each foot swung in a frog arc and splatted the ground beneath her. This time he could not contain himself, and he burst out laughing.

Doubled up in a spasm of coughing Horatio did not see the apparition fade. He did not hear the approach of rapid footsteps. Slowly he sunk to his knees, clutching his chest as he tried to catch his breath.

"Uncle!"

"Horatio!"

They cried in unison, running hard towards him. They bent down, either side of him and slowly raised him to his feet.

"Uncle!"

A young anxious voice reached through to him, and he smiled.

"Take it nice and slow Horatio, we don't want you to do any damage to yourself do we old man?"

Horatio tried to shake himself free from his captors, "Old man?" he spat. "Who do you think you are calling 'old man'? Why you little..."

The other man laughed, "Listen here big brother, if I can be called old at seventy-six, I think you qualify."

"But Uncle Horatio, what are you doing out here in your night clothes and all?"

Horatio Greenway RAN (retired) looked down at his great-niece, straightened himself up and smiled at her.

"Why I've come out to see this..." he turned to face the harbour, and his outstretched arm dropped to his side. "Oh." His body sagged as he took in the gentle swell, the seagulls lazily circling the moored yachts and fishing boats. "I could have sworn that there was a sailing ship out there," he whispered quietly.

His brother and great-niece laughed.

"Sorry old salt," said his brother, "you're a day early. She doesn't arrive until tomorrow."

"But I saw her. She was there. And so was Milly. I saw her, Jack." He turned to his younger brother anxiously, "Milly was there I tell you."

Jack and his niece exchanged looks.

"I saw her on the ship. Do you remember the last fancy dress party we went to Jack? Well Milly was dressed like she was then. Do you remember?" Horatio started to laugh again.

"Take it easy Uncle Horatio. Don't excite yourself. You know what the doctor said."

"Doctor be damned! I saw my Milly on that ship and I'll get excited if I want to!" he said as he allowed himself to be slowly led back to the house.

INVISIBLE TOUCH

Jennifer Lilly

The hair along Blue's back rose and his ears pricked up. He whined and Matthew dropped his hand to rest on his head, feeling the raised hair. He looked up from the newspaper he was reading in time to see the yellowed lace curtains fall back against the windows. He was sure he had closed them.

"It's all right Blue, it's just the wind. Must have come in under the door, or something." Matthew tried to sound convincing, for his own sake as much as to placate the Kelpie which had once more settled down beside him. He watched as the flames from the dying fire licked at the tired piece of wood on the grate.

"Soon be time for bed Blue" he said and returned to reading the sports section of the paper.

In the hall the old grandfather clock chimed eleven. Matthew sighed, rubbed his strong fingers through his now sparse hair, yawned, and eased himself out of the commodious armchair. He ambled over to the fire, squatted down and scattered the remaining coals. He watched as they first glowed bright red and then slowly dulled and frosted before turning black. He scratched Blue behind the ear.

"Fire's out, now it's your turn."

Blue wagged his tail.

As Matthew rose, he saw the photograph of his parents on the dusty mantelpiece. He picked it up and gazed at it and remembered when the house had rung with life. Everyone was gone now. It was just him. Even his nephews' visits were infrequent now that they had lives of their own. He sighed, replaced his parents on the mantle, and moved towards the door, Blue at his heels. He paused in the doorway and looked around the room. A well-worn room that had been loved and lived in for decades was now left forlorn to comfort him after a hard day's work. He glanced at the windows, yes, they were all shut. He turned off the light and padded down the hall. The waning moon shining through the window at the end illuminated the familiar way to the kitchen. The warmth from the wood stove made a cheerier welcome than the greasy dishes which greeted Matthew when he turned on the light. He tried to avoid looking at them as they teetered haphazardly by the sink. They could wait till morning, he thought as he scraped chop bones off his dinner plate and onto an old newspaper. There weren't as many scraps these days either, now that everyone was all gone, Matthew thought as he heaped dry dog food on top of the scraps.

"Come on Blue," Matthew said as he picked up the newspaper corners and, shouldering aside the fly-wire door, carried Blue's tea outside. The dog followed. While Matthew put on his boots Blue raced to where his empty dish lay, barking and cavorting. Matthew fed Blue, chained him up beside his kennel and scratched him behind the ears again.

"See you in the morning Blue," Matthew said and walked back to the house. Matthew took off his boots and went inside, closing the heavy kitchen door behind him. He looked at the dishes, and then at the clock above the stove. He shoved up the sleeves of his handknitted jumper, and set about washing the dishes and cleaning the kitchen for the next day. He smiled ruefully to himself, it was already the next day. He couldn't justify delaying going to bed much longer, not when the cows would be waiting for him before dawn. With the last of the dished put away and the stove stoked for the night Matthew turned off the light and made his way to bed.

The grandfather clock in the hall struck one as a soft flurry of warm air eddied around the dead ashes in the fireplace. A cascade of silken hair fell around her shoulders and down her back as she stood before the hearth. She looked at the photograph of two elderly people, watching them as they watched her. She picked up the photograph and placed it face down on the mantle. She must remember to right it before she left.

She looked around the room. The same tired chintz-covered table near the bookcase, still overstuffed with racing memorabilia and leather-bound books. No additions. Her fingers played along the top of the piano and she wondered if it was ever played now. There had been a few happy moments spent around the old upright. Laughter in the air and a song in the heart. The springs of the sofa protested slightly as she lowered herself into its soft bulk and she drank in the memories. She saw his pipe lying on the coffee table beside his chair. The tobacco tin beside it. She picked up the pipe and caressed the smooth bowl against her palm. She got up and left the room, wincing as the floorboards creaked beneath her. She could no longer remember which ones to avoid. She placed the pipe on the hall stand and silently left the house. An owl called from the old cypress tree, and a dog whimpered in its sleep.

Matthew didn't need an alarm clock. After years of milking his body was attuned to the need of the cows and he was at the dairy as the first of the cows ambled to the gate. They were creatures of habit as much as he, he thought as he switched on the lights, sent Blue out to round up the stragglers, and opened the gate to let the first of the cows in to the stalls. It was comforting to have the familiar sights, and sounds and smells around him as he drifted into full wakefulness. The lack of sleep didn't worry him; work wasn't so demanding now that he had reduced the size of the herd, and was able to cope with the milking on his own. Had there ever been a time when he hadn't been on his own? Even when everyone had been here, he'd still been on his own. Shame and guilt prevented him from consciously remembering when he hadn't felt alone. He wanted to forget.

He jumped back as a cow kicked out when he tried to put the cups on her. He swore and thumped her on the rump. She bellowed and backed out of the stall, causing the other cows to shuffle uneasily in the yard outside. Matthew shouted at Blue to keep order. The cows were fidgety today, and so was Blue. It did not bode well for it being a good day. Matthew couldn't wait to return to the house. Maybe breakfast, and a quiet sit in the lounge with the morning papers and mail would help right the day. He doubted it, but he could always hope.

After breakfast Matthew wandered down to the front gate and collected the mail and newspaper. Blue had not followed him, but had remained sniffing around the front door and along the veranda. Matthew hadn't noticed. He returned to the house and flopped into his chair, opened the newspaper to the sports section and reached for his pipe. Puzzled at not finding it he glanced at the table. His tobacco tin was there, but not the pipe. He couldn't remember taking it out of the room. He wriggled on the chair and took a packet of chewing gum out of his shirt pocket and put two sugar coated slabs into his mouth. Chewing furiously he ripped open the few envelopes that had come in the mail. Nothing interesting. No one wrote to him. Not now. Matthew could hear Blue whining by the front door. He supposed he had better let him in. Better still, he ought to go out and get some work done.

Even though much of the land had been sold off he could still walk around the boundary fence and pretend to be occupied. Or he could always go for a ride. That used to calm his nerves.

Blue's whines were now quite agitated. He got up and walked down the hall towards the rarely used front door, his footsteps echoing across the bare tiles. His foot knocked against the hall stand. He looked down and saw his pipe. Puzzled, he picked it up and turned it over several times. He shrugged his broad shoulders, and put the pipe into his mouth, absently drawing on it.

"Be right there Blue," he called and returned to the lounge for his tobacco. He filled his pipe, felt for the matches in his pocket, then went back to where the anxious dog was waiting outside the front door. Puzzled Matthew opened the door but could see nothing to have caused Blue to be concerned. "What's up fella?" He scratched the dog behind the ears. "Like to come for a ride with me? Come on. Better than mooching around here all day."

Matthew and Blue made their way to the tack shed. Matthew loaded himself up with saddle, bridle, and blanket. "Mustn't forget the oats now must we?" he said, going to the feed bins. Blue whined and Matthew looked around. A small puff of dust drifted into the shed and the door blew shut. "Only the wind, silly!" Matthew said to the dog, reaching into one of the bins and taking out a chipped enamel mug full of oats. He wondered at the strange, yet disturbingly familiar fragrance that seemed to fill the room. He shook his head. "Come on Blue, let's get out of here and go for that ride."

When they reached the horse paddock Matthew's horse was waiting patiently at the gate for him, ready to be saddled. Maybe it was going to be a good day after all, Matthew thought to himself as he lifted himself onto the mare's back and called to Blue.

The morning mist was rising, and patches of clear blue could be seen struggling to pierce it. Soon it would be sunny and it might even warm up. For the first time that morning Matthew began to feel happy. He took the matches out of his pocket and lit his pipe. Blue trotted beside him. As they entered a clump of trees the mare shied. Matthew grappled with the reins and regained control. He looked to see what had spooked the horse, but could see nothing. There was only the slight murmur of the breeze in the trees, and the vaguely familiar smell. He looked around for Blue – he had started for home. Matthew decided that that was where he should be headed too.

After attending to the mare, Matthew went into the house to prepare a late lunch. As he prepared his meal he noticed that the kettle was not where he normally kept it on the stove. He put it on the stove to heat up but it immediately started to sing. Matthew stared, puzzled. He did not remember previously putting it on the hob. It must be the tablets he was on. Normally he wasn't so forgetful. Maybe he should cut back on the dosage. He poured himself a cup of tea and sat down to eat before returning to the dairy to prepare for the evening's milking.

His days were predictable—the same daily going from house to dairy and back again, repeated morning and evening. There was little in his life these days to vary the pattern. Occasionally he might visit the local hotel, but even that had lost its pallid glamour over the years. The owners changed as frequently as his brother changed cars.

Yet, despite this outward monotony, he was becoming increasingly unsettled. Little things kept creeping up and attacking him when and where he least expected them. His trophies were persistently fiddled with. He could never find anything in the kitchen. Doors opened and closed of their own accord. The floorboards creaked more than the changing weather warranted, and the night birds were driving him mad with their incessant chatter. Maybe he was losing his grasp on reality. That is what had happened to his mother before the Good Lord saw fit to call her home. She'd kept forgetting where she put things, and what was what. That programme on the T.V., *Mother and Son*, with Ruth Cracknell, was often too close to home to be funny. Still, he mustn't think ill of the dead. Yet he hoped that he wasn't falling into senile decline. Who would milk the cows if something happened to him? No one was interested in the farm now, and he would certainly never leave it and move into town.

These thoughts flooded Matthew's mind one evening when he was in the dairy and they chased each other in irritating circles.

Thankfully the cows were placid, and the milking went without hitch. The last cow weaved her way out of the yard to join the rest of the herd. Blue followed her. Matthew gratefully set about cleaning the dairy, the more demanding physical work was less conducive to melodramatic thought than the soporific swoosh of the milking machines.

The gate in the yards squeaked. Matthew thought it was Blue and didn't look up. A waft of air rippled the water on the concrete floor, and that fragrance lingered briefly around Matthew and was gone. The dairy door shut with undeniable finality and the skin on Matthew's back crept in waves. He was reminded of Blue's hair bristling the other night. Still, he was a grown man, and he shouldn't let little disturbances worry him. He returned to hosing down and sweeping out the dairy.

When he had finished, Matthew left the dairy and whistled to Blue. Together they chased their narrow shadows over the stony track to the house. Matthew removed his boots outside the back door and placed them side by side next to the worn mat. Recently they had taken to wandering. Every morning it was a guessing game as to where he would find them. He'd thought of nailing them to the floor, but the back porch was concrete. To take them off elsewhere was worse than hunting for them, as he could never remember where he'd put them. At least this way they were always to be found in logical places—by the fire, under his bed, on the shoe box. He wondered where he would find them the next morning.

He rubbed Blue's head and together they went inside. Blue made for the stove and lay down. Matthew washed his hands and went to the fridge for a cold beer. He pulled the tab and sat heavily onto a wooden chair. It had been a tiring day, one way or another, and he was pleased to be finished. He got up and turned on the radio and busied himself in preparing a frugal meal of sandwiches. Suddenly the radio faded and there was silence. The lights remained on so it wasn't the generator. Matthew looked at the radio, then at Blue.

"Well Blue, what do you make of that?" He twiddled the knobs and slapped his hand down on the top of the set several times and tried the knobs again. The radio was dead. Matthew went back to making his dinner. A low murmur caught on the breeze that played through the kitchen. Matthew looked up and the radio burst into life. He gaped. Blue sat up and whined. Outside a kookaburra laughed. Matthew strode over to the radio and viscously turned the set off. He grabbed his plate in one hand, and a mug of hot black tea in the other and strode out of the room and into the lounge. The tea slopped over his hand. He cursed as the scalding liquid washed his fist and spread down his wrist. He put the mug down beside his down-turned parents. He looked at the photograph, and righting it, wondered how long it had been lying flat on the mantelpiece, and how it had got to be like that. He picked up his mug and settled into the armchair. Blue came and sat by his feet, chin on his knees.

"Been an interesting day, hasn't it Blue? What'd you make of it all? Not much cop really, wouldn't you agree? Let's hope tomorrow brings better."

Blue wagged his tail, grinned as only a Kelpie can, and lay down across Matthew's feet. Matthew looked over at the fire. He should have lit it before he sat down for the evening. He felt settled, so fire could wait till he'd eaten though it would be cool soon.

He sighed, picked up his empty things and gently nudged the sleeping dog aside before getting up and taking the dishes out to the kitchen. The radio was on. Matthew frowned. He was sure that he had turned it off. He smiled as he listened to a Beatles song from the 60's. He put the dishes on the bench and, humming *Prudence*, picked up a box of matches, returned to the lounge and lit the fire. The pinecones leapt into flames and crackled in contrast to the spitting of the still slightly green kindling that he had thrown on earlier. Maybe he would listen to records tonight. There was never much on the television these days, he'd read all the papers, and the books on the shelves just didn't interest him. He rifled through the records stacked in the cupboard and selected three old Beatles albums. He stacked them on the turntable, glad he hadn't listened to his nephews' pleas to buy a new-fangled stereo with its fancy knobs and manual change of records, and settled back into his chair, with his pipe, and stared at the ceiling. Slowly he drifted into a blue haze of tobacco smoke.

The records ran their course and came to a stop. Matthew didn't move. Blue's ears pricked up in his sleep then relaxed. Outside a night bird could be heard. The flames in the fire flickered as the front door swayed open. Blue stirred in his sleep, sat up, and looked towards the door. A soft breeze carried the fragrance of spring flowers into the room and a light tread creaked the floorboards towards the lounge. Blue waited; his hair raised.

She appeared in the doorway and smiled at Blue who whined in greeting and settled down again. She walked over to Matthew, searching the face she had once known. Quietly she touched his cheek. His skin twitched and quickly she withdrew her hand, and smiled down at him. A hum could be heard from the radiogram. As she turned slowly towards it her hair flowed out in an arc and came to rest against her body. She knelt down and ran her hand along Blue's back before gliding over to where Matthew kept his record collection. She selected three records and put them on. Matthew, a smile on his face, didn't stop her.

She walked across to the bookcase and admired the trophies displayed there. She thought back to the highs and lows of her life, and of Matthew's. She picked up her favourite trophy, Matthew sighed. Slowly she faced him. He didn't move. She looked at the trophy in her hand. She hadn't been allowed to be there when he'd won that one. With a wry smile she misplaced it in the display, putting it in the front where she thought it belonged. She walked

over to the settee and sat opposite Matthew while the records played
in the background. As the last track came to an end she rose
gracefully and moved towards Matthew. She put her fingertips to
her lips and laid them against Matthew's, letting them rest there
briefly before quietly leaving the room. She paused at the door, let
her fingers wave to Matthew's parents, then to the sleeping Blue, and,
with a last lingering look at Matthew she was gone.

It wasn't until he heard his name being called that Matthew
woke. Blue, at his feet, was sitting up expectantly, so he hadn't been
dreaming. Someone had called his name. He leapt to his feet.

"Who's there?"

The dying embers in the grate winked in reply and a warm
fragrance flowed past him and the front door sighed as it shut.

"Who's there?"

There was still no answer.

"Did you hear it Blue?" Blue wagged his tail. "Come on then,
let's go and see who's about."

Matthew and Blue walked around the house several times,
calling to find the elusive visitor. Dissatisfied, yet having to admit
defeat, Matthew went back inside and prepared Blue's tea. After
feeding the dog and seeing him settled for the night he returned
to the lounge. As he went over to the radiogram and opened up
the cabinet he decided to double the dose of sleeping tablets and
try to get a good night's sleep. He lifted the arm of the player up
and over to the side. Gently holding either side of the records he
went to lift them off. They wouldn't move. He gripped them more
firmly and tried again. They would not budge. He scratched his head
and muttered to himself, glanced towards his parents and mentally
apologised for the profanities he'd uttered. He turned back to the
records and tried again. Nothing that he did would help those
records slide up and off the shaft. He could not raise them off the
turntable. He looked down at the top record. It wasn't a Beatles

record. He'd never seen it before. If the double dose didn't work tonight he'd have to go back to the doctor. Where were the records he'd put on? Frantically he looked around. He was no longer muttering to himself but cursing quite loudly. In desperation he grabbed his parents and slammed their grinning faces to the mantelpiece. He felt better and, cursing more eloquently, continued his frenetic search. Where were they? They could be under the top record, but he'd never know if he couldn't get them off the turntable. He dashed across to the player and, grabbing hold of the records went to wrench them off. Freely they sped up the shaft and flew out of his hands as he lost his footing on the scatter rug. He swore, then silence filled the room.

Matthew sat on the floor among the LPs. He picked up the closest—the one that had been on the top. It was *Invisible Touch* by Genesis. Genesis? Wasn't that a book in the Bible? What was it doing on a record? He'd have to listen to it one day. He heaved himself off the floor and, picking up the LPs, wondered how this particular album had come to be in the house. He took the pile over to the record cupboard and opened the door. Records tumbled out to greet his feet. Matthew left them all as they were, put the guard around the fireplace and went to bed. He was too tired to do any more tonight.

It had been a bad morning, the cows cantankerous and his temper short after another night of little sleep. He had to admit that the strange happenings were starting to get on his nerves. He was alone and for the first time since his parents had died and his brother and nephews had left the farm he was feeling the need to have someone, other than the radio announcer and the plastic people of late night television, to talk to him. There came a time in everyone's life when a dog just wasn't good enough. He would have to go back to the doctor.

Matthew followed Blue into the lounge and eased himself into his armchair. It was good to sit down. He reached for the large envelope that had arrived in the morning's mail. It was more of a parcel than an envelope, and quite heavy. He recognised neither the writing nor the postmark.

"Only one way to find out what this is about, hey Blue?" he said, fondling the dog's head. Blue licked his hand and settled down by his feet. Matthew opened the parcel and read:

Dearest Father,

He sat up, snatched the wrapping and looked again at the address. It was addressed to him. He looked at the date, he knew it wasn't April 1st, but who could be playing a joke on him? He turned back to the letter, his heart beating faster than was healthy.

Dearest Father,

I know this will come as a shock to you.

That was an understatement, he thought wryly.

I know the revelations were a shock to me. Pamela had hoped to keep what I'm sending you for a few more years yet, but time ran out for her. She died last week. I found this among her things and felt that she would like you to have it. There was also a letter which I am enclosing.

Hoping to meet you one day,

Love Susan.

Matthew sank back into the chair, unable to bring himself to reach for the remaining articles in his lap. His eyes stared blankly at the ceiling; his hands played on Blue's head. The grandfather clock in the hall struck 11 and still he sat. Finally he reached for the other letter, looked at the familiar writing and read:

She's yours now. She knows.

He laid it down and picked up the photograph album that had been beneath it. Slowly he turned the cover and tentatively looked at the front page. It showed a small monkey-like face swathed in pale pink blankets. The child's eyes were open and unfocused. A small fist was clenched against her chin. Her rosebud lips were pursed, as though sending a kiss across the page. Below it were the words:

-Susan Roberta Bartholomew Reid. 16.7.1970-

Matthew's eyes filled with tears as he thought back to 1970. The last time he had seen Pamela had been in 1969, just before Christmas.

As he turned the pages he watched Susan grow up and explore the world. Her first steps, Kindergarten, then school. Christmases and school concerts. Always smiling out at him. He wondered what Pamela had told her. About him; why she didn't have a father. Had she said her father was dead? Or that he didn't even know that she existed? His heart ached at the lost years. Why, Pamela? Why didn't you say? But he didn't need an answer to that, he knew. And she would have been right. He turned another page and was at Susan's confirmation. Then more photographs. Of her on a pony. As a proud Girl Guide. Winning races and playing the piano. High school and boyfriends. He found himself envious and jealous of her boyfriends. They knew her, and he never had. The last page showed a proud young woman holding a piece of paper beside a new car. It was Pamela smiling at him. The caption read:

- Susan and her driving licence. 18.7.88 –

So recent. Today was the 10th September. He closed the album and lent his head against the back of the chair and let his eyelids squeeze out the tears. What a fool he had been. All these years when he could have had life and love, enjoyment and a family. Wasted. Did he want to meet Susan? He honestly didn't know. Would he have wanted to meet Pamela again, after all these years? Probably he would have, even though it would have opened up wounds long suppressed and forgotten. Wounds and realisations that even now he did not know if he was prepared to face. The things that he had done in archaic obedience to his family instead of creating his own family. Pamela had tried to show him, but he hadn't been prepared to see. Hadn't been prepared to go against the family. Where had it got him? They had all left him. Did he want to meet a daughter he'd never known?

"Come on Blue, we're going for a ride." Matthew reverently placed the album and the letters on top of the newspaper on the table and made his way outside to the tack room then down to the horse paddock, where he saddled and mounted the mare. In a daze he walked the mare down the track towards the bush. Blue trotted calmly beside.

It was good to feel the rocking movement of the horse beneath him., He leant forward and rubbed his hand along her neck, feeling the warmth. He caught the sweet smell, peculiar to horses, that he loved so much. He'd loved Pamela, but not enough. He wondered how she had had the patience to put up with him and his treatment of her for as long as she had. He marvelled at how much it must have hurt her to leave. She must have known by that Christmas that she was carrying his child, yet she had had the strength, and the loyalty, not to tell. Would it have made any difference if she had? He thought back to that December and shook his head.

No, it would have made no difference. His family were adamant that she was not suitable for him, and he had gone along with them. They would not have wanted to know about the child, and Pamela would have been labelled as trapping him. No, she had done the right thing by leaving him in ignorance. Instead she had born his child, and the secret of his own weakness.

He decided that he would like to meet Susan. See if he could make her understand the agony and loneliness that he had suffered all these years. All these years without even knowing that she existed. All these years where his pride had over-ridden his guilt to such an extent that even after his parents had died, he had lacked the courage to try and find Pamela and make amends. Instead he had hidden his memories and cloistered himself in emptiness, believing that he had a full life, and was in need of nothing. He had thought he had been happy, alone, a man, his dog, and his work. He realised now that he had only been pretending. Maybe he could make it up to Pamela by befriending Susan. Now was his time to be a responsible parent.

He had reached a clearing in the bush. Pamela and he had ridden out here once. He looked around at the tall straight trees with the ferns growing between. The trees had been smaller then, but still impressive. Not that they had really noticed. They had been happy. He was happy now. He listened to the birds as they chattered to each other and watched Blue fossicking in some abandoned wombat hole. Matthew called him. He backed out, muzzle dirty. He looked up at Matthew, a grin on his face and tail wagging furiously.

"Come on Blue, we're going home. We're going to make a new friend."

Matthew turned his horse around, brought his heels that little bit closer to her flanks and started off down the track which led home. Suddenly the mare shied as an early snake slithered across the path. Matthew struggled to control her. Frantically he pulled on the reins. Speaking soothingly to her. The mare reared. Her front legs failed the air as she hobbled backwards. Blue raced around in the dust, yelping and barking encouragement. Matthew cursed the dog and cursed the mare. He pulled on the reins again, trying hard to turn the horse. Instead he hit his head on a low hanging branch.

He fell.

The horse, twisting with the pull of the reins fell and rolled on top of Matthew before she regained her footing. She shook herself, snorted, and wandered off to browse at some nearby grass. Blue came and sniffed at Matthew as he lay on the ground. Matthew didn't move. He licked Matthew's face. Matthew's eyes flickered briefly then opened.

"Hullo Blue" he whispered. Blue wagged his tail and yelped. Matthew winced as he tried to move. "Go home Blue, get help." He gasped for breath and coughed. Blue whined. "Go."

Blue looked at him and turned towards the farm. He stopped and looked back at Matthew, uncertain what to do. Matthew tried to sool him on, but he couldn't move his arm.

Reluctantly Blue left.

Matthew lay there and listened to the sounds which would be his only company until Blue returned with help. Whenever that would be. By twisting his head he could just make out the mare's tail as it flicked at the flies. He whistled to her. She didn't come. He could hear the birds courting in the trees. Maybe if he listened to them the numbness and pain would go away. He sighed and closed his eyes against the glare of the sun as it filtered through the leaves overhead.

When Matthew opened his eyes the sun was lower in the sky. He could hear the cows anxious to be let into the yards. What was he doing flat on his back? How long had he been there? He tried to get up. He couldn't. He sank back onto the ground and closed his eyes again. He had to get to the cows. He had to milk them. Mark wouldn't. Mark never did any work around the farm, and if he did it had to be done again. Mark usually had a reason to be somewhere else, usually with his family, when work had to be done. It was he, Matthew, who did everything, gave everything, but it was Mark who always managed to get everything, have a family, be somebody. Matthew had nothing, was no-one, had nobody. Pamela had tried to show him that, but he wouldn't listen. She had gone away. Where had it all got him?

Now he remembered what he was doing here. The horse had thrown him. That was hours ago. Where was Blue? He tried to call, but his mouth was too dry. He tried to raise his arm to see his watch, but it was too painful, and he gave up. There it was again. That disturbingly familiar scent. He heard the rustle of leaves and then someone calling his name. He opened his eyes and turned towards the voice as best he could. The setting sun hurt his eyes, and then he made out the faint silhouette of a person standing near his feet. He squinted, and tried to speak. No sound came out. The person came closer. The scent grew stronger. Of course! Pamela!

With a pang of regret he recognised that his defences, built up over the years, had indeed succeeded in repressing her memory. That was why he hadn't recognised her perfumed signature when the 'Happenings' had first started to appear and haunt him.

He tried to reach out to her. She smiled. She touched his face with the back of her fingers. How Matthew wished he could clasp them to him. But he couldn't move his wretched arms. He must have broken them when he fell. He was weary now, and his head hurt. Was he dreaming, or was Pamela really there?

She sat down beside Matthew and watched as he grappled with understanding the past weeks' events. And the past twenty years as well. Life had been hard on him. She had only wanted to share it, and help. She reached out and touched his cheek. His skin felt cold and clammy. She smiled at him. Her hair tumbled around her face and the sun cast a halo about her head. He tried to talk, but only his lips moved. He could still hear the cows, but they didn't matter anymore. Pamela was here.

The sun warmed her back as she knelt on the ground. It had been a dreary day. Not even the daffodils in their bright coats had helped lighten it. Her heart felt heavy and the distant roll of thunder echoed the bleakness of the moment. She raised her head and read the inscription on the stone.

Pamela Anne Reid.

1942 – 1988

Wearily she got to her feet and stood clasping her hands in front of her. She turned and watched as a bereaved family walked away from a newly filled grave. A solitary wreath graced the bare soil.

Slowly she picked her way through the cemetery to the new grave. A stone lay nearby waiting to be erected. Her fingers traced the words that her tear-filled eyes couldn't read.

Matthew Robert Bartholomew.

1932 – 1988

Slowly she turned and walked away. "I hope you can be happy together now, Mum, and Dad."

IT'S EITHER CLAIRE OR ME

Norma Smyth

I slammed the car door, fastened my seat belt, and turned on the ignition angrily. I fumed for a while then drove for the next hour, carefully mulling over the thoughts racing through my mind. I loved my husband but he had to realise I was not prepared to stay with him whilst he was involved with another woman. It was a calculated risk on my part, and I had no idea whether I would win or lose. I would give him several days to think about it and then expect my answer. I had always thought our life was bliss and that we would live life to the full.

Until the day I happened upon Jacob being passionately embraced by a small blonde, who gazed up at him adoringly. I froze in shock then walked away blindly, but very aware of her smug look as she saw me leave.

The next day she saw me. "Sally, I'm sorry about yesterday. Don't take it the wrong way. I admire Jacob for his ability and the rapport we share in our work together."

"Claire, I don't believe you. I thought we were friends. Now let's forget the hypocrisy, you go your way and I'll go mine." I turned on my heel and strode away, glancing only briefly at the astonished look on her face.

I had told Jacob I had not appreciated their clinch and would prefer that he had nothing more to do with Claire. I was amazed when he told me there was nothing between them, that he only had respect in her ability, and was happy to assist her in any way he could.

"Sorry, Jacob, doesn't work like that. It's either Claire or me. Over to you."

"Sally, come on!" he exclaimed. "I like the woman. I don't love her, or lust after her. Don't be like that."

I took him at his word, but the next week I heard him saying "Yes I'll join you for coffee. See you at the café tomorrow." I decided to check this out and walked into the dimly lit coffee lounge the next day. I ordered coffee and a lemon slice, and sat unobtrusively at the back of the café. Sure enough, they arrived together, deep in conversation, with Claire's cockney voice grating as usual, and her clutching his arm possessively.

I sat quietly until I could not stay any longer and I walked over to them when they stood up from their table, and Claire threw her arms around my husband.

"Well, well, caught on the spot!"

Claire jumped back and stammered "Sally, hello, I didn't see you here."

"That's obvious," I said coolly. "Having fun, Jacob?"

"Hi, Sally. Claire and I have just been discussing the exhibition she is setting up and we're off to examine the hall and I'll give her a few pointers. See you later."

"Not likely," I said bluntly. "I told you, either Claire or me. You've obviously chosen Claire so I'm off. I'm leaving the city but I'll come and sort things out with you in a while. Bye, for the pair of you."

I almost laughed at the expressions on their faces, but instead stalked out of the café into my car, and sped down the motorway, to visit friends in the country.

After an hour I realised I was close to my destination, and looked carefully to make my turn into the bumpy, winding, farm track up to the barn, where I pulled in, beeped the horn and prepared to wait until the farm dogs settled back into their kennels.

"Sally, love, great to see you. Come out of that car, so I can give you a big hug. Peter is pouring us a glass of wine, and I will be out soon to help with luggage."

I followed Geraldine into their house, where Peter engulfed me in a bear hug.

"How's my girl?"

"Bleeding at the moment, Pete. I've come to be pampered, and helped with decisions."

"Hold on, here's a wine. Sit down and we'll take this seriously," he said.

"Thanks, I need time to relax and think things through. I'll give you some insight into this situation and you can tell me what you think. Do I eat humble pie and stay with Jacob, or do I move out and make a new life for myself?"

"Come on, love, that's pretty serious. So put your feet up. Will be with you in a moment."

I nestled into a very comfortable armchair, and Pete and Geraldine sat together on a deep couch, asked questions, prompted me to tell them or, sympathised with me, then looked at the other side of the story.

"It's not necessarily an affair," said Geraldine. "Because they work in the same areas it may simply be a close rapport, respect, friendship. She's obviously not his type at all. You are!"

"That's what Jacob said. I know he enjoys the company of other women but I don't need him being cuddled before my eyes."

"Mm," said Pete. "Was it him cuddling her, or was she cuddling him?"

"Point taken. I was so angry I may not have seen the whole picture. I asked him on several occasions to stop seeing her. He was very uncomfortable about that but refused to upset her, not taking on board the fact that I was in a real mess, upset, and all set to do them both in."

"Okay girl," said Pete. "Enough of that. Now, Geraldine, how about dinner? A good meal and another glass of wine would be beneficial, and we'll give this more thought. Also, Sally, I've put your luggage in your room."

After the three days I had allowed myself to have with Pete and Geraldine I kissed them goodbye, thanked them for their help and headed back to the city. I concentrated on my driving and finally swung into our drive, then carried my suitcase into the guest room. I moved through to the lounge, turned on the gas heater, made myself a cup of tea, then sat down to read a local paper, when I heard the garage door open. My heart did a flip which surprised me, as I felt cool, calm and very collected. The door was opened and Jacob walked through into the lounge where I was sitting. He looked terrible, his complexion grey and drawn. He put his arm around me and said "Sally, don't leave me, I love you. I don't want anyone but you. Claire is a good friend but I've no wish for involvement with her or anyone else."

"Jacob, I've seen for myself how she wraps herself around you. I've been so upset, particularly when I asked you to break your ties with her, and you wouldn't. When I saw you together in a clinch, I just couldn't take any more. That was it."

"Sally, she sees me as her father figure, likes my advice my input into her work, and I've enjoyed it. There's no harm done."

"But what about me? You have been terribly casual about me wanting you to be with me."

A tear wended its way down my cheek, and I groped for my handkerchief. "I love you, and I don't want to leave you, but I don't want to see any more passionate embraces."

"They were never serious. Claire is just an affectionate little person, and she's no threat to you, but if I must walk away from her, I'll do so. Let's make a new start, lead a new life."

I snuggled into him as he wiped the tears from my cheeks. I felt a strong wave of love and believed we could start a new life together. All I needed was to have Claire totally out of my life. Better still if she would go home to her own father in England, and Jacob agreed that he would listen to me and love me in our new life.

LADY IN WAITING

Jacklyn Harris

This story was written in mid-1980s Australia when there was a general dislike of boat-people and Bruce Ruxton [an Australian ex-serviceman and President of the Victorian Returned and Services League] was very vocal in his opposition to Asian immigration.

It was a still day. The sun sparkled in the cloud dappled sky. A family of magpies chortled in the nearby peppercorn trees and the faint ripple of water told the world that the creek would run for a few more months, despite the lack of rain. A slow hum of expectancy from the little settlement wafted over the bare expanse of the much-misused oval and only added to the aggravation that Phyllis Daintree could feel seeping into her being.

She looked down at her hands. The ridges of her gold and bejewelled rings showed plainly through her cream-coloured gloves as her long and slender fingers drummed incessantly against the steering wheel of her metallic grey Volvo sedan. She looked out the windscreen. That was a mistake, she now realised.

Filthy vermin, she thought. Littering up the country. Just look at them! Scabby lot they are too. Even if they are playing marbles and have scuffed knees, they will never be Australian. Not with their black hair, swarthy skin, and slanted eyes. Poor boat people indeed! Hardly in the town a day and already they own half of it. It wouldn't have happened when I was growing up in the district, that's for certain.

The group of Vietnamese boys that she was watching were clustered around the traditional ally-ring which had laboriously been carved, over the generations, out of the dirt beneath the soft dust which covered the worn path. They were laughing and playing, tussling each other as they vied for the honour of being the winner. Scantily clothed in ragged trousers and shirts, they were barefooted and happy. In another time it could have easily been her brothers playing there.

The interior of the car suddenly became unbearable, the leather upholstery too claustrophobic. She would get out and stand. Besides, she thought, to stand would lessen the chances of getting her linen suit crushed beyond respectability. It is all too annoying. Some people!

Effortlessly she flowed out of the car and stood to let her tailored clothes fall into place about her. She looked at her watch. Thank God she wouldn't have to wait much longer, she thought as she brushed a fly away from her face.

Two young girls, pigtails flying, raced past her laughing and shrieking as they were pursued by a couple of the local boys.

Grubby things, children. No respect for their elders these days, she thought as she looked down at her feet neatly clad in elegant cream court shoes onto which the film of dust was slowly settling. Damn the children! Damn him!

She strode into the building. Oblivious to the immaculate iron lace work and the automatic doors. All Phyllis was aware of as her eyes took their time to adjust to the poorly lit interior was that the station was pokey and draughty; and it smelt. Phyllis stopped herself from wrinkling her nose and withdrew a lace handkerchief from her compact cream clutch purse and held that to her nose instead. What was the smell? It was more than fresh paint and disinfectant. A memory from when she had been a child floated into her mind. An era which she chose to forget, yet today seemed hellbent on haunting her.

Funny how smells bring back memories, no matter how well they have been buried, she thought as she was mentally carried back to a time of bashings and brawls; poverty and pain; anger and anguish. The smell that was now assaulting her nostrils was the smell of Sundays. The dank sodden aroma of grog-drenched debauchery the morning after. And her mother, God rest her soul, desperately trying to get them all ready for church and out of the house. She could still see her father slumped in the armchair, stubble thick on his spittle-flecked chin. The bottles, cigarettes, and newspapers strewn over the stain imbued carpet and the threadbare loose-sprung sofa. The smell of grog and newsprint hot from fish and chip dinners pervaded her memory.

Then she saw the source of the stench. A lone, drunk tramp. Someone's father. Propped up on the only serviceable bench in the cool green waiting room. Limbs akimbo, the pockets of his well-worn grey serge jacket stuffed with bottles, his pathetic, once black boots tied up with mismatched string. His mouth was wide open and his eyes were closed in the luxury of sleep.

Phyllis stood and watched with grim fascination as a fly negotiated its way across the tramp's beard, pausing every few paces to rub its feet together. Phyllis wondered if it was in expectation of a welcome feast, or to rid itself of accumulated grime. With much effort she averted her eyes from his face with its mantle of unruly ginger hair. It was then that she noticed, poking out from behind him, the neck of an old black violin case. Uncharitably she wondered what he kept in it, and walked through onto the platform.

The train had better be on time, she thought vehemently, looking at her watch and starting to pace up and down the creaking loose boards. Even out here she wasn't alone, but had to share the draughty expanse of peeling red paint, rotting timber, and rusting iron. The renovations had not, as yet, extended beyond the ticket office.

Equally uncouth lot they are too, she thought as she surveyed, off to one side, the small group of teenagers talking loudly together. Dressed as though they were going to a fancy-dress party. She looked at them in their striped, oversized jerseys and tight blue jeans; striped woollen hats and ridiculously long striped scarves. Queued up beside them on the platform were wicker baskets, ineffectively loaded with large crepe paper pom poms, rugs, radios and stuffed animals. Really. Children these days. Stuffed toys at their age, and then they will be hollering because they want to be treated as adults! Why doesn't that train come?

Thank God I had enough sense to get out when I did, and that I was able to then help the others too. Not that they would ever thank me. They were all too young to appreciate what I rescued them from. They would only feel compassion for that drunk back there. Compassion indeed! And sentiment. That could be the only reason why Daphne would choose to get married here. Sentiment. Thank God our father is dead, or she would probably have wanted him to give her away. Now where is that train?

Phyllis looked at her watch again. It seemed not to have moved since she last looked. She could hear the church bells ringing now, and by concentrating she could even hear the burble of the guests and onlookers as more arrived outside the little church on the other side of the oval. How much longer will I have to put up with this, she wondered. Hooligans on the platform, drunks inside, and a choice of riffraff outside—ethnic or Australian. Ethnic! What sort of word is that? What's wrong with 'New Australian'? That's what they are isn't it? They say they are adopting our country as their own. Taking over more likely! And all we do is bend over backwards to accommodate them! The politicians tell us that we are underpopulated and need the manpower. Bruce Ruxton, despicable little man that he is, has the right attitude after all.

She shuddered involuntarily and looked down the rail lines as they shimmered in the midday sun, appearing to converge on their way to Melbourne. At their apparent end she could just make out a faint pall of smoke.

Oh no! Phyllis groaned inwardly; she should have guessed. If Damien was travelling by train, it was a sure bet that it would be a steam train if at all possible. She glanced over to the billboards, weathered and warped and nearly obliterated with graffiti. What she saw further fuelled her inner fire of resentment. This weekend was one of the regular weekends of steam travel along this line.

"Typical," she muttered between clenched teeth.

Already the platform had started to fill with rowdy enthusiasts. She shuddered, and attempted to return to the car to wait. Her futile attempts did nothing toward endearing her to the tide of people now crowding onto the small space available. They jostled each other in the most undignified of manners, talking loudly and gesticulating wildly towards Melbourne. They were like a big happy family filled with awe and excitement as they anxiously await a new arrival. Phyllis wryly noted that the uniformly striped teenagers had vacated to the opposite platform. She managed to move towards the end of the platform, away from where the crowd was gathering and constantly growing. She stood alone and aloof. Only a few of the peripheral crowd noticed her and giggled.

Let them laugh, she thought, grateful that she could busy herself with replacing her forgotten handkerchief into her purse. Just because I choose not to indulge in such rash displays. Soon she realised why her position was not popular. As though on cue the crowd broke into a clamorous frenzy and all heads strained towards Melbourne. Next there was a shrinking whistle which nearly pierced Phyllis's ears, and with a sigh the bulky green steam engine laboured to a stop amid hisses and sighs and appreciative applause. A soft plume of soot slowly filtered down and settled over Phyllis.

That was it! Wait till she found Damien She was ropeable. Damsels to the rescue indeed! Next time he needed a ride let him get it himself! She was finished with him. To have to put up with ordinary people was bad enough, but to attend a railway station such as this was just too humiliating, and now, to have a steam train ruin her outfit. It was, it was... outrageous to say the least. The sod!

Contemptuously she watched as a well-dressed young man swankered uneasily towards her, grinning from ear to ear, and swinging a small overnight bag effortlessly beside him. She determined to herself that for once she would not allow that grin to disarm her as it had so often done in the past. Yet, she conceded, he did look reasonably attractive. He carried his six feet well, unlike so many tall men she knew, who would slouch, or who were hollow chested. Not Damien though. He took pride in his body and worked out at the gym at least five times a week. Still, he hadn't managed to control, or even curb, his shock of unruly blonde hair, no matter how often she suggested a certain style might suit him. His sparkling clear blue eyes caught hers and she quickly glanced at her watch, straightened her gloves over her hands and smoothed her skirt, before carefully placing a cold welcome on her face.

"Darling Phil."

She winced at the childhood utterance.

"How awfully good to see you. And don't you look smashing too."

Phyllis chose to ignore his welcome embrace and proffered her cheek to him instead.

Unabashed, he gave her a resounding kiss which brought unwanted colour to her cheeks. It was all she could do to stop herself from slapping him. As if he hadn't already caused her enough harassment, now he was making a public spectacle of them. Really, where was his decorum, she wondered. How shaming for people to see her debased to such a common level of emotional display. The sooner she got him and herself away from here the better.

As the steam train slowly pulled out from the station amid more wild cheering it deposited another offering of soot over Phyllis. She didn't notice as she busily wondered if Damien's car breaking down had only been an excuse for this train buff to catch another ride. Her malicious thoughts were interrupted at that moment.

"Look, I'm awfully sorry about all this, the car didn't really breakdown..."

Phyllis smiled smugly. There, she knew it all along!

"You see it was really the only way that I can get here. By train, you know. I thought that if I told you the truth you wouldn't believe me, or that you would laugh, and, well, it's really rather embarrassing." Damien's voice trailed off.

"Well, what is it?" Phyllis asked.

"It was Mrs. Wilson, you know, the woman who lives next door to me? She lost her husband last year. I did tell you didn't I? Well, anyway, she's been on her own and being a woman like, she's been asking me to help her a bit around the place. You know, jobs that only a man can do.".

Phyllis seethed. She remembered Mrs. Wilson, and how young and attractive she was, and capable too, she was sure.

"Well, this early morning she came knocking on my door. Her cat was stuck up in the neighbour's tree, and could I please help her retrieve it? Of course I said I'd oblige. So off I set forgetting I was only in my PJs. To get to the only tree on the block I had to climb over her backyard fence, either that or walk right around the block and then plead right of entry with the Bikies who owned the place. Much simpler, and quicker, to just scale the fence, wouldn't you agree? Well, there I was ..."

Phyllis looked again at her watch and started to steer Damien towards the now clear exit.

"Moggie under one arm I was getting ready to climb down the tree when I heard the back door of the house squeak open and saw three German Shepherds hurling themselves down the yard towards me. Must have been them that sent poor Rastus up the tree in the first place, I reckon. Anyway I wasn't about to ask them. I hightailed it down the tree and over the fence as quick as you please. Only I got caught on the old fence. Ripped my PJ shorts and got several large splinters in my backside for my efforts."

Phyllis winced visibly, not from the pain, but from his use of such an indelicate word.

"As it's rather painful to sit down, and I knew I could stand on the train, I felt it was the best way to get here."

They had reached the car, and Phyllis watched as Damien, with unconcealed pain, gingerly settled himself into the passenger seat. Phyllis got into the car and hoped that the short ride to the church would be bumpy. She couldn't understand why the delectable Mrs. Wilson hadn't offered to remove the splinters. Maybe she had, and the wounds were still raw. Maybe it was all an excuse to get a ride on the train after all.

Damien interrupted her thoughts.

"Steady on there girl, didn't you see that rut in the road? If I didn't know better, I'd say you went out of your way to hit it on purpose."

Phyllis smiled to herself with satisfaction.

"Good thing I'm the Padre at this wedding. Won't have to sit down will I?" Damien laughed, then winced as Phyllis steered through another deep rut in the road. He looked across at her. There was the suggestion of a smile, but her eyes were quite hard.

"But I want to be able to sit down at the reception. Think you can get the splinters out for me before then, sis? Mrs. Wilson positively paled at the suggestion."

L.O.G.

Leigh Leslie

When my now ex-boyfriend left, he also left Dracula—a cute, cuddly, soft-mouthed female canine. There was no way I was going to call this dog Dracula. She is Boots, because she has this habit of bringing me boots. I thought it cute the first time she came to the door with a saliva seasoned child's rubber boot.

Funny thing is, she only ever brings one boot. Never a pair. In the beginning I'd play at being the prince and try to find Cinderella, but never with any success.

I spent hours peering at people's feet. I even lined the odd boots along my front veranda, then fence, in the hope that owners would recognise their footwear and claim them. But no. I have boxes of boots stacked about the place, and the dubious reputation of being some sort of freak.

Having removed yet another contribution from the porch I retrieved the morning paper from the path. Why couldn't Boots be like other dogs and bring me in the paper, rather than a slobbered-over boot?

"Will you look at this Boots?" I asked, stabbing the offending classified with my finger.

Lonely old guy seeks vibrant young female for company.

"The cheek of him! Who does he think he is?" I threw the paper down in disgust and pulled my laptop towards me and started to punch at the keys before my mood changed.

Dear Sir,

Until today I always considered your publication to be a paragon of literary functionality. Now I find that you, too, have succumbed to the ravages of back peddling into the realms of sexism. How dare you allow your newspaper to carry such disparaging advertisements as that which I read in today's issue? Did you not ask yourself how anyone who describes themselves as a 'lonely old guy' could possibly be of interest to young women?"

I smugly sent it, as an e-mail, to the editor.

The next day, there was my letter, with a response from the editor.

We saw, and still see, nothing offensive in the classified that you found exception to. Surely it is everyone's right to search for companionship, regardless of age, or state.

And so started a three-way conversation in print. The 'lonely old guy', the editor, and me.

Then one day Boots appeared, early in the morning, with her latest acquisition. This was no child's gumboot, nor the usual worker's elastic-sided boot. This one suggested the arrival of a new resident. Here, obviously, was someone 'different'.

The boot was an exquisite masterpiece of craftsmanship. The latte-coloured leather was tooled with an intricate swirled design reminiscent of Mexico. They must have cost a fortune. This was definitely a boot whose departure would be noticed and missed, so when I next sat down to write my regular letter to the editor, I also added a notice:

Found: one cowboy boot.

Unfortunately I neglected to add a contact number, unwittingly leaving myself open to critical comment from my fellow Letters to the Editor correspondent.

It was with interest that I read about the discovery of the single cowboy boot, and was somewhat surprised that my vitriolic correspondent did not find this advertisement, with its lack of contact details, worthy of comment.

The cheek of him! Did he have nothing better to do than scour the newspaper for discrepancies?

So I forgot to add contact details? Big deal. Whoever owned the damn boot, if he wanted it, could surely find out how to get it back.

Obviously the owner of the said boot is not in any great hurry to retrieve the apparel, otherwise there would have appeared something to the effect that the prince had been found, and required directions to the palace. So I do not know why you have suddenly become the champion for the boot-bereft. Let them do their own talking, or walking.

That would show LOG— yes, I'd become familiar enough to give him his own acronym. I was getting tired of the whole thing. Any day now I expected to see a curt comment in the Letters to the Editor column to the effect that the topic had run its last. But no. Instead, in a letter in the paper, the editor asked if we, LOG and I, would like to meet? Person to person. Face to face.

And here was I thinking that Dear Editor was a friend of mine. I whipped out the laptop and my fingers flew "NO THANK YOU." And I didn't care if I was being nettiquetly rude. There was no way I wanted to meet LOG.

Airing my grievances with LOG's inflated ego through the public domain of the local newspaper was one thing. Venting my spleen to an unknown face easy enough, but the prospect of LOG being a neighbour, or someone I met every other day in the course of my daily life was another.

And so it continued, snipe and counter-snipe. I wondered if I could somehow get rid of the ride I was on. It was getting quite puerile, even I recognised that. I decided to give it one last, nail-in-the-coffin letter to the editor.

Dear Editor,

I must applaud you in your judicial refereeing on our slanging matches these past several months, and while I am loathe to call a truce, I really do find Lonely old guy's attempts and endeavours to procure himself a nubile nymph who can only exist in his wildest imaginings to be totally reprehensible. However, as it would appear that his search is totally futile, I cannot see why I should waste my time in correspondence with such a deadbeat. Therefore I painfully relinquish my role as surrogate sounding board to his mad ravings, and suggest that instead of filling this space with garbage, he goes out and gets a life.

I hit 'send' and then sat back. I felt good. A release that one only gets to experience when the door shuts behind a departing ex-partner in the making. Now, if only finding the owner of the cowboy boot could be so easy.

Did I say 'boot'? Silly me, I should have known my smug complacency was an invitation in disguise. That afternoon Boots arrived with the mate. I sighed and turned on the computer again.

Found. Missing partner to previously found cowboy boot. Would owner please arrange their retrieval.

Once again, I hit 'send' and realised, too late, that I had forgotten a contact. Well stuff it, I thought. If they want their boots they can put in their own advertisement.

Sure enough the next edition carried an ad.

Lost. Pair of cowboy boots. Owner grateful they've been found. Now would like to get them back.

A week later, in the Personals column, I noticed that LOG still had not got a life. Below his ad was another:

Plenty places to go, but no way of getting there. Would the person who has my boots please contact me.

This obviously was someone with, not only a warped fashion sense, but also a sense of humour. Definitely someone I'd like to meet. Only this time *they* had neglected a contact point.

Found. Pair of Homeless but not forlorn cowboy boots totally out of place among their rubber relatives. Owners of all lost footwear are invited to came and inspect the collection.

Now I knew why there was no contact number—like me they were a cheapskate—classifieds twenty words or less are free. Well too bad, I was not going to cull any more words.

Boots. Toes cold. Desperate. Finder please phone 379 4675.

I rang. Grant sounded as gorgeous as his boots looked. So I was in quite a tizz on the day we arranged the exchange. So was Boots. Grinning and tail wagging. She kept returning to the boots carefully placed by the front door.

I jumped when the doorbell rang and Boots went crazy. I looked in the mirror and ran my fingers through my hair. Boots fluffed herself up and ran yelping to the door and snuffling the boots.

I took a deep breath and joined her, except for the snuffling. I opened the door, glad of the support that it gave me. He was not barefoot, but he was every bit as gorgeous as I'd imagined, and more.

I am very glad that LOG and I are no longer at loggerheads—my life since meeting Grant has been too busy these past couple of weeks to have been bothered with sparrings in print, and LOG's drivel.

Grant and Boots – members of the same mutual appreciation club – and I have spent all our free time together and I wonder where he has been all my life and why did I waste all that time with LOG when I could have been with Grant.

Oh well, that's all under the bridge now. I still look through the paper every issue though. It would seem that some poor fool has filled the void in LOG's life. Either that or he has given up. I haven't seen his ad for a couple of weeks now.

LUCY'S HORRORSCOPE

Jennifer Lilly

Lucy pushed the sunglasses further up the bridge of her nose as the early sun reflected brightly off the bleached buildings across the piazza. It was promising to be another unbearably hot day.

She flipped over another page of the newspaper. And, not for the first time, she wondered at her sanity in pushing for this trip. Her accommodation, arranged by her firm back in London, was barely sanitary, far less commodious and comfortable. Hardly the type that she had expected to find.

But then again, she should have known that Julie would have gone out of her way to book less than pleasing accommodation. Well, that's what you get for being a business bitch, Lucy thought to herself. If you will try and push your way into a man's world, and not stick with the female fraternity, you cannot expect to be liked by them. Especially when they all wanted to come on this trip, accompanying their bosses no less. Romantic Rome. That was a real laugh!

She sighed as she scanned the newspaper. Unintelligible bold print leapt out at her. Then she saw a few paragraphs, which she thought she might understand. But her heart sank as she rummaged in her bag for the dictionary, which constantly lurked there. She couldn't even decipher which was her horoscope, far less what it may say to her.

She needed all the help she could muster. How many more days did she have till the conference was over and she could return to the safety of her home ground? And she had thought that to represent her firm would be easy. Even in this day of enlightened equality there appeared to be certain bastions of male dominance—and the European Convention had proved to be one of them.

She was the only female delegate, and she was finding it a lonely, rather than an exhilarating, experience. Slowly she scanned the small print, her lips silently mouthing the unfamiliar words, yet she felt compelled to persevere and glean what she could of what the stars had on store for her.

Today is going to be a good day. She could understand that much. At least that was something. Yesterday had been quite unbearable. Then again, if she thought about it, not half as bad as it had been the day before.

The first day. She felt her spirits flag as she remembered that first day, when all the delegates had been milling around, meeting each other, and exchanging pleasantries. Their bimbos latched onto their arms and introduced as 'my P.A. Couldn't do anything without her'. And the ever-present eyes following her, wondering to whom she belonged. But never really belonging at all.

Her brow creased as she stared at the newspaper. Health, work and love eluded her. She riffled through the dictionary: *Don't eat too much*. She looked at the crumbs that lay scattered in front of her. Remnants of an extravagant continental breakfast.

Her hotel, if it could be called that, did not provide meals so she had to venture out into the world of restaurants, trattorias, and the good old 'Bar'. More like a café, really. And here she sat, at such a Bar. Outside on the pavement. A round table with an unfurled umbrella piercing its middle.

Actually, she quite enjoyed eating breakfast here. She could watch the people bustling along the cobbled street, weaving in and out of the vehicular traffic which followed some indecipherable road code. She marvelled that there could be so much chaotic activity and no injuries.

Well, maybe if she didn't have anything further to eat today, she could say that she hadn't eaten too much. She had certainly eaten enough this morning to last, but the selection of pastries had been overwhelming.

She tried to read further. *Many* ... something ... *today for those in business.* Another fumble through the dictionary... many *problems*. Not again? Yesterday had been bad enough. Grappling with multinational businessmen on foreign soil was no longer her idea of a working holiday.

Still, she had only herself to blame. She'd wanted to come. She'd begged to come, anything to get away from the advances of the clerk from accounts. Besides, hadn't she always thrived on the challenge of asserting herself in a man's world? Only she hadn't counted on the cultural differences. Oh well, if the stars had it in for her today she'd be prepared. She ordered another coffee and pastry. To hell with not eating too much, she had a tough day ahead of her.

The stars didn't shine much on love either, *Good sentimental vibes and the chance to meet someone interesting.* After yesterday she felt that meeting new and interesting men wasn't all it was cut out to be. Of all the businessmen she'd had to deal with yesterday only one had treated her as an equal, well, at least not as a sex object, and that was only because he was gay.

She shuddered as she remembered the fiasco the evening had turned out to be. And now the stars were predicting the same fate for today! She couldn't wait till the week was through and she could return to the sanity of London and the clerk from accounts.

Her thoughts were interrupted by the waiter bringing her her coffee and pastry.

"Pleeze, signorina, this is today's newspaper," he said, handing her a neatly folded newspaper. "You are reading yesterday's issue."

MAN-FIRE

Jennifer Lilly

Inside the darkness of the cave the two families crowded together to keep warm. Jasper and Silas, like their fathers and father's fathers before them, sat huddled at the entrance, watching the mountain. Tonight they could see the large figures leaping and twirling in the red and yellow sky.

"Bron and Mathias are dancing again tonight," Jasper observed, drawing a heavy weary arm across his brow.

Silas nodded. "That's the third night now."

"Do you think they know our plans?" asked Jasper. He looked anxiously at his brother. Shadows flickering across his face, etching the worry line deeper.

Silas slowly shook his head. "We've only talked when they're growling. They can't have heard us."

The figures stopped dancing. Jasper and Silas moved closer together as lightning ripped the sky.

Bron and Mathias could be heard to laugh.

"They know," said Jasper.

Silas nodded. "The women must make more sacrifices. And we must move fast."

With a furtive look towards the mountain the men crept back into the cave and their families.

"Did you see their fire?"

"Was it the gods?"

"Are they angry?"

Whispers echoed across the cave as wives and children clamoured for answers. None of them knew what Jasper and Silas had planned, but all were interested in the gods and their fire.

"Yes, we saw their fire again tonight. But Bron and Mathias saw us watching, and yes, they were angry."

Later that night, when the women and children were asleep, Jasper and Silas moved away from their families.

"It has to be tonight. Besides, why should the gods be the only ones with fire?" Jasper whispered hoarsely.

"Yes, but remember how often the others tried, and how angry Bron and Mathias became; and the retribution they rained down upon us. That's why it is only we who are left."

"I know, but if we don't do something, then there will be none of us left. We can't afford any more sacrifices." Jasper rang his hands in desperation. "It has to be tonight."

Fearfully the two men stole out of the cave and slowly walked towards the mountain which loomed high above them. It had to be tonight.

They halted at the base of the mountain and looked up at Bron and Mathias. Thankfully they were sleeping. Their breath condensing in the cold night air.

Silas and Jasper exchanged glances. The stories handed down from past generations mirrored in their eyes. Tales of death and destruction. Intrepid explorers never returning, and then the ones that did – scarred for life both physically and mentally. Telling tall tales of gods with voracious appetites, with breaths so poisonous that they killed on greeting. Of water that bubbled and overflowed, red and yellow, and hot.

And of fire. The one thing which could make life for everyone so much more comfortable. It would bring light, and warmth, and comfort. And protection. See how it protected the gods? Why, it could even make them gods themselves!

Silas and Jasper smiled at each other and slowly walked on, determined to be the ones to return, and with fire.

MRS. CARMICHAEL

Jennifer Lilly

Mrs. Carmichael lived at the top of the stairs. She'd always lived there. Even when my great-grandmother was born, Mrs. Carmichael had lived there, on the top floor, though, admittedly, she had only been a small child herself way back then. She was small, again, now. But she still didn't like being called Mrs. Carmichael. "Call me Fanny" she'd call down the stairs in her russet voice. But we were never allowed to. And Mrs. Carmichael would stand at the top and look down at us with sad and longing eyes as we ran outside to play.

"Mummy, why doesn't Mrs. Carmichael ever go out?"

I looked down at my straw-haired daughter. "Because she's old." I smiled and remembered a conversation generations old.

Mrs. Carmichael, with her translucent skin and blue veins. A fixture, almost, at the top of the stairs.

"But Mummy, you are old, and so is Grandma, and you both come outside, and you play with me."

"Mrs. Carmichael is very old," I told my daughter. But her eyes didn't believe me.

"Mummy, can I visit Mrs. Carmichael?"

"No dear. She's too old." Another conversation from the past. Only my daughter belonged to a new generation. A generation where children were taught to question.

"Why not?" A question I'd never have dared to voice, no matter how much I may have wondered, and I didn't have an answer.

"Because old people don't like to be bothered with children."

"But Mrs. Carmichael has asked me."

I looked down at my daughter.

"When did she ask you?" I asked gently, anxious not to intrude into her make-believe world.

"Yesterday."

"Yesterday? When yesterday?"

"When I went out to play. She was there, at the top of the stairs. I looked up and she called out to me."

I nodded. I knew the scenario well.

"'You can call me Fanny' she said as I waved to her. Mummy, why does she always say that?"

I did not have an answer.

"Then she beckoned me. But I didn't go, Mummy. I didn't go."

I stroked her hair. She looked up at me. "I'd like to go. Can I?"

Hand in hand we slowly climbed the stairs. Mrs. Carmichael watched our ascent, silently. An apparition in the flesh. My daughter's enthusiasm fought desperately to impinge upon the apprehension that dragged at my heels as years of denial clung tenaciously to the stairs, and I wondered what my own mother would say when she found out that I had broken the bounds of discipline and had actively mounted the stairs up into Mrs. Carmichael's domain.

And I wondered, with the delayed innocence of youth, why we had never been permitted to associate with Mrs. Carmichael. Why we had never questioned our parents the way my daughter questioned me. Would anyone remember?

A rustle brought my eyes upward. There was Mrs. Carmichael, waiting for us. A benign smile creased her face as she reached out her hands to my daughter. I stood several steps below the top landing and watched as my daughter floated towards the frail old lady above. Without hesitation she reached up to the welcoming hand and entered a musty embrace.

"You can call me Fanny, if you like." Her voice crackled like autumn leaves scrunched underfoot.

"Why?" My daughter asked in innocence.

We walked into a world totally removed from reality. Mrs. Carmichael's home was a child's fantasy —feathers and lace rippled in the soft scented breeze that played throughout the room to the trill of panpipes. Fluted light filtered through the decades and fell softly on a myriad of memorabilia, which lay precisely on top of antiquated antiques. My daughter ran from one cabinet to the next, exclaiming in delight at each new treasure—generations of miniature lives in fragile porcelain. I gazed in equally rapt wonder. This house was living history. Along with the furniture and furnishings that appeared to have survived a century of living were the bric-a-brac of a lonely lady's collecting.

"You can call me Fanny, if you like." Mrs. Carmichael stood before me. "Please." Her eyes were twinkling and pleading.

"Why?" I echoed my daughter's, earlier, unanswered question.

"It would make an old lady so very happy."

I digested the simple response, but my expression betrayed me. Mrs. Carmichael laid her spindly hand on my arm.

"No one calls me Fanny anymore."

I looked at the frail fingers on my arm and knew that one day mine too could be like that. But would mine be as strong, I wondered? I doubted it. My arm was in a relentless grasp. So why couldn't I call her Fanny? She nodded her head in understanding. She knew, and accepted the fact that my upbringing was waging war with her request. She led me to an old upright, horsehair filled chair and left me. She glided into another room and returned with a pale, jointed, papier-mâché and porcelain doll in one hand and a huge tome in the other. The doll she passed to my daughter, the book she placed in my lap. She then stood behind me like a schoolmarm of her own era yet not quite mine, but I felt the spell. Slowly she leant forward and opened the book, and her history fell out.

"I'm going to see Fanny," yelled my daughter as she raced up the stairs.

It was so nice to see her go, and to know that, at last, Mrs. Carmichael could enjoy being called Fanny.

"Give Fanny my love," I called after her. Funny Annie. A childhood taunt which settled to stay, and be loved and lost as friends and family left and the strictures of correct upbringing forbore any familiarity with landladies or the older generation.

MY BEAUTIFUL GINA

Norma Smyth

With a terrible fascination Gina Compton watched the bright red stain spread across the crisp white perfection of Connor Major's white dress shirt. Gina had been practising her knife throwing skills and, at her last throw, Connor had cracked a funny joke, and she had doubled up with laughter, but her aim was not true. She sat down hard on the floor and gave serious thought to what she should do next.

She had been asked to rejoin the crack Secret Service Squad with whom she had been a very high-ranking and skilled member, and had recalled she needed to hone her skills, hence the knife throwing.

During her last assignment she had met Connor, who was one of the new but experienced group, and they had admired their fatal attraction for each other. She had not meant it to be quite so 'fatal' and now, as she calmed a little she dialled another of her team. She requested that a doctor be sent immediately, then she ran back to Connor and knelt down beside him. "Connor, darling. I'm so sorry. I've rang for help and the doctor will be here shortly."

He opened his eyes and peered up at her. "Can you ease the pressure on my shirt? I feel like death."

Gina stood up, kicked off her gold sandals, hitched her cream satin sheath high, got down on her knees again and started to undo his shirt buttons.

"Just a moment." She ran to a bathroom cupboard to get a roll of cotton wool and some gauze. "This will help staunch the flow." She eased the pressure off his shirt and was able to withdraw the knife relatively smoothly. Connor gasped and swore, closed his eyes, his face was pale and a look of anguish had crossed his face.

"Can we play solitaire next time?" he gasped. "It would be safer."

Blood welled out of the cut and Gina pressed a pad of cotton wool and gauze against his shirt.

"Help will be here soon," she breathed, and mopped her cheek with a tissue. "Hang on there, love. I missed the fatal spot so you will recover."

Connor more or less chortled at her comment and said "I think you've missed the plot. I thought we were going out tonight to have a wonderful surprise, go for a very nice meal, be dressed in our best, but instead you're killing me."

A knock on the door and Gina rushed to open it. A tall, dark man strode in, surveyed the scene and in turn knelt beside Connor. He removed the pad checked it and Connor closely and said "You've done a good job, girl."

"I know!" said Gina, her voice was hard and cold. The doctor swivelled his head towards her, and Connor lifted his slightly up from the floor. Both were startled to see Gina, her back against the door, a Glock pistol turned on them, and a grim expression on her normally beautiful face.

"Okay, you two. I mean business. Doc, move away from Connor. Connor, my love, it's time for us to part."

Connor's mouth fell open in astonishment. "Gina what on earth are you up to? Why are you acting like this? I thought we were getting married, not killing each other."

"We were," agreed Gina, "But I got a better offer. I'm going over to the other side. You and I have had some good times, but now it is time for me to go. Doc, sorry you had to get involved, but you are too important to be left at large so it's goodbye to you too."

The doctor by this time had climbed to his feet, and he started across the room to Gina.

"Hold it right there." She waved her pistol in his direction. When he didn't stop she aimed for his knee, he screamed in pain and fell to the floor.

Connor was getting weaker by the moment and watched helplessly. Gina moved over to him, kneeled down and kissed him passionately. "Bye darl!" She stood up and moved to the door. As she reached for the doorknob the door burst open and two more members of the team burst in, holding her against the wall. They surveyed the scene briefly and turned as she was aiming her pistol at them. They meant business and she realised she was outnumbered. Quickly she pushed the pistol under her left breast and pulled the trigger. The blast of sound filled the room, and a red stain spread across the front of her cream dress.

Gina smiled at Connor, "Tonight, Darl, we played snap." And she crumpled slowly to the floor.

A quick telephone call, to another doctor to come as soon as possible, and life would go on.

"Why were you guys so slow?" queried Doc. "Another doctor is needed here, and we should question Gina."

The four men turned to look at Gina and watched coldly as the lifeblood ebbed from her wound, and the woman they thought as their crack operator died before their eyes.

"Don't worry about my beautiful Gina," groaned Connor. "She doesn't exist. It's me I'm worried about."

By the time the second doctor arrived, the necessary team members were able to assist, and Connor was hurriedly taken off to hospital. A sad, lonely, and totally disillusioned young man.

NEW BEGINNINGS

Rita Middleton

Maria sank back into the deep seat of the SUV, glad for the blacked-out windows. She didn't want to look out and she certainly didn't want to be seen. She was glad for the refuge, and the anonymity, that it afforded her. She was too frightened to process anything right now. They had promised her a new identity and with it a new beginning. She had been reluctant to accept it at first, but after the explosion, she would go along with anything they offered. It seemed to be the only way out. She wasn't sure if she would ever see Andre again or even if he was still alive. Shame. She had really liked Andre. It was he that had kept her going during the last few desperate weeks.

Maria let her eyelids droop as she settled back in the SUV. They had pulled away from the curb and were moving smoothly along the boulevard. But instead of respite, she was right back in the thick of things, feeling absolute terror. She could smell the acrid smoke as the building collapsed, and the smell of gas was everywhere. How had she been so lucky to have been out of the house when the tank exploded? She had just stepped out to look for the cat before she settled down for the night. The sirens blared, as she was rushed to the SUV. The agent who had helped her into the vehicle was kind enough, but very impersonal. Still, she should be grateful that they had been keeping her under surveillance. She wondered if she would ever see Tabby again. At least she was sure he had not been in the house, but she worried who would care for him.

Her mind flicked back to the night it had all begun. She had been hurrying home after a quick trip to the dairy. She had heard a shot ring out somewhere to the left, and had glanced down the alley, in time to meet the eyes of the biggest brute she had ever seen. He was bending over a body, trying to pull it further down along the alley to a waiting van. The menace in his look sent a chill down her spine. The jagged scar on his left cheek just added to the impression of danger. She hurried on her way, hoping he was not following her. When she reached home she had carefully locked the door, and turned off the lights, hoping that if anyone had followed her, they would not be sure which house she had gone into. But she still felt uneasy as she was heading off to bed. From her bedroom window on the second floor, she had peered out onto the street below, only to see a van cruising along slowly as if they were looking for someone. It looked like the same van, but she could not be sure in the darkness.

The next few days were a bit of a blur. She had seen the request for witnesses to please come forward to the police after a murder in the neighbourhood. She realised that that was just what she had witnessed but was reluctant to report it to the police. Would it increase the danger she felt she was in? Two days had gone by and so far, nothing had happened. Perhaps she was just being paranoid. The next day as she was heading for work, she could not shake off the feeling that she was being followed. She had seen the white van in her rear-view mirror as she turned out of her driveway, and it had still been there when she parked up outside the office. She had hurried into the building, keeping her head turned away so she could not be seen clearly. In the back of her mind, she realised this was useless. If they were following her, they must have a pretty good idea that she was the one who had seen what had gone on in the alley.

After worrying about it all morning, she decided that she had no option but to go to the police. Not sure if the van was still watching the building, she decided to call rather than to go in, in person. When she had said what she was calling about, she had quickly been put through to a senior officer. She could sense from his attitude that he was concerned for her safety. After describing being followed to work that morning, his concern was even more evident, only increasing her fear. It was decided that it was too risky for her to go to the police station. It was also too risky for the police to come to her office. Finally, it was decided that she would go with a friend to lunch and would be met by a plainclothes officer in the café.

As they slid into the booth, Maria had looked around nervously, but had not spotted the van in the street. Moments later, a big man in a grey suit stepped up to their table. He pulled his badge out and flashed it, before insisting that Maria must go with him immediately. This was not at all what Maria had expected. She hesitated, just a few seconds, and suddenly chaos erupted. She ducked under the table as gun shots were fired. The man beside her crumpled to the floor. She felt strong hands pulling her from under the table, and towards the door. She screamed but immediately felt a strong hand clamp over her mouth. She looked back and caught a look of shock on Susan's face. In the same instant, she realised that there was blood spurting from Susan's left shoulder. She felt absolute helplessness as she was dragged out the door. She was shoved roughly into a late model car, which took off with its wheels squealing. A few moments passed before the driver spoke to her. "I am sorry I was so rough with you, but it was imperative that we get you out of there immediately. Your life is in danger." Maria remained silent, not at all sure that she was safe now. "Who are you?" she muttered, "I thought you were the bad guys."

A dry chuckle, and then he replied. "I am not surprized! I didn't exactly introduce myself. I am Special Agent Michael Turner of the FBI. It appears that you have witnessed a gang killing and will be needed as a witness." Maria was confused but she kept her thoughts to herself. She had contacted the local police, not the FBI. She was meant to have met a detective and been taken to the police station to give a statement. Where was she being taken? Who was the man who had met her in the café? How had they known about the arrangements to meet in the café? As she glanced out of the car window, she realised that they were leaving town.

A few moments later they were pulling up outside a long low building on a secluded campus. She was ushered out of the car and into the building. It certainly had the feeling of a government building. It felt completely sterile with dull tones of grey, and no artwork on the walls. She was hurried along a corridor, and into an office. Agent Turner indicated that she should sit, as he shrugged out of his coat and settled himself behind the desk, his holster with his pistol now plainly visible. "Now Maria, I will need you to tell me exactly what you saw on Monday night at 9:30pm."

Maria was shocked at the abruptness of his question, after what she had just been through. As if reading her mind, his tone softened. "Would you like a cup of tea? You have had quite a fright."

"What will happen to Susan?" she asked. "She was not involved except to accompany me to the café. She was injured in the gun fight."

"Point taken," replied the agent. He picked up the phone and spoke curtly to someone on the other end. "Can you get a follow up on what happened after I left the Lazy Dog Café? There was an innocent bystander injured. Is she getting the help she needs?" A pause, "OK get back to me."

With a cup of tea in her hand, Maria could focus more easily. She recounted to the agent, the scene she had witnessed three nights earlier. She described the man she had seen in the alley trying to move the body. She shuddered as she remembered his malevolent look and the jagged scar on his cheek.

"Do you think you could recognise him if you saw him again?" the agent asked.

"I am sure I could," Maria replied. "Although it was dark in the alley."

Before she knew it, she was sitting by herself in another office, looking through mug shots. After going through countless books, she finally spotted the man with the scar on his left cheek. Just then Agent Turner came in.

"Thought you might need this," he said as he handed her a sandwich. "Any luck?"

"Thanks," Maria replied. "I think I have found the killer."

In some ways, Maria was surprised that she had not been allowed home after her interview with the FBI agent. She had been kept in the witness protection program, in a safe house. Of course, she agreed at the time, because she was afraid to go home, but it was certainly an abrupt end to her former life. She had lost her job, and not been able to contact friends or family. Once the trial was over, and the killer had been incarcerated, for life, she had insisted on going home. Look where that had got her! Now she was facing another change in her life. The person who had kept her sane during her time in witness protection was Andre. He had even lived in her house and looked after Tabby. She had grown quite fond of Andre, but he had always kept it on professional level.

When Maria woke up it was in an apartment that she did not recognise. Strange. She did not remember coming here. The rooms were very quiet, and quite tastefully decorated, with thick plush cream-colored carpets, and teal blue drapes. The furniture was a blond maple, but quite standard, nothing to distinguish it from the average hotel room. Maybe this was a hotel. She looked around more carefully, but could find no evidence of branding, no brochures, no 'In case of an emergency' poster on the back of the door. She crept out of bed and started to explore. Looking out the window, she was startled to see that she was several stories up. The street below looked quite narrow, not at all like the New York streets she was used to.

In the lounge, she found the television, but it took a while to locate the remote in a drawer in the coffee table. Switching it on, she was alarmed to realise that the programs were in a foreign language. She listened carefully and found that she could make out a few words in French. Flicking through the channels, she found that there was only one channel in English, and it was screening a children's program. She was beginning to panic. Where was she? She hadn't realised that she might be relocated out of the country. Suddenly she remembered that she was meant to be given a new identity as well. She wondered who she was. Looking for her handbag, she found a black calf leather shoulder bag, not too different than the one she usually used. Reaching in she pulled out a passport, which was in French. The address was Apt. 401, 1493 Boulevard de La Place, Lyon, France. OMG! Now she was in total panic! Just then the doorbell rang. She found the intercom system and buzzed. A familiar voice asked to be allowed in. A few moments later, she opened the door to find Andre, with a big bouquet of roses. Next thing he had swept her into his arms, his lips on hers.

"Andre?"

His gently put his finger on her lips. "Non, Non! You must call me Jacques" he whispered in her ear.

And so began her new life.

OH, ELI!

Jennifer Lilly

She had loved Eli, but lust had killed him, and look what it had done to her! Stephanie cautiously made her way along the wooden floorboards as her right slipper dragged fractionally behind what would normally have been her footfall. If she didn't remember to slide her right foot along the floor, she was apt to trip over the loose sole and slop even more tea than usual into the saucer which she carried in her hand. Stephanie looked at her feet. She really ought to buy a new pair of scuffs, she thought ruefully as the gaping mouth of her slipper smiled up at her.

Her buttocks rolled in synchronized waves as she cautiously advanced into the sitting room and set the cup and saucer down on a small occasional table beside a worn armchair. A white cat, coiled in the hollow of the seat cushion opened an eye and leapt to safety as Stephanie sat heavily into the warm chair, and the particles of dust caught in the dim mildewed light which caressed the chair, slowly subsided into their lazy dance again.

She smiled to herself as through a filigree of cracks in her Salvation Army Thrift Shop glasses she looked at the memorabilia around her. Years of living stared back at her from out of tarnished photograph frames, and dust cloistered the trophies and nick-knacks of a lifetime. She pulled the frayed ends of her hand knitted shawl closer around her ample bosom and clutched at the fond memories of her past. An era when laughter and life eddied around a lithe young woman. A life dripping with jewels and beaus. She had been the belle of all the balls and the queen of many a quest. Her life had been gilded and her career in the forefront of the public eye secure.

"Oh Eli." Stephanie sniffed, "why did you have to die?"

The dull tock of a clock could be heard marking the minutes in a quiet forgotten corner of the room. It had been a present from the cast of some long-forgotten production. As tears misted her eyes her body was abruptly racked by a rasping cough. She delved into her cleavage and withdrew a wilted tissue and she waited for the attack to die.

Exhausted, she slowly slumped back into the folds of the chair and once more drifted back in time. The public had loved her. Once. And so had Eli. She peered through her glasses, searching the dark clutter of the room until she found the sepia photograph of a stiffly smiling couple. She smiled and remembered their wedding day, and the glorious, heady days, and years, that followed.

She'd been proud to successfully juggle a family and a career, long before it had become fashionable, or an economic necessity. Maybe she ought to consider herself a forerunner for the Women's Liberation Movement. She laughed emptily to herself. A feminist she definitely was not, nor had ever been.

Now those years were only memories. She reached out for the yellowing scrapbooks that littered the table, and threatened to capsize her teacup. Her fingers erupted in vast folds of flab either side of the conglomerate of rings which strained to encircle her fingers. As she tried to balance a book across the rolls of waist held in check by a loud floral print housecoat, the pages fell open to reveal a glamorous hourglass girl.

For decades the critics had raved. And she had basked in their acclaim. Now they were all silent. All that was left were her memories, and her scrapbooks. They were her only friends. She ran her wedding ring across her tongue - a subconscious action from which she always drew comfort. She caught sight of her reflection in the fly-specked mirror that hung on the wall next to her wedding photograph, and tears once more welled up in her eyes and spilled down her puffy cheeks creased with old foundation and rouge.

"Oh Eli," she snuffled, "I loved you. But lust killed you. And look what it has done to me!" Sobs broke through her composure and unsettled the scrapbook on her knees. She let it slip away, unnoticed. The cat considered the loose pages disdainfully and stalked out of the room. "Oh Eli!" Sadly she shook her head, "Why did you let your greed for power destroy us?"

Stephanie reached up to her glasses and with a sniff removed the arms from behind her ears and methodically rubbed the lenses between her thumb and finger before replacing them on her nose. She dragged the sleeve of her housecoat across the tip of her nose and sniffed again, then leant forward for yet another scrapbook. This one she opened out on the table, and, poised precariously on the edge of her chair, she slowly turned the pages. She came to one page and hesitated. She tapped her finger over an article pasted onto the page. That was when it started, Stephanie thought to herself. It had all started with *The Avenge of Beauty*.

It had been a well-written play, by a young playwright, and she had enjoyed the part. But the play had been doomed, or so it seemed, from its inception. It had appeared that everyone in connection with it was to suffer, somehow, from its production. No one was left unscathed, though, at the time she thought that she had survived the onslaught of disaster.

How wrong time had proved her smugness to be. This was the play that Eli was to direct, by default. He was not a man of the theatre, leastways, not in its production. For sure he had become involved with the machinations since meeting and marrying her, but up until that time his only association with the theatre had been as part of the audience. Now his time had come. The director had fallen foul of the playwright, as had the previous two directors, and suddenly Stephanie found her husband flung into the role of directing *The Avenge of Beauty*. Surprisingly, he did extremely well. And so did the play.

Stephanie peered at the page and read the review. Nothing had prepared her for the metamorphosis that was to follow *The Avenge of Beauty*. While she had been adored by the critics and public, and had basked in their adulation, her feet always remained firmly rooted.

Eli, on the other hand was a changed person. No longer the gentle, supportive man she had admired and married, but a man totally swept up in, and possessed by, the adulation and power of popularity. A man demented with a lust for the limelight and the power of telling people, albeit actors and production crew, where to go, and what to do. And money. He became increasingly more demanding of her, both at home and at work. He took control of her career, and insisted on directing the productions she was in.

Stephanie heaved a weary sigh and turned the page of the scrapbook. Their faces smiled up at her. Hers, and Eli's, and a despicable little man whom Eli had met at some bar and whom he had insisted should become their adviser. Now what was his name? She thought that she would never forget *his* name. She leant back in the chair and closed her eyes.

"Stephanie, love." Eli had said, as he came up to her where she sat at the mirror in her dressing room one rehearsal.

She smiled at the memory. It was always nice when Eli would come into the dressing room. She hugged her shawl closer to her. It was their secret time together. A time when they could share a few moments, alone. She would lock the door, and then... Then a scowl creased her brow.

"Steffie. This is the man I was telling you about yesterday. You remember?"

Stephanie remembered now how she couldn't recollect even seeing Eli the day before, far less talking to him, or him to her.

The newcomer's smooth, slicked-back hair gleamed in the reflected light, and his smarmy grin caused her gut to cringe. She didn't really want to turn around and meet this person face to face, but another look at Eli and she knew that she had to.

Her first impressions of... Jethro. Jethro McLeod, that was his name! How could she have forgotten? Her first impressions, and she was one to stand by first impressions, were not enhanced when he stuck out an insipid hand for her to shake. For goodness sake, the man didn't even have the acumen to know that a gentleman always waited for a lady to offer her hand in greeting. Not that she would have offered her hand to that leech. And a leech he proved to be too. He stuck to them as a leech to a leg in long wet grass; only neither salt nor flame would remove him. And she had tried. On more than one occasion. But all that had done was to increase his tenacity and Eli's resolve that they needed him.

Needed him! The only one to need Jethro McLeod was his mother, and then Stephanie even had to doubt that his mother would have wanted, or needed him. A shark, shyster, fraud, these were all words not strong enough to describe Jethro McLeod. Together, he and Eli spiralled down a path of destruction, and she, and her career, had been passively pulled along in their wake, flotsam in the fall.

And now Eli was dead. And so was her career. She laughed. Her career! It had started to die the minute Eli started to have input and impact on it. But she had been too much in love with him, then, to notice. Or if she had, to do anything about it. Slowly, in his lust for power, he had eroded away her fans, and suffocated her talent under the guise of experimental art.

Experimental? Pah! Degraded decadence, which Jethro McLeod had convinced Eli was the way to go. No one in their right mind would pay to see the trash they put out, and no one did. More and more Eli and Jethro would leave her in her dressing room to find her own way home while they 'discussed business'. It was always some dodgy transaction which had to be dealt with in some seedy bar. And always after closing time. And she was never told.

By the time she allowed herself to wake up to the reality of what was happening her credibility had been totally destroyed and no self-respecting producer or casting director would even return her calls. And she was damn sure that she would not participate in another of Eli and Jethro's 'productions'. Not that they were interested in her anymore. They were looking at younger, and more nubile talent now. The sleaze of the streets. But that didn't bother Eli. Oh no. All he was interested in was the money that the now blatantly pornographic films brought in. And the girls.

Stephanie shuddered as she remembered the girls. Each year they would get younger, and each year Eli and Jethro would ogle at them at auditions, dirty middle-aged men with middle-aged spread straining at their belts. Stephanie had often wondered how many years it would take before they started to visibly salivate at the parade of flesh. But it hadn't happened.

She shuffled her feet in her shonky slippers and twittered in glee. Jethro McLeod had had his come-uppance. He had been caught, with his pants down, as it were, and the parents of the under-age girl were not pleased, not at all. But it was too late for Eli. By then Eli was well and truly hooked, and without his supplier he had rapidly drifted into a gibbering mess, and then one day it ended.

She sighed, then turned the pages to his obituary. With tears misting her eyes and fogging her glasses she smoothed the newspaper cutting down with the palm of her hand.

"Oh Eli. Why did you have to die? I would have helped you; you knew that." Stephanie sniffed and rummaged for her tissue. She dabbed it around her nose and sniffed again. "It wasn't your fault. I understood that. It was that Jethro man. It was he who turned your head. He, and lust. Well, you fed your lust, and it took control of

your life, but together we could have made it good again. I know we
could have. Oh Eli, why did you have to die?"

ONE HOT SATURDAY

Lynia Antram

The hot summer weather had long since become monotonous. The strong sun traversed daily the cloudless sky, its heat-waves bored into every vestige of life struggling with the dryness created on the earth below.

The hungry birds had tired of the struggle for food and hung about the garden waiting for free handouts offered by humans. The cattle stood motionless by the gate, looking hungry and depressed, the only sign of life being the rhythmic flicking of the tail to deter the restless flies. The daily ration was due for delivery, freshwater and grain. It was a long time since they had enjoyed the taste of fresh sweet grass.

In fact life had become a mental nightmare from which no inhabitant of the Bush was exempt.

Bushfires roared in the distance, a threat becoming more and more likely as the restless heat continued.

Saturday morning began hot and dry. The air was heavy with smoke from distant fires. The atmosphere smelled of burnt plant material and particles of ash floated above. A gentle breeze wafted spasmodically about the yard, quietly lifting the feathers of the king parrots gratefully drinking the cool water especially placed on the dilapidated table on an equally dilapidated deck. The temperature soared to 50°. About the heat level of a hot bath.

Life in the Australian Bush is simple, laidback and unpredictable. Weather patterns determine what is done today and what remains for tomorrow.

In the yard an enormous bundle of cut gum was randomly stacked. The result of the removal of trees deemed too close to the dwelling and now nestled amongst an overgrown garden and now the wood supply for winter yet to come. The top foliage, small twigs and masses of loose leaves lay within the confines of two redundant corrugated water tanks where time would take care of them. No other means of disposal exists in this dry heat-ridden environment. No dump facilities. No means of compost if your product is so full of oil only burning obliterates it. A method unthinkable in such dryness.

The eucalyptus leaves don't lie and rot, they dry and blow. Windrows develop against all solid structures and beneath the tall straight trunks of the vast varieties of the same species – great fire fodder and death sentence where conditions mesh to create an out of control raging inferno.

The Creek is just a smidgen of its former self. A thin line of coolness. A ribbon between the long arid grass and the endless confusion of gums and scruffy undergrowth. A large petrol driven water pump is obvious above the man-made pool catching the cool clearwater and is insurance against any breakaway fire. Over the parched lawn, on a fire hose is sprawled a giant snake with its mouth focused on the dwelling and the array of outbuildings dotted about the yard. The breeze lifts the wind dust which once was lawn and blows it like a veil over the barren landscape.

Radio commentaries give conflicting reports and updates of the pending devil raging in distant areas. There is an element of concern for fellow Australians battling the raging hot enemy.

"It's bloody hot out for some," they declare.

The latest report implies that the front is heading in the opposite direction due to a wind change. For some, not good news. Hard to understand when the smoke levels appear to be increasing. Some locals with children hedge their bets, tired of the thick air and the heat they make the decision to head for the city.

Generally the bush looks tired. Foliage was silver and transparent, lacking moisture and the leaf cover was greatly reduced – survival it's called. Large strips of bark hung like redundant Christmas streamers dropping at intervals to the forest floor.

Smoke formed a very eerie backdrop to a very worrying situation. A thick layer of leathery leaves and old plant-litter covered the undergrowth and bush floor. Tinder dry and highly flammable. Great starting material for an indoor domestic fire and fuel abundant for the fast moving fire front of the dreaded screaming red devil of a wilderness fire.

Locals began to congregate in clusters to share concerns and relay plans. Advice on fire skills was willingly shared. Those prepared to stay and fight regardless spent time clearing debris from roofs and damping down the area where the water supply allowed. Sacks were soaked in precious rainwater conserved normally for domestic use.

Inevitably the conversation turned to the accuracies in the information broadcast; the lack of timeframe supporting given updates; the shortcomings and poor predictions provided by the local shire in the event of disaster; the fact that great promises were made by Federal Government after other major fires, and how quickly they were forgotten after the event.

By late morning it became obvious from the increasing smoke levels that the fire was moving ever nearer. The smoke began to inhibit breathing. Stress levels soared whilst the making of decisions, gathering of precious belongings being stowed in vehicles and the damp downs became more frantic.

To leave or to endeavour to protect a lifetime of personal material goods was a question posed wherever a group assembled. Many who were nervous, several of the elderly, and those responsible for children in their care, made the call to race to the safety of the city. While others in similar situations opted to stay in the belief it would never affect them.

Others had great faith in God and were confident the faithful radio – the Bush dwellers' friend – would give them plenty of warning and keep them safe. How wrong they were. Nature controls their environment and mere mortals are but pawns on her board.

Suddenly and within a very short space of time it became obvious that the breeze had not only increased to a wind, but the direction had changed.

Incredible noise associated with fast moving fire, the denseness of the smoke and the change of its colour from grey to orange spelt disaster for all those still in the area. Small spot fires ignited randomly, generated by burning debris wafted by the wind and dropped onto the parched earth.

Rapidly the noise increased. Distant trees became fireballs. Explosions filled the air and the heat increased, and smoke become a dark red. The noise was deafening, the echoing roar of an out-of-control bushfire screamed through the valley, the flames destroying almost instantly every vestige of civilization in its path.

A split-second decision needed to be made, to stay could mean death. The noise was deafening. The fire-breathing dragon was too close for comfort. The dire situation became suddenly worse when a shift in the wind broadened the fire's hold to three fronts.

The only escape was the road out. The smoke was red. Without any communication the survivors raced to their cars and headed up the dirt track to the hardly visible strip of seal which was the only escape. The red smoke was like a wall on three sides making it difficult to see ahead.

To hasten was out of the question as every living creature be it human, or animals both domestic and wild, were racing down the same narrow strip in utter confusion. Buildings close to the road were burning fiercely. To hit a cattle-beast or a kangaroo would be disastrous.

Twenty kilometres seemed an eternity. Eventually through the screen of smoke the outline of the Community Hall appeared. A few vehicles had gathered from all directions. A brief discussion ensued and the decision to drive on was made. A convoy of well laden dirty mainly four-wheel-drive vehicles began their long journey to survival. The passengers frightened dejected men, women and children.

What a horrendous journey. Red hot embers showered down upon them. The intense red smoke, in reality flames within the smoke, swallowed up not only vegetation but all things created by human existence. The heat within the vehicles was hardly bearable, children made pathetic mutterings as they sensed the fear. Where and how would it end? Who would they never see again? Would they have to suffer the loss of all familiar belongings? Could they ever return to a much-loved area so familiar and once safe after such a horrendous happening?

Eventually the sad convoy noticed the change in the smoke. It had returned to orange. At last they were ahead of the fire.

What a relief to reach Yea with its wide streets and tree lined central plots. Safety at last. How they cried, hugged and shook hands with friends who were last seen prior to the fire. A gaggle of tired, stressed and despondent survivors dressed in anything from bare feet to gum boots with an assorted array of clothing anything but coordinated. Time did not allow for colour coding or a quick change. Facial expressions told it all. Tears flowed unashamedly for some. And others were pallid and trembling, eyes wide with an expression of absolute hopelessness. Lungs full of smoke rebelled and loud bouts of coughing reverberated along the plots. Children moaned or whined not fully understanding why they were in such a place.

A large assortment of animals of varying gender stood silently relying on their owners for safety. The caged cockatoo, its white feathers stained by smoke called "Have a great day or bugger off" which caused an odd slow smile on an otherwise stressed face.

As darkness dropped like a blind the smoke levels diminished slightly. Survivors laid down side by side along the central plot of this tiny organised town. What will tomorrow bring they wondered. Communications, were as usual sparse. However the odd straggler who had defended his patch with stoic heroism and then sought refuge, reported loss of life and property beyond belief.

As the long night travelled slowly and comfortably on, whispered conversations could be heard.

"How you going mate?"

Don't know how bloody safe we are here."

"Who knows where the bloody fire will head next."

"If the wind blows this way we're all done."

Dawn broke, and the day after began. The tired, fragile, disjointed throng rose from their hard earth beds and prepared to face the unknowns of yet another day. Fire fighters from the city sent support to the existing contingent of brave men and were greeted by clapping and cheering. Their faces just visible under their helmets, it was obvious the news was not good. It transpired many communities had been ravaged by fire. Not nameless people read about in the morning daily but mates, or the neighbour last seen hurtling down the river track on a dirt bike.

Utter despair embraced the pathetic homeless group. Looks of horror stamped the once happy open features. 'There's little left', was the repeated message. No passage back before authorities have investigated the damage to property and the loss of life.

Names, addresses and information on the whereabouts of others were written on a clipboard being passed about.

The future had begun, but the direction unsure. Some opted to be with friends and to remain in the area. Others went to family in the big city never to return. Dedicated bush dwellers vowed to return as soon as possible, to rebuild lives with a new beginning. The elevated heat levels, the stress and the uncertainty drained their energy. Sleep was spasmodic and disturbed. To think or function at normal levels impossible. Every day brought more sadness. Sadness and need were to be repeated. Unbearable emotion took over and a surge of anger and despair again reared its head.

When at last the brave returned to the homes they'd left in such a rush the trauma began again. Many returned to nothing but memories, others found a home still standing amid the ash. A remnant of what there once was. Rotting fruit in fridge and freezers. Badly scorched areas of cladding, and useless water tanks, smoke tainted interiors an everlasting reminder of that dreadful day.

Some lost family members. Where children once waited happily for a school bus there was now only a dream. The community regained its strength.

The wealthy, the workers, the sick, the unemployed, the elderly and the outcast of society worked together sharing the pain and helping each other. The local Community Hall still standing became the welfare centre. Supplying the immediate needs from the truckloads of donated goods. Much of which was brand new. What incredible kindness the greater community expressed. Furniture, food, clothing, tents and bedding for those in need.

Of almost 400 homes only 40 remained. Tents sprang up everywhere and the rebuild began in earnest.

From the ashes life began again. The area today, some four years on, defies belief of such tragedy.

Homes have been replaced, wildlife has returned, the gums have regenerated, the grass is green and lush and the gardens and trees are well established. The only evidence of fire are the blackened trunks of the trees for mile after mile. The huge black beech with its massive tall trunks stands even taller and greener than before. Bush fires are its salvation.

PLAYING HOOKY

Jennifer Lilly

George woke to the sound of magpies in the yellow gum tree which grew outside the back door and helped camouflage the lopsided out-house with its mantle of geraniums interspersed with blackberry canes. The perfume of the nearby honeysuckle pervaded his room as he drew aside the tattered curtains and looked out onto a perfect spring morning. Just the kind of day when the fish would be lying, beckoning any intrepid truant.

Delighting in the day George made haste to complete his morning chores. Without a fuss he collected the eggs and chopped the wood before carrying an armful into the kitchen where his mother was preparing breakfast for his father and two older sisters; George slid into his seat and listened earnestly to their tales of dropped sales and increased queues, George really wasn't interested. The sun was shining and there was food on his plate, and all the children these days had bullseyes on the seats of their pants, and most everybody's fathers spent their days queued up outside the Labour Exchange.

In the distance he could hear the clatter of the night-man returning from his rounds. Soon the mill would sound its shrill cry, calling the lucky ones to their shift. Then it would be time for him to grab his leather satchel and try to escape the kitchen undetected. Slowly he sidled to the end of the form.

"Where do you think you're going?" His father bellowed from behind the newspaper. His elder sister snickered.

173

"That's enough from you Mavis, haven't you got a job to go to? I'm quite sure that if you don't turn up at the store on time you won't have a job to go to tomorrow."

George felt better as he watched the soft flush rush up his sister's face before she dashed out the door.

"Well, are you going to answer me then?"

"I'm just on my way to school pa."

"Not before you..."

"Leave the boy alone Bill, it's not his fault that you've got sit around all day counting the flyspecks on the ceiling. He's got an education to attend to."

George made for the door, and, grabbing his hand-me-down boots, ran out into the yard.

It was good to get out of the house. He made his way around the side and banged through the rusty old front gate and into the street. It was going to be a hot day. Even the horses knew that, as they meandered, heads down, pulling the jinkers along the road. The cicadas had already started their chorus, and the dogs were lying in the morning shade, tongues lolling and too tired to scratch their fleas.

George joined the haphazard gaggle of children wandering towards the old wooden schoolhouse, the boys in long grey flannel shorts held up with braces and the girls in plaits and shapeless frocks. They all wore their shoes or boots tied together and strung around their necks, their bare toes making patterns in the soft dry dust of the main street.

"Psst, George!"

George looked over to where Podge was hiding behind the dilapidated palings of old Ma Brown's side fence.

"Come over here George, the fish are running at the weir - the swaggy who dossed down in our barn last night told me this morning."

A quick look at the sky, and a further look up the street towards the school with its massing children was all it took for George to scramble through the gap in the fence and follow his friend into the thick undergrowth that surrounded Ma Brown's house.

"Better keep a look-out for Harry," said Podge as they passed the lifeless eyes shaded by torn brown blinds. "Remember what happened last time Fred and Charlie came through this way? Scared as hell they were. Reckoned they'd never come this way again."

George shivered and looked around. Nothing but dried brambles and pine needles here. Not even a whiff of Harry. Maybe he was lurking around inside the house, following their progress from behind the closed doors and shaded windows. He could see a soft pall of blue smoke erupt from the kitchen chimney. So Ma Brown was just up and fixing her breakfast. They would have to be careful.

Ahead of them they could see the wire netting marking the boundary. Not much further now and they would be out into the open paddocks, and freedom for the day. Eager to achieve that freedom and get away from the possibility of Ma Brown, or Harry, catching them, they broke into a slow run, their clothes catching on the clawing fingers of the straggling saplings. An unheralded screech set their short hair on end and shivers ran down their spines. George and Podge stopped and waited. Ma Brown had seen them. They knew what would be next.

The two boys heard the bang of the wire door closing behind Harry as he ran towards where they were cowering in the dry pine needles and mouldering leaves. Long seconds lapsed before they could summon their legs to flee, and they crashed their way out of the undergrowth and tore across the remaining few yards of relatively clear ground in an attempt to outrun Harry. For his age he could sure run. He was so close now they could smell him. What a pong!

The sound of the blood pounding in their ears drowned out Harry's raucous howl of rage as George and Podge clambered over and through the netting and lay panting on the other side. Harry viewed them from inside.

"Ugly things Bull Terriers," said George, puffing to catch his breath. "I wish Ma Brown'd give him a wash."

The two boys stuck their tongues out at the dog and, picking themselves and their bits and pieces up, disappeared into the adjoining paddock, laughing as they heard Ma Brown calling vainly for her dog to come back into the house. She sounded funny without her dentures in place.

In the distance they could hear the school bell. George could see in his mind's eyes ginger-haired Charlie O'Grady with his checked shirt, buttons missing, and upturned nose crinkling with the pleasure of calling the other children into line as he manhandled the bell in arcs through the air. Charlie was so small that he needed both hands to ring the school bell. He was bell monitor this term and delighted in being important. He was too stupid to know that nobody, except maybe his mother, liked him. Oh well, there would be two boys short in the Grade Four line this morning. George wondered what Mister Pilson would say. It would be the fourth time this month that Podge had been absent. His first. He hoped that his mother wouldn't hear about it. Good thing his sisters had left school.

Podge threw a clod of dirt at George and jolted him out of his daydream.

"Race you to the edge of the wheat paddock," he said and started to gallop across the dry grass before George could answer. Spindly brown legs leaping haphazardly under a rotund body. It amazed George that a person as overweight as Podge could be supported by such thin legs. But that was Podge.

George took off after him, determined to catch up with him before they got to the fence. If he didn't then Podge was just as likely to go ploughing through the wheat, rather than around it. Wagging school was one thing, but ruining the wheat was something else entirely.

With a rugby tackle that would have done the local team proud last season George halted Podge's progress. The ensuing tussle was injury-free and friendly. Afterward the two boys lay panting on the ground. The dust settled over them. They coughed and gasped for breath. Two magpies flew over them and landed in the nearby gum tree.

"What can you see in the sky?" asked Podge.

"What do you mean, what can I see in the sky?" George answered, squinting above him.

"Well, I can see plenty of things. I can see the future, and the past. I can see castles and dragons, and kings and queens. What can you see?"

"All I can see are spots of black, dancing crazily when I close my eyes," said George. "And that's from having looked at the sun too long, and that's what's the matter with you, Podge. Come on or those fish'll have been caught before we even get to the weir."

George jumped up and kicked Podge in the ribs. "Come on. Race you to the river." And he ran off down the side of the fence. He could hear Podge pounding along behind him. At least it would keep him out of the wheat. When George reached the end of the paddock he stopped. Ahead of him he could see the sprawling river red gums, majestically dotting the river flats and providing shade and shelter for the straggling sheep and coloured lorikeets.

With the clear blue sky, it made quite a picture. He was glad he had wagged school. This was much better that sitting in a stuffy old school room, the air thick with chalk dust and the smell of carbolic. George could hear the drone of the teacher's voice and see the flies lazily circle above the bent heads of the children as they worked at their slates.

Podge collided into him.

"Oomph! Why'd you stop for? This ain't the river." And he ran ahead.

George shrugged his shoulders and raced after his friend. Podge would never understand. Small craters pocked the dirt track while their bare feet sent tufts of dust into the air as they raced towards the river.

They reached the river below the weir, and they waded up the bank, their toes squelching in the yellow clay, the tussocks scratching their bare legs.

Podge bent over and scratched his leg. "Reckon it'll be a good day for fishing, look at all those midges and the ripple rings in the water. Come on, beat you to the top."

George poked out his tongue and chased Podge up the grassy incline to the side of the weir. Already Podge was making his way to the retaining wall.

"Where're you going Podge?"

"Across the other side. The fish always bite better in among the reeds on the other side, you know that."

"But why didn't you cross over below? You can't cross here on the wall." George looked at the wall. The weir had been made by the locals just before the Great War. They had gathered together all the broken bits of concrete from the old bridges in the area, along with old pieces of pipe and timber and stones that they had lying around. Since then it had created a haven for the youngsters in the town. Now they had a permanent water hole to swim in and fish. But you didn't cross on the wall. His sister Mavis had known a boy who had tried once, he hadn't tried again. George looked at the sheet of clear water rolling over the slime covered, uneven surface of the wall. He didn't want to try.

"Podge, don't do it. You'll kill yourself."

"Don't be daft. You're just a sissy. Come on."

Podge was already a couple of feet out on the wall. The water banked up against his thin legs, changing the tone of the water as it slipped over the edge and disappeared down the wall, tumbling haphazardly over the conglomeration of masonry. George didn't like the idea of crossing over, nor did he want to be called a sissy and end up spending the day fishing on this side of the weir by himself. Shifting uncomfortably from foot to foot he tried to summon up the necessary courage to follow Podge.

"Come on," called Podge from the middle of the wall.

George looked over to his friend balancing precariously in the middle of the spillway, a forlorn scarecrow abandoned in a field, arms at right angles, balancing, spindly legs stuck out from underneath baggy grey shorts and disappearing into water above his ankles.

A long piece of bark was floating lazily along the surface of the water, heading straight for Podge.

"Look out!" shouted George.

Podge swung around. The bark snagged on one of his legs. His arms started to windmill as he tried to balance himself, but his feet could not find purchase on the slippery rock beneath them. George stood transfixed and watched the expression on his friend's face change from one of cocksureness and taunting to one of realisation and fear.

"Podge!" shouted George as, amid screams of terror, thrashing of limbs and the churning of water Podge disappeared over the wall and into the depths of the swirling water below the weir.

George ran back down the incline and raced to the edge of the river. The water was a murky yellow at the base of the wall where the water flow unsettled the clay bed of the river. For what seemed like hours George could not see any sign of his friend. Then, further downstream his peripheral vision glimpsed a blotch of grey.

"Podge!" he called, running to where his friend was, "Podge! Are you all right? Answer me!" He slipped out of his braces and shorts then stripped off his shirt. So what if he ripped the buttons off? He waded out into the cold water and started to thrash out toward Podge. The current was stronger than he'd thought it would be, but finally he was beside his friend. Podge was lying face down in the water, George turned him over. His eyes were closed, and his face was a horrid shade. George frantically kicked and splashed his way to the opposite shore.

He dragged the sodden Podge up the bank behind him and, turning him on to his stomach started to wallop his back to expel the water from his lungs. He didn't know if he was doing it right, but he had to do something for his friend. What would he do if Podge died? How could he explain to his mother, and to Podge's mother, what they were doing at the weir, instead of being in school? That he had stood by and watched his best friend drown?

He thumped into Podge's back even harder. His own breath was coming in sharp bursts and he could feel a stinging in his eyes. He dropped his head onto his forearms to rub his eyes, he couldn't leave off his thumping, and was surprised to find his arm, which had dried with the exertion, wet again.

Podge's arms and legs started to twist and shake in a grotesque fashion.

"What the dickens do you think you're doing? Trying to kill a fella?" spluttered Podge, coughing and struggling to shake George off his back.

George sat back and stared at Podge glowering beneath him. He was alive! He'd done it! He'd saved his friend! He gave him another thump between the shoulder blades before falling back on the grassy bank to catch his breath.

"Is that all the thanks I get? I nearly drowned myself to save you, and all you can do is yell at me."

The two boys lay on the bank, chests heaving and both coughing spasmodically. The sun warmed their bodies and a fine steam rose from their wet clothes.

"Well, we sure ain't dead," said Podge, scratching himself. "There ain't no ants in heaven. And we've still got the rest of the day to go fishing."

George looked across at his friend. He couldn't believe it. How could he lie there so blatantly oblivious to the narrow escape he'd had from death, and carry on as though nothing had happened?

As the boys lay there in the sun recuperating and planning the rest of the day they didn't hear the soft rustle of the rushes and scrunching of dead leaves.

"Mister Pilson! Look what I found!"

George and Podge both rolled onto their stomachs and watched as Charlie O'Grady beat a hasty retreat towards where the school children, and Mister Pilson, could be seen making their way toward the weir. The two friends looked at each other, flopped back onto the grass.

"Who forgot that today was an excursion to the weir?" snarled George.

Podge grimaced. "And to go fishing too," he groaned.

RAINCHECK

Leigh Leslie

Phoebe regarded the telephone warily. Since childhood she would, every now and then, get a flash of inspirational foresight. She was getting one now. She just *knew* who was holding the handpiece at the other end of the strident wailing. And she did not want to pick her end up.

It could only be Lyle Fisher.

Why was it that every unappealing man thought he was God's gift to womankind, and to her in particular? She was sure that he had a wonderful personality. But in the real world it was looks that counted. Lyle Fisher. Overweight, pear shaped, balding blob. And that was being kind to him on a good day. Okay, she would grudgingly admit that she was no longer any great shakes herself. In all honesty, these days she tried to avoid the mirror. But at least when she sat down her knees still met.

"Hello Phoebe." Lyle's voice grated in her ear.

"Lyle. How are you?" She eased herself into the armchair by the phone.

"Just fine. I was wondering what version of *EverNote* you had on your computer."

"*EverNote.* I don't think I know that one."

"You know, that program that lets you copy and paste."

"No Lyle. I don't know, so I guess I don't have it."

"It's really good. Quite handy in fact. You can do your copying and pasting with just a click on your tool bar. You don't need to open other windows. Would you like me to install it for you?"

"That's quite alright Lyle. I don't think I need it." She stifled a yawn.

"Oh but you do," he enthused. "You do. I use it all the time. Don't know how I managed without it before. Have you seen any movies lately?"

She blinked and sat upright. That was a quick change of direction. "Er, no." What had possessed her to give him her number? Then she remembered that she hadn't, it had been her sister Claire who had done that.

"How about we go then?"

"I tend not to go out much these days, you know."

"All the more reason to go. What about tomorrow?"

"I have no idea what's on."

The rustle of paper filtered down and into Phoebe's ear, accompanied by the inevitable wheezes that went with any physical activity on Lyle's part. Why on earth had Claire thought that they might be a match? Didn't Claire realise that after years as a single parent, followed by years of caring for their aged father, she might just like to be on her own?

"Okay, there is ..." he listed what she could only assume he imagined she would like. All chick flicks, nothing with substance. Just went to show how little he, or Claire, knew her.

"Is *Casino Royale* still showing? I haven't managed to see it yet." She felt sure that he would have already seen it, and it would be a safe 'out'.

"It's a good movie."

Excellent! Phoebe thought, but then her euphoria was dashed.

"Wouldn't mind seeing it again. It's on at 5.40. Shall I pick you up?"

"That's okay, I'll meet you there at, say 5.30?"

"Good-o. It's a date! See you outside the cinema at 5.30 then. Bye, and thanks."

Going to the movies was *not* a date. And there would be NO dates, not with Lyle anyway. She had not liked him when they were at school together, and she still didn't like him. Why had Claire given him her number? More importantly, why had she agreed to go to the movies with him?

Phoebe stared at the handpiece in her hand and groaned. She could not believe it. She had agreed to go out with Lyle! Then she chided herself. Lyle was all right. He simply was not for her. She replaced the phone and wandered into the garden. The weeds greeted her with a profusion of green. She smiled. A weed was simply a plant in the wrong place. A bit like Lyle.

The phone rang again, and she rushed inside to answer it. No premonitions this time, so she was taken quite by surprise.

"Phoebe? Lyle again."

Maybe he was going to beg off?

"Only, I don't know if I thanked you."

Thanked me? What is with this guy, she wondered. "Thanked me? Sorry, can't help you there. Wouldn't know. If you did, then I didn't notice, if you didn't, it didn't register." Ouch, she thought, but apparently Lyle didn't notice the insult.

"Yes, for saying that you'd go out with me."

"It's only going to the movies, Lyle."

"I know, but...I'm really pleased that you agreed. I've been wanting to ask you out for a long time now..."

"It's okay Lyle, I'll see you tomorrow." She hung up. She did not want to hear anymore.

Geesh, what was it with some guys? Smile and they think it's an invitation to bed. She really would have to be careful tomorrow. There was no way she wanted to give him the wrong idea, but somehow she felt that she already had. She yanked at another weed and tossed it onto the growing pile of wilting greenery beside her.

Tomorrow. What could she say to quell his ardor? Assuming, of course that that is what it was. Oh yes. Another weed hit the pile.

He was desperate. She could tell that by the sound of his voice. She may not have had a beau for a decade or two, but she was, after all, a woman, and women knew these things. They could tell when a man was on the prowl. Pity that men were not as perceptive to the vibes. She really could kill Claire. She was simply, not, interested. She had her children and grandchildren to keep her occupied.

Grandchildren! She sat back on her heels. How could she have forgotten? She had a baby shower to go to tomorrow evening. And her eldest son was calling in on his way home to load *Skype* onto her computer. How could she have forgotten?

Then she remembered Lyle's second phone call, and how desperate he had sounded, wanting to ensure that he had thanked her for agreeing to go to the movies with him. While she might not want to go to the movies with him, there was no way that she would allow herself to feel sorry for him. But she still felt bad about having to let him down. Yet there was no way that she could go to the movies with him, not tomorrow. Not now. Not ever.

She brushed the dirt off her hands and struggled to her feet, arching her back to get the crinks out. She looked ruefully at the weeds still in the garden. "You'll keep," she said with a shake of her head and went indoors to phone Lyle.

She was still trying to reach Lyle on the phone at 5 o'clock the next afternoon. Just typical. Whenever you want a man, he can't be found. She stormed about the house, flinging her things together. Drat the man, there was nothing to do but leave a message for her son and go and front up to Lyle and tell him that she couldn't go.

Phoebe arrived at the cinema at 5.25. She had thought that if Lyle was as anxious to go out with her as he appeared to be, then he would have ensured that he was there waiting for her. But he wasn't. By 5.45 her face was tight from the congenial grinning to the patrons streaming into the cinema while she stood outside and waited.

She turned swiftly at the sound of hurried footsteps behind her. A retort ready. But it was a stranger who stopped in front of her. She felt her stomach do a flip. His face lit up as he smiled and her stomach did another flip.

"Are you Phoebe?"

She nodded, not trusting her voice. Now if Lyle had looked like this.

"Oh good. Sorry I'm late, but..."

"But you're not Lyle."

"No, Lyle couldn't get away. His mother, you know. She's taken a turn for the worst. I'm Alaine. Alaine Underwood. My mother is in the next room to Lyle's mother, and... Well anyway, Lyle couldn't get here, and he wasn't able to get to a phone, so he asked me to come and apologise for him. He suggested maybe another day?"

Phoebe gulped. "Well, I'm only here because I couldn't get hold of him, I was going to ask for a raincheck."

Alaine Underwood looked at her and raised an eyebrow. Phoebe wished that her stomach would behave. She hadn't felt such flutters for many years.

"And you'd like to make that a permanent raincheck?"

Phoebe blushed, not trusting her voice.

"Like a coffee?" his eyes twinkled. A thrill raced through her, her chest tightened and her voiced squeaked "I have to get home, but..."

"A raincheck maybe?"

"Yes please."

They both laughed, and Phoebe knew that this was one raincheck that most definitely would be redeemed.

SOME MEN CAN BE BASTARDS

Leigh Leslie

The patchwork of clouds was quickly coalescing and threatening to spill over into rain as Janice and Muriel sat in the car watching the hearse slowly negotiate the rutted path up to the stone church.

"An appropriate send off for Lionel, don't you think?" Janice mused.

Muriel guffawed. "You mean the weather?"

"That, and the uneven ride. Bet you anything Mavis would be getting her boots on ready to dance a jig, if she only knew what was happening."

"Poor Mavis. Don't suppose there's any chance she'll be here."

Janice turned the key and switched the wipers on to clear the windscreen. "What point would there be? Other than for her and her carer getting wet."

"Such a shame. She was such a lively lass."

"No thanks to him. Do you know what he did?" Janice asked.

Muriel creased her brow, wondering what incident in particular Janice was referring to. "You mean after Bert died?"

"Yes, Bert was hardly in his grave before Lionel was there with a comforting arm around her shoulders. All sympathy and offering a lending hand."

"After Bert's money was he?"

"Well, yes. Bert had been quite the astute investor and had left Mavis very comfortably well off. Thankfully the boys, you know one's a lawyer? Well, when things looked like nuptials were on the horizon David made sure that his father's legacy was securely out of reach of

Lionel's hands. And a good thing too as it turned out. Mavis's now being well cared for."

"You mean that Lionel wasn't responsible for financing where she is now?"

It was Janice's turn to laugh. "You can't be serious? Lionel? Look after Mavis? He was hoping that by marrying her he'd be living in clover. When he learned that he couldn't get his grubby hands on the money all the lovey-dovey pantomime flew out the window. Do you know, they'd go to the cinema and he'd take a book to read during the intermission?"

"Never!"

Janice nodded her head. "Yes, and then ... Do you remember that time when she had laryngitis? Well I was with them at a meeting, and the adjudicator asked Mavis to read the minutes. Lionel stood up at the back of the room and, twirling his finger around the side of his head as if to indicate insanity, yelled out that it was stupid to ask her as she couldn't read. Then, to add insult to injury, he laughed."

"That's awful. Did Mavis say or do anything?"

"You bet she did. Gave him quite the evil eye, *and* an earful. As eloquently as her laryngitis would allow, she read the minutes to a silent room. Everyone applauded while Lionel stalked out."

"Good on Mavis. Hope he didn't get stuck into her when she got home."

Janice shook her head. "I don't think he ever laid a hand on her in anger. At least I never saw any evidence, nor did Mavis ever mention anything. Besides, growing up with multiple brothers, and a background in jujitsu, she could look after herself well enough."

"I didn't know that she did jujitsu. Mind you, I've not known her as long as you have."

Janice watched the wipers sweep back and forth across the windscreen.

"But that's not all. I was out in the car one day—this was before Mavis had been diagnosed with dementia—and I saw her. It was mid-morning and she was out walking, barefooted and in her PJs. That did make me wonder. Anyway, I stopped and gave her a ride home. When I got to their place Lionel was sitting there on the front porch reading the newspaper. Do you know what he said?'

Muriel shook her head while Janice caught her breath.

"I can still hear him." Janice pitched her voice in a perfect copy of his squeaky voice, "'Oh, you brought her home, did you?' and he continued reading. It was me who took her inside and helped her to get dressed."

The two women sat silently for a few minutes, noting the sombre people, presumably friends of Lionel, as they straggled along the path and into the church. Janice looked at her watch.

"I suppose, if we are going to attend, then we ought to make a move."

"Guess so. It's the least we can do for Mavis. Good riddance I say."

Janice gave a little giggle. "Yes, at least if we're inside we can know for sure that he is no more." Janice turned the wipers off and took the key out of the ignition before undoing her seatbelt. She turned to the back seat and hoiked her umbrella out from off the floor behind her. The two friends got out of the car and once both doors were closed Janice locked the car and they headed towards the church.

"For me the worst incident, and I witnessed this one myself, was one day in one of Mavis's more lucid moments – she does have them you know – Lionel turned up with a parcel for her. A few weeks previously I'd been visiting and noticed that Mavis's knickers were in tatters. I know, I could, and I should have, gone and bought some news ones for her, but ... well, I didn't. Instead I suggested to the staff that they ask Lionel to bring her some new ones from home. After all, he was her husband."

Muriel looked across at Janice.

"Oh yes, I knew Mavis would have had more at home."

Carefully the two of them picked their way around the puddles. Janice laughed.

"I was there when he brought them in. You know, the knickers. He almost threw the plastic supermarket bag at Mavis where she was sitting in the chair. She just managed to grab the bag before it slid down off her knees. But not in time to save the contents from tumbling out and onto the floor. You'll never guess what he had brought."

"What?"

"I bent down to pick up the knickers, only to see that they were his."

"You're kidding!"

"Oh yes. His Y-fronts. Old, and I mean old, they were grey, thread bare, and holey. I was speechless. But while I knelt beside Mavis, she, the darling soul that she is, looked up at Lionel and lashed out at him with her walking stick."

Muriel cupped her hands over her mouth and laughed.

"Yes, and she copped him a beauty. Must have left quite the bruise. In fact, with that one swipe she succeeded in being instrumental in us being here today."

"You mean, she killed him? With a walking stick?"

"Not exactly, but the force of the blow inflicted sufficient vascular damage that the clotting precipitated, eventually, the heart attack that ended him."

Muriel stopped at the open church door and looked at Janice. "Well, good for Mavis. That's all I can say. Are we going in or what?"

Janice and Muriel linked arms and smiling, entered the church and sat down.

"Unbelievable."

Janice looked at her friend, eyebrow raised in query.

Muriel nodded in the direction of the coffin at the front. "That man is totally unbelievable."

"Oh, you'd better believe it, he was that, and more. Some men can be bastards."

SPINNER OF YARNS

Leigh Leslie

Johnny Buchanan stood at the entrance of yet another new school playground and sighed. Would he ever get used to being the 'new kid'? Would things be different this time? Please, please mum, don't hold my hand, he thought and held his breath as his mother's hand moved from his shoulder. He looked up at her and mustered a smile. Life simply was not fair for a ten-year-old boy to have a father who moved his family every couple of years.

The two of them walked up the path to the school office. Johnny could feel eyes glancing in their direction and then move away, back to the clusters of cohorts scattered around the playground. Typical. This school would be no different to the others. He would quickly become forgotten as a nobody. There was nothing he could do to change that. He didn't excel at sport or at exams, and with his knock knees, unruly red hair, buck teeth and freckles he had no charisma. He would never be a teacher's pet, nor anyone's friend.

The bell announcing the commencement of the school day had rung before the enrolment procedure had been completed so the halls were empty and quiet as the principal led Johnny to his classroom.

Johnny stood, shoulders back and stared blankly at the display of artwork on the back wall opposite him, ignoring the disinterested students sitting in front of him as Miss Gillespie introduced him to the class, and admonished the children to be helpful to the new boy. There was a shuffling of feet on the wooden floorboards. He thought it interesting that she should say 'helpful' and not the usual 'kind'. Even his new teacher could see no potential in him, he thought as she directed him to a desk at the front. At the front where he would be invisible to her as she glared at the disruptive students at the back, but in the line of sight of those behind him all too ready to whisper about him, or use his head as a target for spit-balls until the novelty wore out when he didn't respond.

That first week's assignment was the turning point in Johnny's existence. The class was to go home and find out something about their family. Preferably something noteworthy. Johnny had rushed home confident that there would be someone in the family whose exploits would give him kudos sufficient to provide him with friends and confidence.

Such hopes had been shot down with the proverbial flames. In fact, both his parents had laughed at him even suggesting that the family would have any skeleton of worth lurking in forgotten cupboards.

Feeling utterly dejected, and hopelessly despondent he retreated to his bedroom, lay on his bed with his hands behind his head and stared, unseeing, at the ceiling where his collection of model aeroplanes silently swayed at the end of their fishing line tethers. It had been stupid of him to have entertained the notion that ancestral acclaim would redeem him.

As the war planes came into focus the foundation of the lie was formulated. Johnny bounced off the bed and grabbed a book from the shelf above his desk. If his family could not help him, then he would create his own family.

"My grandfather," he announced the next week, chest puffed out with pride, "was an officer on the *Lusitania* when she was torpedoed. *He* saved Alice Lines by pulling her into a lifeboat by her hair." No one can beat that, he thought, his smile almost a smirk. And no one did. The remainder were a catalogue of pub-owners, policemen, dressmakers and the like. More to the point, having claim to a war hero elevated him to the status of 'someone of interest'. However, for this popularity to be maintained Johnny needed to elaborate on the exploits of his grandfather, and other members of his extended family.

If Johnny was to be believed, and he was, his deceased aunts, uncles, and cousins for generations past were all people of notoriety. Never fully in the limelight, but always active in the periphery, and nearly always on the right side of the law—he had thrown in some renegades for colour and variety—it would never look good to not have the occasional black sheep, that always seemed to appeal to the girls.

By the time Johnny left school and entered the workforce he was not only accepted by his peers but lauded by them. His belief in the heritage he had created boosted his confidence and he not only wore the fantasy with pride, but he imbued his own family with it as well. His own children would quickly jump in and defend their history, quibbling with anyone who dared to dispute the facts as they knew them to be.

The lies that had started when he was just a lad had become so much a part of who he was that he had long forgotten that the stories were all make-believe. They had been born out of the need to belong. To be accepted. Even to stand out. And they had grown from there and become a part of his entity. And now, after all these years, here was a little flibbertigibbet standing in front of him who was calling him out. Him, John Buchanan, respected member of the community and local tycoon now found himself at the peril of his favourite granddaughter.

Amy had come home from school the other day all fired up over a history assignment. She was to research her family history and see if she could find anyone in her ancestry worthy of note. Of course she had been tempted to put her hand up there and then, she told her grandfather, and recite what she already knew to be true. But the teacher had said that any claims to fame had to be substantiated with accurate references, and suggested that the students forgot about family folk lore and started from scratch. Confident in what she already knew Amy had gone home and duly researched the undocumented but well-known family ancestors.

"Don't worry Pops. I promise not to tell anyone about your fabrications, but I am going to lay claim to having royal forebears. Fancy no one knowing that your family tree links in with the likes of the Habsburgs."

TAXI

Jennifer Lilly

She saw the taxi driver looking at her in the rear-vision mirror. She smiled briefly and looked at her watch.

"It's all right pet, plenty of time yet. They'll be asleep for hours."

Her head flicked up as though she'd been shot. He was grinning at her via the mirror. What did he know? She took a furtive glance at her travelling companions. They didn't stir. She wriggled uncomfortably and wished that the traffic along Swanston Street wasn't so slow.

"Been doing this long have you pet?" The driver shot her another white smile, only this time he turned around, so that she caught the full effect of his white teeth and charismatic face. She continued to stare ahead, preoccupied, reading the bumper stickers on the rear window of the car in front. They were stopped at traffic lights. She wished the driver would turn around.

"There, there, don't get upset. Bob and Roy are good mates of mine. I've been through this lots of times."

Her teeth were clenched as firmly as the hands in her lap. If he didn't turn around and stop talking soon, she'd ... She didn't quite know what she could do. Still, it was rather reassuring to hear Bob and Roy mentioned. If only she felt more at ease. Under different circumstances, she would quite enjoy the challenge of flirting with the driver. He wasn't bad looking and she'd like even to go out with him. But not now. It was her first delivery, and she was nervous.

The taxi jolted forward as the lights changed. She quickly looked at her companions. Mrs. Beatty sat in front with the driver. She could see her rinsed curls bobbing every time the taxi jerked forward. She smiled to herself and leant forward as far as her seatbelt would allow to see the woman's mouth had dropped open, dark tongue lolling like some stray dog's.

"She's all right pet. Don't fret yourself over our Mrs. Beatty."

She sat back with an angry jolt. How dare he read her mind like that. What else was he privy to? Pink fused up her cheeks.

"You look quite cute when you are ruffled like that. Not like old Mrs. Death there. Now, there's a name for you!" He burst out laughing as he slammed on the brakes. She spun her head to the left to look at the woman sitting beside her. What possibly could she have done now? But the woman was sitting there perfectly poised. Gloved hands in her lap, fur collared coat, with a small posy of violets attached to the chest. The fine lines around her mouth ran to join the rivers and ridges that coursed down her neck, before being engulfed with fur. She could see nothing wrong with Mrs. Death. Miss Phillips, on her right, was sliding down on the vinyl seat. Her skirt was rumpled up around her thighs, revealing pudgy pale flesh oozing over the tops of her stockings. A dribble was wending its way from out of the corner of her mouth where the lipstick was blurred. Of all the women, it was Miss Phillips that she had the most pity for. The other women were of the world. Miss Phillips was the epitome of weak character. All too ready to follow along with the stronger characters of her sisters.

"Strange one to have on board that one," said that the taxi driver, looking in the mirror briefly and jabbing his thumb over his shoulder at Miss Phillips. He was totally irritating in his manner, and not for the first time she wished the trip over. In fact, she wished that her need for money had not been so great that she now found herself in this position. She must have been mad to answer the advertisement, and madder still to accept the assignment. If only she had not needed the money. She wriggled uncomfortably under the reflected scrutiny of the driver.

"Not your usual occupation is it? Still, I can't imagine you walking the streets. Did you need the money?"

God! She wished he would shut up. The traffic was thinning now as they left the city behind then and headed out of Melbourne. She tried to pull Miss Phillips' skirt down, but the weight of the sleeping woman was too much for her.

"This isn't the way to the airport!" she exclaimed, as the taxi sped past the freeway entrance. "We're going to the airport. I told you that when I booked the taxi, and when we got in." She was starting to get a headache. Late nights and early mornings did not help when she was under the stress of today.

"I refuse to pay the extra fare, if you don't take us the shortest route to the airport. We have a plane to catch."

"Don't worry pet. Bob and Roy are friends of mine."

She sat up straight and looked in the mirror. For once the driver wasn't looking at her. She took a closer look at his eyes, and the set of his head. He wasn't from the same mould as Bob and Roy's other friends. But maybe that was because he was more in the public eye. Maybe he didn't know them.

"How do you propose to get these three sleeping biddies out of the taxi and into the airport, far less the plane, by yourself?"

"I'll manage," she said through clenched teeth. She hadn't thought of that, and neither Bob nor Roy had mentioned it. How would she get them out, and on board? "Just get us to the airport." She looked over at the sleeping women. Maybe Roy had doped them too much. They should be only groggy. Enough to warrant assistance through customs and immigration, and on to the plane. Then her part was over. She could then go home and pay off her sister's debts and even have a bit left over for herself. She looked up and realised that the taxi driver was looking at her expectantly.

"I'm sorry, what did you say?" Why was she apologising? He would collect his fare at the end, there was no need to engage her in conversation.

"I asked if you were sure you want the airport, and not the hospital? The one in here with me looks in more need of a doctor than a flight. She is quite high enough as it is."

She leapt forward, but was stopped by her seat belt. She unclipped her belt and leaned over the front seat. Mrs. Beatty was slumped against the door. Her face was very white, her breathing shallow, and her pulse was visible as a slight, slow flutter at her temple. She felt quickly for her pulse. What was she to do? Would there be a doctor at the airport, or should she make a detour to the nearest hospital?

"Well?"

"The hospital."

She sank back into the seat and sighed. All that money. She wouldn't get it now. Even if she left Mrs. Beatty at the hospital and took the other two women to the airport she still wouldn't get paid. It had been an all or nothing deal. And it had seemed so easy. Escort three dopey women onto a plane and collect $10,000. Do not pass go, do not collect $10,000, go straight to jail. That's where she'd be going as soon as the doctors took a look at Mrs. Beatty. She wasn't too sure what racket Bob and Roy were into, but a racket she was sure it was. Why else drug three old ladies before bundling them into a taxi and taking them to the airport? The taxi driver was still looking at her in the mirror. God, she wished he'd stop. What was his name and number? She'd report him when she got home. Unsavoury types like him shouldn't be allowed to drive defenceless ladies. She looked for his license. It was too tattered to be legible. That figures, she thought to herself as the taxi pulled into the casualty entrance of the hospital. Furiously she struggled to get out of the taxi. But she couldn't get past Miss Phillips on the one side as she had slipped down too far and was blocking the door. She couldn't get across Mrs. Death to get the catch. The taxi driver, seeing her plight walked around to open the door for her. Mrs. Death slid out of the car into a heap on the road. An orderly from the hospital came to assist.

"No, not her, the other one." She frantically gesticulated to Mrs. Beatty sitting regally in the front of the taxi. "The one in the front."

The orderly looked at her sprawled across the recumbent old woman in the tatty fur and raised his eyes to the taxi driver.

The driver shrugged his shoulders. "I think they had all better be admitted," he said, and helped her to her feet.

She shrugged out of his grasp and brushed herself down. "Get your hands of me! I'm sick of you and your interfering. You were hired to get me to the airport. Nothing more. And you can't even do that for me. What am I to do?" she wailed as he manoeuvred her inside the hospital behind the three women.

"Now suppose you tell me your name and the names of these three women. And while you are about it, you may like to tell me about Bob and Roy as well."

She looked at him. "I thought you said you knew them."

"Ah, yes, I know them. But only as names, behind a drug racket."

"I'm not telling you anything."

"I think you are," he said, showing her his identification.

"You're police?" she managed to gasp.

He grinned, patted her hand, and nodded.

She turned pale and slowly collapsed into his arms. He liked the feel of her resting against his chest, before a passing nurse, seeing his predicament, attended to her in her faint. Maybe she could turn crown witness and be reprieved that way. She certainly didn't give the impression of being a hardened criminal. Besides, he liked her spunkiness and the soft warmth of her as she had fallen against his chest as she collapsed. He took out his notebook and pen and wandered to the phone. He'd think about that aspect of this morning's work later. For the moment duty demanded his whole attention.

THE BREAKWATER

Jennifer Lilly

He loved to walk along the beach in the early morning, before the sun became unbearably hot and the sand littered with bronzing bodies. A most unhealthy habit he had always thought, and now, weren't the medicos saying just the same thing? A man born before his time. That was what he was. He kicked a dead jellyfish aside with his sand-shoed foot. If they were in the Bay it would be a sure thing that today more people would be on the sand than in the water. Before breakfast certainly was the best time of the day to be on the beach.

He put his hand against his chest and felt his heart pumping. Not too fast, so he was doing all right. He looked ahead. It wasn't far to the breakwater now. He would rest then.

One step at a time.

That is what his mother used to tell him, so many years ago, and when she had stopped, his wife had taken over the task. It should have been his motto. One Step At A Time. The breakwater was closer now. He could reach it easily. Why had he doubted his ability? Just because everyone kept telling him that he could no longer do things, he was starting to believe it himself.

He must be getting old. He smiled and a throaty laugh bubbled up inside him. Getting old! Why he was only seventy. Still a chicken. His Dad had lived to be ninety-six. There was plenty of go left in him. Still, his Dad hadn't been wounded in the war like he had been. No. His Dad had been down the mines since a wee tot, had fought in the Great War, smoked all his life and had worked hard. Oh well, there was that theory scotched.

One step at a time.

The breakwater wasn't far away now. He could make out the individual rocks which had been cemented together to make a safe sailing harbour, so many years ago. He could remember playing on the foundations as a kid. Getting in the workmen's way. How they had yelled at him and his mate George. George. Now what had happened to him over the years? Where was he now? He'd gone away to war too. Had he come back? It was damnable not being able to remember important things like that.

He looked up at the breakwater again. He could see the twinkling of the flecks of mica in the granite, the sun must be rising above the red sandstone cliffs which were behind him. He still had time. It would be another good thirty minutes before Mabel would be up and wanting him to eat his breakfast and swallow an apothecary's selection of pills. Damn pills. He could not go anywhere these days without taking along a rainbow of pharmaceutical concoctions. And how Mabel loved to remind him. It brought the Charge Sister out in her. Once a nurse, always a nurse. Still, she'd been a pretty little nurse. A regular sight for sore eyes that one had been. All dolled up in her starched white uniform. A real prim and proper battle-axe, until you learnt how to get around her. Then she would show you her true heart of gold. They used to call her the Velvet Lady. Not the Iron Lady, the Velvet Lady. She was a real sweety underneath her tough exterior. Still, that's how she would have had to have been to have survived and got her job done, surrounded, as she had been with the regurgitated remains of soldiers from battle fronts.

She had been his ward Charge Sister for the three months he had been there. Then she had become his penfriend for another three months, agreeing to marry him on a whim one summer evening before he returned to active duty. Neither of them had thought that he would return, and he often wondered if she had only married him to get rid of his advances and because she had felt sorry for him. He'd never felt sorry for marrying her. And they had had a wonderful life together. Still, she was rather enjoying her role as a nurse again. He laughed, then grasped his stomach and started to cough. Breathe deep, and slow.

Deep and slow. That could have been another motto of his.

Deep and Slow.

Mabel thought he was a deep person, and slow. She'd laugh with friends and say that his courting of her was so slow that she'd just about decided to propose herself, she'd gotten so tired of waiting. Deep and slow. He'd been in a deep coma and had been slow to rally. But he'd made it.

Deep and slow.

The coughing spasm stopped, and he once again looked at the breakwater. Another few steps and he would be able to touch it. He could see the roughness of the rocks above the high tide mark, where the water never reached and so never weathered the rock into a smooth, uniform surface.

The tide was out this morning, so he'd have to walk some distance beside the breakwater before he could reach a point where he could ascend to the top of the breakwater wall. Once he was on top he would be able to look back over the distance that he had come that morning. He would see where his feet had pocked the wet sand, and where the advancing waves had obliterated his presence. He would look beyond his footprints to the red cliffs which jutted out into the Bay. When he had been a lad they had seemed to tower ever upwards, challenging him to scale their dizzy heights. He could remember the exhilaration he had felt the first time he had succeeded. How wonderful it had been to stand on top of the world, the Bay dotted with sailing boats, lying at his feet. He had clasped his imaginary telescope to his eye and scanned the horizon for pirate ships and enemies. Little had he realised how prophetic those innocent boyhood gestures would become.

Slowly he made his way along the cold sand. He could feel the roughness of the rocks under his steadying hand and smell the salt which had dried on the lower rocks. Or was it just his imagination?

The sharp pricks of the periwinkles hidden in the cracks and on the cement were real enough, he thought as he absently leaned his weight against a particularly vindictive one. This morning he didn't feel like clambering over the breakwater. He must be getting old. No! He wasn't allowed to think like that. Still, he would walk up to the end, and around it. Mustn't stop till then.

One step at a time, that was all it needed. He picked his way along the wall, not allowing himself the luxury of rest. To attain the objective was the aim.

The sun was just lapping the end of the breakwater where it dipped into the waves as he rounded the land end and slowly made his way along the further side of the wall until it was the right height for him to lean against and still see over. No standing on the top today, but he would still look back and survey the terrain which he had that morning conquered.

He leant heavily against the breakwater, moving his body until he could find a reasonably comfortable position. The sun was inching its way towards him. He had until it reached the land end of the breakwater before his curfew would be in jeopardy. His fingers absently traced patterns in the sand which lay on top of the concrete slabs that ran along the top of the breakwater. He blew at the sand in front on him and watched as the grains danced and tussled with each other in their haste to escape the draught. He shifted his weight from one foot to the other. He still had time.

He looked up to the cliffs. He could still see the entrance to the cave which he and George had started to carve out. They hadn't dug very far before they outgrew the novelty and the reality of life had taken over. They had gone off to war, as had all the boys he'd gone to school with. But he remembered George the best. Had George come home? He must remember to ask Mabel. Dear Mabel. What would she be doing now? Probably up and dressed and fussing over his breakfast. She'd squeeze him orange juice and prepare a grapefruit, being careful how much sugar she put on. Then she'd count out the slices of wholemeal bread ready to be toasted. Proportioning the butter so there would be no way in which he could sneak an extra smear onto his toast. He smiled. How he loved Mabel, and all her fastidious ways.

Barbara, their daughter was just like her in so many ways. Fastidious, and a Velvet Lady as well. Only a few knew it. To most of their friends, and hers, she was known as the Woman of Steel. Not only capable of most things, but generally a darn side better at them than any male who tried to help. Himself included. Barbara hadn't always been like that though. It had been a matter of necessity with her. Having to battle and bring up her family the way she did.

He watched, fascinated, as a small yacht sailed into view around the base of the cliff. Someone out for a morning sail. There wasn't much wind where he was, but there was enough out beyond the sheltered cove to fill the mainsail of the yacht. As a boy he'd come to the rock pools at the base of the cliff and had sailed paper boats fashioned from the pages of old exercise books. Sailing had come a long way since then. So had the cove. He looked along the beach. Until recently about twenty brightly coloured beach boxes had jostled with the tea-trees that edged the sand. They had been a good innovation, and he missed them. People had called them an eyesore, and dilapidated, and had demanded their removal. They had been removed. Now families had to lug all their beach things to and from the cove every time they wanted to come to the beach.

He'd been to the beach one day several years ago when it was hot, and he had watched as family after family had struggled down the worn steps of the cliff face. Every member laden with beach paraphernalia. Dropping hats and towels and food and books along the way. Sending little Johnny or Sally back up the path to collect the missing articles. He'd watched them as the babies had become progressively hotter and fractious, the littlies redder. He'd sat smugly under the umbrella which Barbara had stuck into the sand for him and had thought of how much easier it had been when every family had had a beach box. Especially when it came time to go home. Everything had been piled into the beach box, willy-nilly if Mum wasn't around, and there it had stayed till next time you came to the beach. You could then scamper up the cliff unhampered with everything but the sunburn. Mind you, you had to be particular to whom you lent your box to, otherwise you might find things missing next time. He'd lost a comic book that way once. And the last visit of the summer was always a pain. For one thing Mum always said it was the last time, but it wasn't, and you had to bring everything back again. Or then again, opening it up for the first time of the season, and you'd find forgotten socks gone mouldy, and rat muck festering in a corner. Then, as you got older the boxes were always good places to come to in the middle of winter with your mates, or girlfriend. He smiled at the memory. Maybe that was why people had objected to the boxes.

He laughed, sending a flurry of sand across the concrete. Oh, it was good to be alive. And to have such wonderful memories. He looked over to the tea-trees which covered the cliff and lined the beach. You could no longer tell that there had once been beach boxes along here. And now there were smart asphalt steps and a handrail leading down from the top of the cliff. Funny how he had never considered the tea-tree cliff to be a cliff, yet it held the same geography and adventure as the bare red cliff which dominated the little cove.

The sun had reached him. It would soon be time to move and go home. He took a deep breath. He was sure he could taste the sea. How he loved the sea. He was so pleased that he had always been able to live near it, even if he could no longer see it from the house. It was the same house that he had grown up in. Mabel had come and lived with his parents after they had married. Then when he had been de-mobbed, he had returned home too. It seemed the sensible thing to do, to stay with his parents while he looked for work and saved for a house of their own. Then Barbara had been born, and his mother had died. Naturally they couldn't leave his father on his own, so he, Mabel and Barbara had stayed. Mabel hadn't minded, she'd said it was just the same as having a house of their own, without all the hassles of a mortgage.

Practical girl that Mabel. Just like their daughter Barbara. She'd come home too. She'd gone nursing. She'd got married. She'd married a soldier. Only her wedding hadn't been a quick, quiet wedding in a registry office. Their war had not come until after they were married so there was no hurry. She was their only child so they had done things in a grand way, and Barbara had been the most radiant bride that anyone could have wished for. Then all too soon Bob had been sent to Vietnam and then Barbara had come home. Barbara and Melanie had come home. Bob didn't. Practical girl Barbara. She left Melanie with Mabel and went back nursing. Made a new life for herself, and Melanie. He'd been able to show Melanie all his secret trails, and caves, and the rock pools at the base of the cliff. He'd never missed her not being a boy. But she was as good as one any day. But not today. He wrinkled his brow. It worried him that he could not remember why today was different.

A movement at the base of the cliffs caused him to draw his sleeve across his misty eyes and he swallowed several times. Someone was walking along the beach. His beach! In the mornings it was his beach. He became agitated at the intrusion. He watched as the person followed his footsteps, one step at a time. He could feel a pain in his chest as his muscles tightened. Breathe deep.

Deep and slow.

One step at a time.

Deep and slow.

Breathe deep. He closed his eyes, and slowly breathed deep. Maybe when he opened them again the person would be gone. Maybe they were only an old man's apparition.

One step at a time.

Slowly he opened one eye. That was a cunning trick. He'd learnt that one from Nelson. See? There was no one there! Then he opened his good eye. The person was there, and they had been walking the whole time he had had his eyes closed. They were closer, and impinging even more on his territory. It was a girl. She was running. She was waving. The pain in his chest rose and flew out of his hands as he started to wave in reply.

He knew that girl. It was Mabel. Why wasn't she at home making breakfast? He neither knew nor cared. She was here sharing his morning beach with him like she used to do when he'd first come home and they were still newly married.

Breathlessly the girl ran towards the breakwater. Her fair hair spilling out about her face. She was calling something which he couldn't hear. He heaved himself away from the rocks and started to slowly move towards the end of the breakwater. The girl reached him before he got there.

"Grandpa! Mum's frantic. She says that if you don't come home now, she will never get everyone ready in time, and you'll miss out on giving me away this afternoon."

THE LETTER

Jennifer Lilly

The other night I set meself down like in me favourite chair and I figures on how it woz probably 'bout time I wrote to me brother Fred. I'z hadn't written him for a while like, I never woz much for writin', and well, him and me, we never really saw eye to eye, him being so much younger. Anyhow, as I sat there puffin' away on me pipe, I kinda figured as how I ought to write.

Well, I ambled over to the old bureau—remember the one that ma used to keep her books and things in? Well I still got it 'ere. Still standin' in the same place. Nothin' much has changed over the years, though I reckon on howz you'd notice a change. Anyhow, over I ambled and thumped the drawer a bit—it sticks in winter you know—and after a bit of paper shuffling I found this 'ere bit of paper. Hope you don't mind the roses none. Well, next I had to find me pen. Things never stay where a bloke leaves them these days. Anyhow, way at the back of the drawer I found this 'ere old pencil stub. Not that you'd know it's a stub. Chewed to billy-o around the end it is. Musta bin left over from when we woz kids.

Remember them days? The old one room school, crammed with sweaty kids and chalk dust? And old Mr. Cruikshank? He never could git used to us lot. Thirty-eight of us there woz when I started, an' 'bout the same when I left, eight years later. Don't know if it did any of us much good. We all stayed on at the farms and worked, and went off to war. Some got ourselves killed. Only you seemed to fare better. It musta bin the war what done that. Better teachers after the war. Fewer kids in them classrooms too. Do you remember the old fireplace in the school room? And how the chimney used to smoke? Nah, you wouldna remember, unless someone else stuffed dead possums down it like Stringy Mackrell used ta. He was older'n me. Bought it in the trenches he did. Poor Stringy.

But this ain't gettin' the letter writ. Where'd I put me glasses? Can't do much without 'em these days. Used to be real good at seein' things when I was younger. I can remember one day out rabbitin' with me Dad. That's me real Dad, not me stepdad, which woz your Dad. I was out rabbitin' with me Dad, an' ol' Tugger from up the track some. We woz up in the back paddock, "Hey Dad", I sez, "Wot's that comin' up the track back home? Ain't that the parson?" Dad never saw nothin'. Wasn't till we woz back home some hours later that ma said that the parson'd visited. I seen him come. That's how good me eyes were. Not no more though. Now I can hardly see where to pee without me glasses on.

Got to git meself comfortable. Ma always used to say you gotta be comfortable to write, otherwise the letters don't come out proper. The springs in these dining chairs still shoot out at ya from all angles. It's like them bleedin' snipers, never know when or where you're gonna get hit.

Ha! Just licked me pencil lead. Remember Maggie Mitchell? Cor, didna she grow up to be a beauty? She always sat in front of me, bein' in a grade lower'n me. Red hair an' freckles. She used to go home with blue tips to her plaits when I woz in Grade 4 an' we'd started to write in ink. She woz still usin' pencils. Mr. Cruikshank used to always tell us not to chew our pencils, so we used to lick 'em instead. Had to get the thoughts runnin' somehow. Anyhow, this day Maggie got to lickin' her pencil. She went home that afternoon with blue tips to her plaits and a red tongue. She'd bin lickin' her indelible pencil! Geez we laughed. We called her Indelible Maggie for a whole week after that. Now where woz I? Oh yes, gotta write this letter to me brother Fred. Why does writin' always make me 'ead itch? There's me glasses! Now I'm ready.

Dear Fred,

How are you? I am fine...

Fine? What's fine? The only thing about me that's fine is me hair on me 'ead. Can't git much finer than that. Dad always used to say he wished his sheep'd grow wool as fine as me hair. And the sisters! How they used to carry on about it. They all had wiry straight hair. Mine was fine and wavy. I remember once when Rose went and cut me hair an' tried to paste it onto her 'ead. She musta been 'bout ten, nah, older'n that 'cos I knows she was seein' a fella on the quiet. She wanted to have nice hair for him to run his fingers through and thought mine'd do better'n hers. She told ma that I said she could, so I got the wallopin' for lettin' her. I musta bin 'bout six at the time.

I hope you and Mabel are well and that your ulsa ain't hurting too much these days. How are Mabels' corns going?...

Corn! Remember the ol' swamp paddock down near the milkin' shed? Well a few years back this 'ere cocky from Collins Street come up round the district tellin' us all how to run our farms, well he reckoned on how that paddock ought to be drained.

Told him ain't never been drained in all the years I bin on the place, and it ain't bin missed. Well he reckoned that he knew a chap down at one of them University places who'd like to try an experiment on it. I said he was welcome to it, weren't no good to me. Next thing you know, this chap comes on up, loaded with all manner of contraptions I ain't never heard about. The paddocks bin growin' corn ever since. He gives me a couple of bushels every season. I ain't got the heart to tell him I's allergic to the stuff. Makes me randy it does, and that ain't no good for an old geezer like me with no one about to share it with. I use 'em for the fire in winter. They smoke a bit and sure as hell make a bang or two, but what else'm I supposed to do with it all?

Thank you for the socks you sent last Christmas. They keep my feet nicely clothed...

Better go an' get a cuppa, all this writin's fairly makin' me parched. Don't know how he can do it all day, every day. They must pay him heaps. You wouldn't catch me doin' it. Farmin' weren't good enough for him. He didna like to get his hands dirty. Used ta cry if he saw blood. He'd stay inside with his 'ead in a book while the rest of us would be workin' our guts out outside. And what used to really get me was that ma let him get away with it. I loved you ma, but I could never understand why you always treated Fred different. Him and Gloria.

She didna want nothin' to do with the farm neither. You let her go ta town and get a job in some Beauty Salon and then she married some city slicker. Never seen her no more after that. We wasn't good enough for her and the likes of him. Funny how they all ended up leavin' the district and gettin' married.

It's always the war. It changed everythin'. Me olda sisters was already married by then. They were all on farms, and doin' nicely too. Me older brother, he had a good 'ead for motors and was snapped up into the army. I was proud to go off an' fight for me country, only when I got back Indelible Maggie Mitchell had gone off an' married some cocky farmer from up north. Never found no-one to quite match up to Maggie. Still, Shirl was a'right till she croaked it a few years back. Only I stayed on the farm an' looked after it. Not that I is complainin' like. It's treated me real good, and I wouldn be doin' anythin' else. Not that you'd understand Fred. The feel of dirt under your nails and under your feet. There ain't nothin' like it.

Damn those chooks! They will get outta their yard, and now they've set the dogs barkin'. Guess the letter'll have to wait a bit whiles I chase 'em back through the hole in the fence. Nah, let 'em wander a bit, they won't go too far. If I leave off 'ere I may never git back to writin'. Now where woz I?

Last week I got a baker's dozen of eggs from the chooks...

Nah, I'd betta scratch that out, they wouldna be interested.

Last week I got a postcard from Dorothy's youngest. He's holidaying some place called Bali. Had a nice picture of palm trees on it...

Palm trees. Saw plenty of 'em in the islands, the beaches an' women didna look like they do now though. Didna see many women - the native men kept them well hid. Don' know if it woz from the Japs or from us! Guess I was lucky in that way. I got home, twice. And what thanks do we get for it all now? Guess I'd betta get on with this letter. Why is writin' to Fred so hard?

Fred, it's like this...

Damnation! Who uses the front door of a farmhouse? Some twerp from the city no doubt. Don't suppose they'll go away an' let me finish this letter. There goes the bell again. Didna know it still worked. I'll have ta remember ta see to that. Rotten sound. Any visitor worth havin' knows to come to back an' yell.

"I's comin' keep a hold of yer shirt." Stupid door, never did open proper like. Ar geez, this letter ain't never goin' git writ now! An' it'd've been a goodun' too.

"G'day Fred, hullo Mabel, yer gonna come in?"

THE MALDAPE

Nolan MacKenzie

"We need him, and we need him now. I don't care how you get him, just do it."

The younger man nodded in acquiescence and walked to the door. "And Fletcher ..." He turned, hand on the door handle, and once more regarded the time-worn man seated behind the large mahogany desk. "Remember, the government is not to be in any way implicated. We will deny all involvement with the matter."

"Yes sir." Fletcher walked out of the office.

Five months later the Prime Minister, in the course of his routine paperwork, endorsed an application for a delegation of East German scientists to attend a conference on *The Adaptation of Sonar Technology in Modern Medicine.*

***

The night was windy, and eerie. The girls found themselves suddenly enshrouded in a white, damp darkness. Clusters of snowflakes flung themselves against the bare heads of the two girls as they hunched their shoulders and pulled their parkers closer to their bodies.

The snow continued to fall and the wind to rage as the girls trudged on, gloved hands in their pockets. They sang loudly to cover their fear. Suddenly, Rachel gave an involuntary shudder. Mary caught the movement and turned to her, concern flickering in her eyes. Between mouthfuls of snow, she asked, 'What is it?'"

"Can you feel it? The closeness of the night? You don't think ...?"

"You too? How much further to the main road? Surely it's not much further now?"

Suddenly the wind ceased, and white silence fell. Chill. Quiet. Bright darkness. Only the scrunch of boots compressing powder snow against mother earth, interspersed with frosty harshly caught breath, broke the air. The girls looked at each other and quickened their pace.

Quietly at first, a low moan rent the air. As it increased in strength, so too did the girls' grip on each other's arms. A scream, followed by a cry of utter anguish stopped them in their tracks. Rachel and Mary looked at each other, turned, and ran. Rachel tripped, and fell. Mary dropped down and dragged Rachel to her feet. Together they blindly stumbled forward.

Thump! They fell unceremoniously to the ground.

The bundled heap of two girls looked up from their nest in the snow to discover the cause of the unwelcome, ungraceful and abrupt cessation to their flight. Up, and yet up again, the girls' eyes rose. Blinking through the fine, receding snow they saw what could only be the dreaded Maldape they had heard about. But it was not the living creature that the whole town was buzzing about. This was a robot.

"Well, what do you make of that? After all these weeks of terror the Maldape is a fake!" laughed Rachel.

"Sh! Listen."

The girls listened through the softly falling snow, into the darkness.

"Where the hell is that robot? It must be around here somewhere."

"It's not a robot I tell you. It's a highly developed microprocessor. But I must say it was a good idea of yours to make your local aboriginal monster legend a reality."

"I don't give a fang what it is. It's necessary, it's a nuisance, and now it's gone haywire and taken it into its whatever of a brain to go walkabout. Just like a Maldape! Now where is it?"

The girls looked at each other, nodded, and quietly manoeuvred away from the now silent Maldape. The sound of footsteps scrunching in the snow nearby called a halt to their retreat.

"Hey Harry! We've found him! Over here!"

The footsteps passed the girls in a flurry of snowflakes disturbed from their resting places on the overhanging branches. Rachel and Mary held their breaths and waited, no longer aware of the snow and dark which had suddenly become their friend, as they stared after the disappearing figure of the new local police sergeant.

"Yes, and look what else you've found – someone's been here. We can't afford that. Gustav'll be most unhappy, not to mention the other people involved in this affair. Whoever was here now knows the Maldape's a robot. They must be stopped. Michael, he's your baby, stay here and do what you have to to get him operational again. I'll follow these tracks. Tony, you backtrack and find out where they came from."

Harry hadn't been out here for a sinecure, he was special. He knew his function, but was not paid to ask questions. Just do his job—knowing that the operation was paramount to Australia's defence programme. It still didn't make sense. Pulling his jacket more tightly about him he picked his way through the snow and scrub, back to the old stockman's huts which were accommodating his VIPs.

A motley lot they were too. Scientists, psychiatrists, military personnel, doctors, an assortment of public servants, and even a pilot. A real weird bunch for sure. All busy amongst themselves but with some common connection with whoever was in the main hut. Someone whom he had not yet met. The man they called Gustav. Oh well, the quicker they were done with, the sooner he could get back to Melbourne and away from these strangers with their secrecy and mechanical animals.

The Maldape—the monster meant to frighten the locals enough to keep them away from the area—had, despite its perpetual 'chip' problems, been successful in its task until tonight. Thanks, no doubt, to the aboriginal legends, which Tony had nurtured. But whatever, the locals were keeping well away. Ironically, they kept asking him what he was going to do about tracking down the Maldape.

By the time the sergeant had found where the girls had rested they had gone, their tracks leading very clearly to the main road. Harry raced to the road but all he could see was a set of taillights rapidly fading into the night.

Rachel and Mary had been lucky enough to reach the road as a car approached, headed for the township. In their state of obvious anxiety, combined with the weather, it hadn't been difficult to thumb a very timely lift.

***

Richard Ibrahim sat facing the door, eyes glazed, thoughts far away. His last visitors had left and he still couldn't believe it. Six weeks since he had first become involved in this farce. Two since the police first called, and now today.

In mid-June the organizers of some medical conference had approached him, what the hell was their name? Would he be amenable to hiring out his Cessna 210 for three mid-week days? The organizers of the conference would like the delegates, some from overseas, on a short air tour of the more scenic sights of the state.

Richard saw no problems. He often hired out his plane; in fact, he'd rather it be flying than picketed on the ground waiting for him to use it. Then four weeks ago the police had knocked on his door, his aircraft, on the last day of the tour, had been listed as missing, thought to have crashed in the densely forested mountains behind Melbourne. They were looking for it now. That hadn't really worried Richard overly as the insurance would cover the losses, it was more all the time he had put into the accessories, many of which were his own invention.

It wasn't until after the police had left, and several days of intensive searching, even involving Airforce recce planes, with no sightings reported, that Richard started to worry.

He knew the pilot, and he was good. He would have done everything to save the plane. Besides, in that particular plane Richard had installed a Very High Frequency survival beacon system which was automatically armed when the ignition key was turned on, and could not be disarmed until the ignition was turned off. Any deceleration forces out of the ordinary and the beacon was automatically triggered. There was no way that his plane could come down under any but normal circumstances, and not let the world, or at least a search aircraft, know about it.

He went to the police. The local station was amiable but referred him to the search headquarters. There he received the usual assurances, nothing concrete.

Today the police had called again, to let him know that the search had been called off. The case closed. He was free to start proceedings with the insurance company to recoup his losses.

Shortly after they had left Richard had two more visitors. They weren't so friendly. These men, without offering any credentials, made it known to him that they had the means, power, and immunity to carry out their unspoken threat. The plane was lost, so were the pilot and passengers, so forget it. Don't interfere.

Damn them! Who did they think they were? Who did they think he was? His plane had made a normal touchdown, somewhere, and he would try his darndest to find it.

Richard looked at this watch. Good God, it was three hours since his last uninvited visitors had left. He recalled that an old friend had a shack near the area where the plane had last been reported, with a disused crop-dusting strip nearby. He'd start there. He'd take his girlfriend's car as his was being serviced, she wouldn't mind.

Being a freelance photographer, it was very easy for Richard to get away for a period of time with the minimum of fuss. That evening saw him on his way to John's shack, key in his pocket. Rounding a sharp corner in the road he was startled out of his lassitude with the appearance of two very shaken and agitated figures waving frantically by the shoulder of the road. Their obvious distress, coupled with the foul weather, prompted Richard to waive his usual policy of never stopping for strangers.

"Please, hurry! Away from here. We'll explain in a minute."

The girls looked behind them as Richard accelerated off. There was a gasp from one of them, then a shot rang out and ricocheted off the car. The car responded with an unheralded burst of speed. But not before the figure Richard could see in the rear-view mirror had obtained most of the car's details.

After several warming cups of coffee, and with the fire well alight, Rachel and Mary exchanged their experiences with Richard's. It certainly sounded as though there could be a connection. The two girls would be able accomplices in his investigation, with their enthusiasm, and knowledge of the area.

***

Early next morning Richard drove to the airstrip and found evidence, despite the snow, of recent use. And there was something odd about the dense patch of bush about ten metres off the end of the strip. On closer inspection he made a startling, but not totally unexpected discovery. His plane was very professionally camouflaged with military type netting and patches of the surrounding bush interwoven to give the appearance, at least from the air, of a small stand of native bush. The aircraft's paintwork was different, and so was the registration, but his safety beacon was still intact.

Rachel and Mary were going to meet him for lunch at the Railway Hotel in the town, but after his discovery, and remembering the incident of the previous evening, Richard felt that he could not wait till lunch time. But could he afford to drive into town? Chances were that they, whoever they were, had a description of the car, and then possibly also Mary's glove which she had lost somewhere. It was probably best to leave the car and walk into town. He moved the car further into the scrub and covered it with a tarpaulin that he found in the boot. Then hurried back to the shack where he was staying, then on to town, thankful that it wasn't too far.

***

The first thing agent Harry Porter, alias Police Sergeant Porter did in the morning was to have a check run on the car he'd seen the previous night, and also see if it was anywhere in town. Then there was the other lead, the glove that Tony had identified as possibly belonging to a Mary Rowland.

Harry was calling Melbourne Motor Registration Branch as Richard entered the township. By the time Harry had ascertained that the car was not in town, nor had it been sighted passing t through, the check had been run on the car. It belonged to a Cynthia Phillips, address in East Malvern. He walked out of the Police Station to interview Mary Rowland as Rachel, Mary and Richard left town in Mary's car.

***

"If this area of bush is so lonely, what were the two of you doing out there last night?" Richard asked.

"We'd been out to keep a check on some young seedlings which the Forests Commission had planted out last year. It's a new species for the area and Rachel is writing her thesis on it. We got rather engrossed in it all and stayed longer than intended, and took a short cut home."

"And you really think that this Gustav and his men are holed up in these stockman's huts you were telling me about?"

"Oh yes, for sure," Rachel nodded enthusiastically, "I'd never thought about it before last night. But it all fits. All the reported sightings, or rather hearings, when you map them out, have all been in that general area. With that new policeman involved no wonder we've had no co-operation in tracking it down. Rather ironical don't you think? How he must have laughed!"

Mary pulled off the road into a layby and the three got out, crossed the road, and silently disappeared into the bush.

***

Bill was inspecting the plane, a function which he carried out each day, more to break the boredom, but also to ensure that when he was given the word, the plane and he would be ready. He looked up as the squeal of brakes and splatter of gravel announced the arrival of one of the outfit's cars.

Tony yelled out the car window. "Jump in Bill, we must get out of here and fetch Harry. I'll drop you off at the camp and you can alert them there."

"Why, what is it?"

"Someone's been here. Their car's over there under a tarpaulin, and there's footprints everywhere. They even go down to the plane. It's a wonder you didn't see them. Though I guess you aren't into that kind of detective work. You pilots are all the same, just one love and thought in your life – your mechanical bird. You're as bad as Michael and his mechanical robot! Chaps like you ought to be grateful to have ordinary people like me around."

***

The car came to a screeching halt outside the Police Station just as a dejected Harry was emerging. After a quick conference Tony and Harry were speeding out of town in the police car.

Harry inspected the car under the tarpaulin. It was the same car, and he could see where the bullet had ricocheted off the bumper-bar. A quick, but comprehensive look around, and they were off again down the road that led to Melbourne.

"That's Mary's car," Tony called out as the police car sped past a layby. Harry slammed on the brakes, swung the wheel and headed back. He pulled off the road, and the two men jumped out and crashed into the undergrowth.

Stealthily Richard and the girls approached the perimeter of the stockyards. They could see activity. People moving from one hut to another. Closer to the perimeter were other men, obviously on guard duty.

"Well, what do we do now?" Mary asked.

"Not sure, let's stay put and watch for a bit," Richard said, then a firm hand was on his shoulder and he could feel something blunt in the small of his back. He turned his head around, swinging wildly,

"Bill!"

And then oblivion as the pistol whipped across the back of his head.

A short time later Richard groggily opened his eyes. They hurt. And faces, he could make out faces swimming in front of him. He shut his eyes and opened them again. This time the faces were clearer.

Rachel and Mary either side of Bill were standing in front of him, and a second man, a policeman, stood a bit behind them.

"Sorry Richard, I was already in full swing before I saw it was you. Hope it doesn't hurt too much."

"What are you doing here Bill?"

"Well, I could ask you and your charming friends here the same thing. They wouldn't tell me a thing. Not after what I did to a friend."

"No, we won't tell them a thing," Mary said.

Rachel nodded her head. "Why should we? They won't tell us anything."

"Bet you're glad to see the plane in one piece, hey?" chimed in Bill. Harry glared at him. "No point in denying it Sergeant, you can't fool a pilot, or airplane owner, like Richard here. No matter how much you change it. Right Richard?"

"Would someone mind telling me, no, us, what all this is about? Bill? The three of us are rather perplexed, to put it mildly, and in some respects rather irate to boot."

"Sorry Richard, it's all very 'hush-hush'. Besides, I don't know it all myself anyway. I'm only an outsider. Porter, here, is probably better able to explain it to you," Bill said, thumbing over his shoulder to Harry.

"Not me! But still. Security being what it is, and you three getting so far, and from what I've heard about you Richard, unless you're told it all, you'll just keep trying on your own. I guess you'd better meet Gary Fletcher, the mastermind behind it all. I know he certainly wants to meet you three. This camp has been sheer bedlam these past sixteen hours."

***

"So there you have it," said Gary Fletcher, spreading his hands expansively over the blotter on the table. "After the tragic, and still suspicious, deaths of two of our top scientists involved in the development of the Sonar Buoy, we need the expertise of Gustav von

Humbolt, now to be known as George Haiter, to bring the project to fruition.

"Because of the nature of the device the Australian Government could not afford to be seen to be involved in the defection, or even to 'pick the brain' of such a man as George. So a conference was the ideal ruse to get Gustav into the country, and an air crash, with no trace, not such an unlikely occurrence in this terrain, and a new identity was the ideal means of ensuring that we got our man and George stays in the country.

"Unfortunately, he *had* to be flying your aircraft, with your confounded fail-safe device. Damn good idea all the same. It would certainly help in Search and Rescue in the event of a real crash. Ever thought of marketing it? I'm sure with an oath of secrecy from you and the girls we could arrange, er, suitable government assistance in its development."

THE OUTSIDE AGAIN

Jennifer Lilly

Brian looked out the window and wondered what would go wrong this time. It didn't matter what he did, it always seemed to go wrong, and he'd end up back in here. Everyone knew him, laughed as he left, and welcomed him back like old friends when, like the proverbial bad penny he would return.

He sucked in his spreading waist and gazed out the window. It had been a long time now. Maybe this time would be the rising of his star. No more foolhardy heroics, he exhaled, and his body sagged. He was really getting too old for it now anyway.

He sighed and slowly stepped back and peered at his reflection. Limpid blue eyes blinked back at him from behind thick glasses. His sallow skin blending in with his lacklustre hair. He ran his fingers through the thinning hair and massaged the back of his neck. Once, long ago, his hair had been thick, and hung in waves down to his shoulders, and in his dreams of wealth and fame the girls would run their fingers through it. The corners of his tight mouth twitched.

"You poor bloody sod," he said softly to his mirrored self and he turned around. Dreams, that's all they ever were. The plans he'd made had been methodically stripped of reality. Slowly eroded to nothing. What did he have, now, to look forward to? His mates had left him long ago. They had all succeeded. To them had gone the laurels that were his due, along with the girls.

Girls no longer looked at him.

He wondered, when he was outside again, if he'd even bother looking at them. He shrugged his shoulders. It was too bad, really. All the missed opportunities. Once, when he'd been young he'd had illusions—delusions his mates had called them—of winning all the girls. But as he had approached puberty, and passed through its torturous doors, he had come out, not as every girl's dream, but as a pathetic excuse for a man. He supposed, retrospectively, that he should have expected little else for his parents were no great shakes in the glamour department, nor would they have been anything but overlooked in the crowd. But he, in his innocence of youth, and on a diet of macho magazines, had envisaged the life of a bronzed Atlas

He could hear measured footfalls coming towards him, and he knew that it was his turn to try again. Would he succeed this time? After all, the years had hardened him. He wouldn't be foolish enough to get involved this time. He straightened his shoulders and flexed his non-existent muscles. He was a man with purpose. The footsteps were nearly upon him, and his body drooped as he looked round the room. Already it had resumed its anonymity. He may never have been there. He shrugged his shoulders and bent down to pick up a small overnight bag that was lying by the bed.

It was a sad world, he realised, when your worldly possessions could be collected together into an overnight bag. So much for materialism. He laughed and the silence of the room was broken by a high-pitched squeak. He covered his embarrassment in a hand-contained cough. His escort was outside the door.

Slowly, in silence, they walked the length of the empty corridor. Brian could catch a glimpse of the outside through the small window in each room that they passed. A room for every time he'd been inside. Vividly he remembered each one. Shoplifting, fighting, conversion, brawling, breaking and entering, another fight, the rooms went on, and the last, the worst, rape. There had been such finality with that as the door had slammed behind him.

He really hadn't believed that he would see the outside again. Yet here it was, coming closer with each step. Should he rejoice? Or simply be resigned to returning? His mind waged battle with itself.

For too long he had accepted the falls that fate had provided him. For too long he had tried to compensate his physical inadequacies with pseudo gallantry. Oh, for sure, he had been a success with his fists, but that had not brought the girls. Only the cops.

No! Enough was enough. This time, he decided, it would not be the outside again. This time it would be the outside forever.

He stood at the door and drew himself up to his full height and took a deep breath. It felt good to be on the outside, again. Too good to ever think about intervening on someone else's behalf just on the perchance that he may gain recognition and praise. Next time he would let them fight their own battles. He'd had enough broken bones, bruises and burns, on other peoples' behalf; his body couldn't take any more.

He turned, retrieved his meagre valuables from his escort, bade the collection of well-wishers a sincere, and final, goodbye. Then with his head held high, and his back straight, he walked down the steps of the hospital determined, this time, to stay outside.

THE SOCK

Jennifer Lilly

Going back to nature was all very well in summer, he thought, but now that it was approaching the middle of winter the appeal had become somewhat tarnished. He peered over to the lightly covered windows and saw, with something approaching dismay, that the magnificent view was obscured by minute crystalline patterns which he knew would slowly dissolve into one another and run down the pane. He sighed, and great billows of condensation erupted from his lips. It was not going to be easy to get out of bed this morning; and he was sure that the water he had left in the jug for his morning ablutions and cup of tea would be frozen.

Steeling himself, he leapt out of bed, discarded his pyjamas in a heap where he stood and shoved his limbs into the waiting clothes. Socks. Where were they? He eyed the two in his hands. One red, and one yellow. Not even the colours of a decent football team. And they looked as though they could walk out of the room without his feet in them. That could only mean that he would have to wash today. He put the mismatched socks on and strode into the living area of his shack. The water had frozen over, and the fire, which he had banked the night before, had gone out.

Sometime later he made his way down the track through the peeling limbs of the bush, to the small creek which ran near his shack. There he would wash his clothes. There was a slight breeze, and the sun was peering weakly through the tangled canopy. The washing would be able to dry.

Coming to the bend in the creek he followed the bank till he came to a backwash. Here he let his meagre bundle of clothes drop before he squatted down at the water's edge to wash them. The creek was shallow and clear as it raced over smooth rocks. The gentle gurgle of the water over the rocks further upstream created a pleasant background to the songs of the wagtails and wrens as they flitted through the saplings that lined the creek. Now that he was over the initial shock of the cold morning he could enjoy the pleasures of nature, and he was pleased that he had chosen this lifestyle over his previous hectic pace in the city.

His hands and fingers were numb from the cold of the water, but he did not mind, the water was soft, and the Velvet soap was in a rich lather. He looked down at the sock that was in his hand. It was the mate to the yellow one that he was wearing. Maybe he should wash it too. He rolled up his trouser leg, took off the offending sock and dropped it beside the rest of the clothes. He looked at his other foot; then, rolling up his other trouser leg he took off the red sock and deposited it among the clothes beside the water.

Once more he squatted down, trouser legs rolled up to his knees, and, grabbing the bar of soap in one hand and a sock in the other, he started to manhandle it into the water. Slowly the sock started to fill with water and expand, like a windsock struggling to fill with air on a blustery day. He watched, fascinated as the foot, filled to capacity in a way that his own foot had never achieved, flailed around like the fish he had beached the other day.

Suddenly his numbed fingers could no longer sustain the drag of the water in the sock and the sock slipped out of his soapy hand and fled downstream. He leapt to his feet and plunged into the creek.

Pale hairy pistons in lubricated motion pounded through the water in hot pursuit of the yellow sock. His yells drowned out the chorus of the smaller birds as he splashed and danced his way down the creek after the renegade sock. As he disappeared around the bend a kookaburra broke into song.

He could see the yellow sock ahead of him, darting furtively between snagged branches and water-churning rocks. He followed, cavorting through the cold water. The stones had always appeared rounded and smooth when he'd sat on the riverbank and fished. Now they cut into his pasty flesh, each stone leaving its own brand of pain. Slowly the cold of the water seeped deep into his feet and legs and numbed the pain to his bare soles. Still the sock remained elusive. It would wave encouragingly to him from a quiet backwash, only to laugh and slop away as he reached down to grab it. The kookaburra continued to laugh as he splashed his way down the creek.

Mental images of the sight he was creating caused him to stop and double up in laughter. His trousers were now well below his knees and dark waves of water had crept up the wrinkled cuffs and were seeping up the legs. His jumper was flecked with tiny orbs of water, each reflecting the sun as it sprinkled through the trees overhead. His breathing came in fits and bursts as he tried to regain his composure and still the laughter continued to bubble up inside his chest. He'd never catch the sock at this rate.

Off he stumbled again. He could hear the babble of the small waterfall ahead. He wondered if he'd reach the sock before it plummeted down the fall. The pool at the base of the waterfall was deep, and another creek also entered there. Would he ever retrieve the sock? At least, being yellow, he was able to see glimpses of it as it played hide-and-seek with him. The red one may have been harder to follow.

There it was, caught in another snag. He could see it, flailing frantically. Waving to him as it tried desperately to free itself. He was nearly there. Only a few more steps and he would have it. He made a final lunge at the sock. His foot slipped on one of the rocks and he toppled sideways. He thrust out his hand to save himself from falling fully into the water and dislodged the sock. It slipped silently away, dancing over the lip of the waterfall and falling into the deep pool below.

He scrambled down to the lower pool and sat on the hard bank to wait for a glimpse of yellow in the effervescence of bubbles and monkey soap as the water churned over in the depths of the dark pool. His sock was flirting with him. Allowing only the occasional sighting, keeping hidden below the surface as it flounced in the current. The kookaburra was still laughing. A couple of wrens flitted about the saplings on the other side of the pool—flashes of dull brown and bright blue, weaving in and out of the green foliage, mirrored the antics of his yellow sock in the brown pool.

Suddenly the sock sank. He jumped up, arms waving wildly, his legs leaping up and down in unison with his arms. A marionette on strings of sunlight. The wrens flew away in fright and the kookaburra was silenced. His sock had died. It had slipped away. He could almost hear its laughter fade and plaintive screams of terror rise as it was pulled down to the unseen rocks at the bottom of the pool. Would he ever be able to salvage the sock?

Frantically he scanned the surrounds of the pool. He grasped a young Black Wattle sapling and wrenched it from the ground, ripping its roots away from their bed. He thrust the young trunk with its tangle of leaves deep into the pool. The movement further shattered the surface and scene below. He was searching blind, sweeping the sapling in arcs before him. The weight of the water dragged at the leaves. He slipped on the bank and struggled to hold the sapling. It was worse than trying to land a grandfather trout. What had started almost as a game had taken on the proportions of a battle. He wondered if the sock was worth it.

He continued to wrestle with the sapling and the water currents. Suddenly he slipped and slid into the edge of the pool. The sapling sprung out of the pool, spraying an arc of water behind it, and there, caught on the peripheral branches, was his sock. He watched as the sapling reached its zenith and started to sway back into the water. The sock hung briefly, then dislodged itself, and continued to soar through the air. It landed with a thud on the rocky bank behind him.

He clambered out of the water and clawed his way up the bank to where his sock lay, sodden and broken on the ground. He picked it up. It was heavy. Heavier that just wet, and there was a bulge in the toe. Gingerly, he felt along the foot of the sock, fearful of what might be waiting in the toe. Whatever it was, it was hard, and broken. It didn't feel too dangerous. He slipped his hand down into the clinging sock. It felt like fine sand, accumulated on its journey. In disgust he flipped the sock inside-out and shook it to get rid of the silt. He stood and watched, his mouth gaping open, as a myriad of tiny lights burst in the sun and a fine shower of gold fell to the earth.

He sank to his knees and let his hands drop to the damp ground. It was gold! Where had it come from? He leapt to his feet and stared at the pool. The creek cascaded over the fall and seemed to beckon him. Inviting him to join the swirling water. Was it hiding more gold? Unconsciously he rubbed his hands together and his tongue licked his lips. His eyes filled with hunger as he moved towards the pool. He tripped on a sharp stone. He looked down at his feet. They were blue, and his trousers felt clammy as they clung to his tingling legs. He would be a fool to venture into the pool at this time of the year.

He turned back to where his yellow sock lay, abandoned, on the ground. He took off his jumper and removed his shirt. He bent down and scooped up as much of the gold dust as he could and put it onto his shirt, along with the yellow sock. He started to shiver. It wasn't much fun putting a wet jumper back on, but it did offer some warmth.

He stood and looked longingly at the pool. He would be back, as soon as the weather warmed. He then stooped down and picked up his shirt with its precious cargo of fool's gold and headed back up-stream. He started to whistle, and a kookaburra laughed by the pool.

TRADITION

Jennifer Lilly

Jeremy slowly climbed the three worn granite steps and sighed. Just one morning, just one, he would like to arrive here to find the door open. He slid his key into the Yale lock and turned it, leant his shoulder against the massive oak door and pushed his way into the chambers he shared with George Love, Edward Sons, and the ghosts of generations past. Dust motes danced before him in the early light as his feet floated over the rich red pile of the recently laid carpet strip which wound through the warren of rooms and would eventually lead him upstairs to his office.

Children, he thought, as he slowly climbed the stairs, trailing his right hand along the highly polished banister, ignoring the array of faded photographs that marched up the wall beside him. He didn't need to be reminded of the legacy of large families formally arranged and unsmiling that came before. It all came down to children. It was a problem that had been bothering him all night. Where were they now, when they were needed? Not trapped on the walls behind glass. Somehow it didn't seem right that destiny should have chosen the three of them to play this cruel twist on. The three of them. George, Edward and he had grown up together. They had gone to school together, learnt and loved and fought together. And now there was, just the three of them.

With just the suggestion of a gasp, he stopped at the landing and took a deep breath. He could smell the history of the firm. A subtle blend of beeswax and cigar smoke. Still evident despite the long absence of both commodities from the premises. He gazed out the small diamond of clear glass in the tall stained-glass window and, not seeing the distorted view across the house tops, dreamed of the absence of children. He rummaged for his handkerchief to dab his eyes and was glad that there was no one there to witness his sentimentality.

Slowly he walked towards his office. More photographs lined the walls of the hall. Grotesque huge frames holding in huge sepia families. Parents seated and swamped by curly haired miniature replicas in breeches or skirts. Even the more recent contributing ancestors, less stiff and starched, but still dressed to kill, were large families. Suddenly he stopped, stepped back and took an overall look at the array. He shook his head in disbelief and walked back to the landing.

Slowly he walked past the display again, taking a headcount as he went. He guessed he'd always known, but it had simply never registered before. There was, definitely a partiality toward boys. He allowed himself to smile, not that preference had anything to do with outcome in these instances. Still, it hadn't helped any with this current generation of solicitors and barristers.

Here they were, the eldest son of the eldest son going back five generations, and now no sons to take over from them. They didn't even have any nephews. Oh, they had nephews, but none trained to follow them. What with the tradition so firmly entrenched that it was only ever the eldest son who studied for the Bar. The others were all allowed to pursue their own particular interest. But not so the eldest son. And daughters simply didn't count. Not that any would have been allowed the opportunity to enter Law School. He could still remember the storms that constantly brewed and blew during his youngest sister's last year at high school, when she had said that she wanted to go to university. His parents simply could not understand why she wasn't happy to train as a teacher, or a nurse, like her sisters, mother, aunts and cousins. There were some good fights that year, and his sister had won, but she had not been allowed to study Law. He doubted if she ever would have wanted to. No, she had gone on to become a Chemical Engineer of all things.

Sadly, he entered his office and prowled over to the huge teak desk almost hidden by a mound of files all neatly folded in half lengthwise and tied in pink, legal tape. He sat down and stared vacantly at the leather-bound bank of green blotting paper in front of him.

Children. That really was the problem. Whistling from downstairs caused him to look up and he saw the dark panelled walls of his office and recalled how, as a child, he had meticulously drummed over each panel of the entire chambers, and with his fingernails had tried to prize them apart, convinced that they held secret panels and passages. But there had been none.

He wondered if children today, with their electronic games, P.C.s, T.V. and videos had the capacity for such imagination. He doubted it. Earthy adventure books seemed to have been superseded by the mechanics of a generation obsessed with political correctness, space, war and maniacal fantasy. Maybe he would ask his partners if their children had ever been awed by the sobriety of the firm and dreamt of hidden passages.

He thought of Edward, and his children. Five girls. Not much chance there for adventurous spirits. They had all been Barbie dolls, frills and lace. He shook his head. Somehow he couldn't imagine a life without boys, he had had plenty of brothers and cousins around him, coupled with George and Edwards' brothers. Maybe he shouldn't ask Edward. His lack of sons was a great shame and torment to him. And who could blame him? Edward Sons with none of his own? They had thought about adopting a boy, but by the time Edward and Hilary had given up trying for one of their own they were too old to adopt through the usual, and more legal channels, and Edward had cooled off the idea somewhat when he had come into professional contact with adoptees and their multiple parents, and then of course there was the continual argument over nurture verses nature, and he decided that he would settle for his family of females. And he was happy. So long as no one mentioned his lack. Snide cracks had well and truly worn thin. And not just with Edward, Jeremy thought ruefully. Of all of them, he himself had probably suffered the most, but one learned to live with it, eventually.

George's son was a possibility, maybe he would ask George if his son had ever tapped the panels. He was imaginative and sensitive. A strange boy in many ways. Not like his father. George was tall, and robust. A good all-rounder. Now there was a word to date him. Who was an all-rounder these days? Or was it simply that the word itself was an anachronism? George had had it all—looks, brains, physique, admirers. Even at Primary School he'd had his own following of fawns. Then why had he lucked out in marriage and family? The love in his marriage had died with the birth of his only child. A sickly boy who had grown up to be a pale replica of his parent's blend. Here was no rugger player, no tennis star, no sporting all-rounder. Not even an intellectual. There was no way that Damien would achieve more than a rudimentary secondary education. Instead Damien chose to paint. Closeted inside all day he had lived his childhood in a world of abstracts. Splotches of colour and streaks of light which his mother would frame and rave about. He might have imagination and be sensitive, but Jeremy couldn't see him playing swashbuckling pirates or musketeers. Maybe he wouldn't ask George. Damien was such a disappointment to him, asking would only bring further pain.

Which brought it back to him, and children. A very sore point, seeing as how he didn't have any. Leastways none that he knew of.

"You all right?" George asked from the doorway.

"Fine" He smiled wanly and gave a wave.

"You sure?"

"You know, the usual. I didn't have a good night"

"Another night out with Nancy?"

Jeremy could only nod his head. He didn't want to talk about it. That was all the three of them ever did. Talk about 'It'. If it wasn't Nancy it was some other woman that he was taking out. He was starting to get desperate. And it was getting to him. Pressure never helped any romance. And pressure was what he was living with, constantly now, and had been for the last ten or so years. It wasn't that he didn't like the women he dated, or that they didn't like him. It wasn't that he didn't want to get married, it was just... Anyway, no one performs well under pressure. He knew that the fate of the firm was dependant on him. George and Edward had done their bit, if not their best. For heaven's sake the Anglican faith was founded on the premise that a man must have a male heir. But no, now it was all up to him.

"Oh well," George said as he moved down the hall, "You can always try again, or another. Still plenty fish out there."

Yes, thought Jeremy, but not time. That was what was of an essence. Time. While he didn't have a biological clock to hurry him along, there were the three looming retirements.

He pushed his chair back and stretched his arms above his head, yawned, relaxed and looked at his watch. An old-fashioned fob one which he had inherited from his father along with his position, on the occasion of his father's retirement. A family tradition. There was that word again. Family. He looked at the pile of files on the left of the desk. They were all family files. There was no such thing as the sanctity of marriage anymore. Maybe he should just look to having a child without the trappings. If it was all right for women to seek out men to be duped into fatherhood, why not the other way round? He chuckled to himself. *That* was a whole lot easier said than done. The man need never know that he'd been duped, but a woman? And if he couldn't get a woman that he loved and who professed to love him to marry him, what hope did he have of her agreeing to have his child? It was a hopeless case. He shook his head and cushioned it on his desk with his arms.

"Bit early for a catnap, isn't it?"

Jeremy raised his head to find Edward lounging in the doorway with a grin fit to split across his face.

"Or is it a hangover?"

Jeremy sat up and scowled at him.

"Sorry. Only asking. But really you look like death warmed up. Nancy say no again?" He straightened himself up. "I'd give up on her if I were you."

Pity George hadn't said that, thought Jeremy, then I could have really spat something at him, but not Edward, he could not be accused of not trying, and besides he and Hilary were as in love now as they had ever been. No, it was George who had lucked out in love. George Love in a loveless marriage from which he could find no escape. No wonder he was so taciturn. Still, none of that helped the situation any. The damnable thing was that he really loved Nancy. Oh he'd loved the others too, but somehow Nancy was different. More mature, interesting, accepting. Except on one point. He'd tried to reason with her, but she was adamant. And he guessed that she had a point, and it wasn't totally unreasonable. It was a point that he was loath to bring up with the other two because he knew how they felt about tradition. The same as he did. And he was all for tradition.

"Oh dear, we are in the dumps today aren't we?"

Jeremy's secretary drifted into the room, her arms filled with pieces of paper which she promptly started to lay out in front of him. She picked up a fountain pen, unscrewed the lid and jammed it onto the base before handing the pen to Jeremy to sign the letters she'd typed for him. As each letter was meticulously signed Jeremy would turn it over and smooth it over the blotting paper before passing it up to his secretary.

"I don't know why you don't just get a biro like the rest of us," she said as she shuffled the pages together, and Jeremy screwed the cap back on the pen.

"Tradition."

"Can't understand why she keeps turning you down," his secretary said, "I know I wouldn't."

Jeremy looked at his secretary and blinked. "She does not like my name."

"Why ever not? What's wrong with Jeremy?"

Jeremy silently took the signed letters from her and laid them down in front of her, then slowly ran his finger across the letterhead. He looked up at her and smiled.

In big bold letters across the top of the page were the words:

LOVE, LUST AND SONS.

Barristers and Solicitors.

"Oh," Jeremy said, feeling very sheepish.

TUESDAY SHOPPING

Leigh Leslie

It was quite a hot day when Marge and I found that we had to once more venture into town. One of those unfortunate incidences where a number of small things break or can't be found. Or are found to be finished. I'd been busy in the workshop when the first mishap occurred. I was overhauling the motor on the old ute, reached over for the spanner and knocked the can of oil over. It had to be the last can too. Then the spanner broke, and oh, I don't know, it just wasn't working out.

Marge back in the house wasn't doing any better. I found that out when I went in for solace. She was fair tearing her hair out. She'd been baking and had had to think out her recipes again to accommodate the ingredients on hand. So over a cup of tea we went about making ourselves a shopping list. It was stupid really. We shop on Thursdays, every second Thursday to be exact. Today was Tuesday. The first Tuesday.

Don't get me wrong. There's nothing bad about going into town. Not if it's a second Thursday. The first Tuesday, like today, well, it's just not comfortable. The first Tuesday is for overhauling the motors about the place, and getting the gear in order for the week, and for Marge it's baking day. But, I guess if you must break with tradition, today was as good a day as any. It certainly proved to be an entertaining one for us, one way or the other.

We scrubbed ourselves up, fixed up a thermos and a bit of tucker so's we wouldn't have to waste time waiting to be served in a café, then made sure that there was nothing missing from the list before we piled into the car. A near new Statesman. Very proud of the car we are, it's nice and comfortable, and roomy. That's what we liked most about the car, it's roomy. And so is the boot.

Well, about two miles out of town this cat, big feral bastard it was, fairly hurled itself out of the scrub and at the car. I couldn't do a thing but collect it. I pulled up smart quick. Ripped open the door and raced to the front of the car to check for any damage. There was none. Marge, well she raced in the other direction to check on the state of the cat. Unfortunately, it hadn't fared as well as the car. It lay in a mangled sprawl on the side of the road. Marge wanted to know what I was going to do. She didn't think it funny when I asked "why me?". She thought it even less funny when I suggested that we get back in the car out of the heat and continue into town. That is how we ended up with a dead cat in our boot.

I don't understand women sometimes. You see plenty of dead animals on the side of the roads. Native animals too. So why in blazes did Marge want a proper burial for a feral moggy? She couldn't even give me an answer to that.

So there we were, driving down the main street in our Statesman with a dead cat in the boot. It lay there nicely wrapped in an old supermarket 'never know when it might come in handy' bag which Marge keeps in the car for occasions such as these. Mind you, I'd insisted that it first be shrouded in newspaper, after all, it wouldn't do to get blood on the carpet. We always keep plenty of newspaper in the boot. Not for such occasions as this but to protect the carpet from grease, and grime, and dirt and other nasties which cling to cargo these days.

It felt a bit funny, I can tell you, walking behind Marge and the supermarket trolley knowing that there was a dead cat in the boot. And we had to try very hard not to look at each other, for fear we would burst out laughing. Especially when we were passing the parade of pet foods. We were co-conspirators relishing shared secrets, but never having the courage to actually share them. I mean, have you ever tried to talk, I mean have a really meaningful conversation with someone you love and not look at them? It doesn't make sense. It becomes very impersonal and almost farcical. Believe me, I know.

Well. By the time we had our groceries securely stashed away in the boot we reckoned we deserved a breather. There's a nice spot not far from the shops which has picnic tables and overlooks the lake. We often stop there on Thursdays before heading home, so it was just natural that we should drive there today. Being Tuesday, and not Thursday, we were able to pick and choose which tree to park under, so I parked under a shady gum tree and we got out. I opened the boot for Marge to get the basket with the thermos and tucker out and she suggested that we leave it open, that it might help to keep the shopping cool. So we left the boot open and carried the gear across the carpark to a nearby table. There was a faint breeze blowing and we sat back to enjoy out stolen time together.

There were a few people around. Young mums with strollers, a couple of over-weight joggers, an elderly couple walking an equally old dog, and there was another person. A middle-aged woman. Nothing really distinctive about her except the purposefulness of her walk. Marge saw her first. Well, I mean she had to, she was facing that way. 'Look Harry,' she said, 'is that what they call power walking?' I turned round to look where Marge was facing. And this woman burled right along and passed our open boot. Nothing unusual in that you say. And I agree. Only she scooped up one of our shopping bags and kept walking. It all happened so fast that neither of us even thought to call out. Marge raced over to the car and I scooped up our things from off the table.

"Harry," Marge said as I dumped the basket into the boot. "She's taken the cat!"

I slammed the boot shut. "Quick, this I've got to see," I said and grabbed Marge by the arm. Now we really felt like conspirators, as we tried nonchalantly to follow the power-walking woman in the manner of all good undercover agents. I doubt if we would have won any T.V. awards, but the woman never knew we were there. We followed her back to the shops and into a café. She sat down at a table in the corner. We chose a table for four by the window. That way we could sit corner-to-corner and both face her without being obvious. We were getting good at the shadowing game and were really starting to enjoy ourselves.

Lightfingers Lolita—that's what we had called her as we had followed her from the car—placed our shopping bag on the floor beside her and took a handkerchief out from her pastel-blue tracksuit pocket. She unfolded it and studied the design carefully. I said that she was confirming her superiors' directives. Marge told me not to be so stupid, that she was reading the laundering instructions before soiling it with makeup. We argued for a bit while Lightfingers continued to scrutinise the square of linen in front of her. Then she folded the handkerchief in half and patted her forehead with it. Obviously a signal to her accomplice as at that precise moment the waitress approached her table.

The waitress nodded her head several times before writing something on the pad in her hand. She must have found the cipher hard as she scratched her head with the end of her pencil several times and asked Lightfingers some questions. Finally the waitress left, ripping off the top piece of paper and scrunching it up into a ball which she stuffed into her apron pocket, then she attacked the pad with the pencil again. It was easy to see that we were dealing with a novice here.

We feigned interest in the menu, heads together as if in conference over what to order, but in actual fact we were busy keeping Lightfingers under surveillance while debriefing each other. The underworld is full of shady characters and we agents have to take every opportunity to re-appraise each case with our fellow agents.

A movement caught our attention. Lightfingers was bending down towards our shopping bag. An expression of triumph crossed her face as she peeled back the wrappings. Marge grabbed my arm and we both leaned forward to see better. The woman let out a scream which brought the management and staff running. But they did not get there in time. The woman recoiled in horror, fell from her chair and cracked her head on the next table as she slid to the floor.

Marge and I joined the circle of anxious onlookers as the ambulance men carefully lifted her inert form onto the stretcher and fed her into the back of their vehicle. They then equally reverently placed the shopping bag on the stretcher beside her before closing her world from our view. Marge and I rushed in silence back to the car, to collapse in near hysteria once we were safely inside.

By jingoes it would have been good to have seen her when she woke up in the hospital to find the dead cat still with her. Or to hear her explain how she came by it in the first place. But she must have managed to talk a plausible way out of it as there was never anything about it in the papers, no matter how hard we looked.

Still reckon that every second Thursday is best.

UNCOOL HERO

Jennifer Lilly

"Hey Shrimp-face!'

Aloysius cringed.

"Big day huh?"

"Yeah, sure," Aloysius muttered into the mirror, as his big sister waltzed past his door.

"Good one bro."

"What's so good about it?" he asked his reflection as his brother, head over a pocket calculator ambled past his door.

Aloysius kicked his bedroom door shut, not that he had any more brothers or sisters to disturb him, but he just didn't want to face the world today.

He looked at himself in the mirror and squirmed as the blood rushed to his face. It was so uncool to blush. "Damn hair' he said, running his hand over it in an attempt to make it lie flat. Maybe he could gel it down. Nah, gel-flattened hair was so uncool. Everything about him was uncool.

He stuffed his fists into the pockets of his 'hand-me-down-two-sizes-too-big-he'll-grow-into-them-shorts' and stared down at his new knee-length school socks.

Why couldn't his brother have been one year younger? That way he'd still be wearing these shorts, and his socks wouldn't have worn out. Worn out socks was preferable to baggy school shorts. Funny how his mother didn't mind him wearing baggy shorts to school, but he wasn't allowed to wear his mufti-shorts baggy like all the other boys. Life simply wasn't fair.

"Aloysius!"

He made a face at the mirror.

"Aloysius! Are you ready yet?"

Why did his parents have to call him Aloysius? Why couldn't he have a regular name like his brother Michael, or sister Bridget? Who was Aloysius anyway?

"Aloysius, breakfast dear."

He guessed he'd have to go. He tried again to smooth down his errant conservatively cut red hair—no 'number ones', undercuts or ponytails for him—but it just fell into cowlicks again.

"Aloys..."

"Coming Mum!" he yelled as he left his room and wandered towards the kitchen. Dumb name. Dumb kid. He kicked at the carpet as he walked.

"Don't scuff the carpet dear!"

Damn mothers, they knew everything. He walked into the kitchen and the family fell silent. He could feel himself blushing again.

"Now don't you look smart?" his mother gushed and came to give him a kiss. "Martin?" she said to her husband. "Doesn't he look smart?"

Mr O'Malley looked up from his breakfast and looked at Aloysius over the top of his glasses. He pushed his chair back and stood up.

Oh God, not another lecture, thought Aloysius as he tried to reach his chair. His way was barred by his mother on one side and his father bearing down from the other. He looked to Bridget for help. Fat lot of good that did. Bridget was busy grinning at him fit to burst.

"Well smile, Shrimp-face."

He looked at Michael. He wasn't much better. "Yeah bro! What'd you know?" he said, thinking he was smart.

Aloysius gave them both a sickly smile and waited for his father to pounce.

"Big day for you, hey son?" Mr O'Malley ruffled Aloysius' hair.

"Yeah, he's a turd* now!" screeched Bridget. Aloysius glared at her. He didn't need reminding.

"High school's an important step in any young man's life," continued his father. "This is where they separate the boys from the men. Why, I look back on when Michael started High School." He looked at Michael and was rewarded by a grunt and a grin. "When Michael started High School I knew we had a winner. Same with Bridget. They both knuckled down and worked. And look at them now!"

Aloysius did as he was told and looked at his older siblings. Bridget with her bleached hair and painted nails and a couple of earrings in each ear smiled sweetly at him. She'd wanted a nose stud too, but her parents had drawn the line at that. Besides, nose studs, or any piercings other than ears was against the school's regulations. They tolerated her other excesses because she was a brilliant student. He didn't know how she could be, she was always out with this boyfriend or that.

Michael also had a gawky smile on his face, but it was hard to tell. What with his thick glasses and cultivated pimples, anything could be hiding there. But at least his hair did what it was told.

"We, your mother and I, expect the same from you." His father ruffled his hair one more time then returned to his seat and breakfast.

"Yes Aloysius." His mother nodded her head. "Our baby is about to make his mark at High School. Oh ..."

Aloysius knew what was coming and tried to duck into his place at the table, but his mother was quicker.

"Oh, we are so proud of you Aloysius." She grabbed him in a bear hug. "So very, very proud of you. We were proud of your sister, and your brother, and look where they are now – top students! And we are going to be proud of you too!"

Bridget nearly chocked on her cereal. "Shrimp-face? You expect to be proud of him? Mum, he's just a dreamer!"

Aloysius turned beet red again and squirmed out of his mother's embrace and took his place at the table. One day he would show them. He didn't know how, but he'd dream of something and then he'd show them.

The first day at school was hot and horrid. The other kids avoided him, and he couldn't really blame them. Michael ignored him, and everyone else. And Bridget? Well she seemed to delight in going out of her way to call out "How ya doin' Shrimp-face?" at every opportunity. Then there were the teachers. They all expected him to be a brainwave like his nerdy brother and brilliant, popular sister. He sat through his classes as inconspicuously as he could, at the back and away from the rowdy boys. And he'd looked out the window and dreamed.

It was the first period after lunch and the teacher was droning on about something or another, and all kids in the class were diligently following every word, even the rowdy ones. All, that was, but not

Aloysius. He was watching the flies hovering near the naked light on the walkway outside the classroom. There were three of them, and they'd take turns at landing on the globe and probing it with their legs. One flew away and he followed its path.

That was how he came to see the wisp of smoke puff out from a classroom across the field. He watched as it slowly increased in volume and then, suddenly there was black smoke belching out. He jumped up, sending his desk clattering to the floor, and everyone turned around and looked at him. But he was too worried about the smoke to blush as he pointed to the smoke.

"Look!" he shouted. Everyone looked, even the teacher who had been busy reading down the roll trying to work out the name of the disruptive student. "There's a fire!"

"Fire!" Everyone took up the call and clamoured to be the first out of the classroom and to join the rush across the field to gawp at the flames.

By the end of the day Aloysius was everyone's hero. He had saved the tech wing from destruction, and suddenly it didn't matter that his sister called him Shrimp-face, or that he was un-cool. He was a hero, and everyone knew that his name was Aloysius O'Malley.

*Back in the day, the first year of secondary school was known as the Third Form and the students were called, by the more senior students 'turds'.

WHAT A WAY TO GO

Norma Smyth

The morning was cool and overcast with heavy rain and the trio at the breakfast table were all subdued. Sandy had brought Jake up to date with Anna's news and he sat quietly, trying to absorb the fact that this would probably be the last time he would see the attractive little brunette sitting across from him. Anna had become very close to him ever since he had married her friend, Sandy. She was like a sister and it tore him apart even thinking about her dilemma. Anna and Sandy made idle conversation until finally Anna rose to her feet and said "Okay guys, smile, up at the edges, can't have you down at the mouth. We know what we've meant to each other and we've had great times together. At my funeral I want you to drink bubbly and reminisce about the good times, a celebration of one's life I think is the terminology."

"I'd take a photo but this weather wouldn't produce very good results. Anyway I don't need a photograph to remind me of you. I don't know whether it will be in heaven or hell but I'm sure we'll catch up whichever way it is. Now, one last look at this fantastic view – well it is when the sun is shining. It's almost fantastic now though the rain does dim it somewhat."

She peered out the plate glass window at Lake Wakatipu, barely visible through the rain, across to Kelvin heights, with its barren upper slopes, an increasing number of houses clinging to the lowest slopes, and the golf course constructed at the far end of the Heights.

"At least I've had the benefit of the view on all the lovely sunny days there have been. By the way I do believe in an afterlife and I feel surprisingly calm about it all. Someone up there will be looking out for me." She hugged them closely in turn, then headed for the door.

"Your luggage?" asked Jake.

"Packed in the car. I'm all set to go so don't come out or you'll be soaked. Love you both."

Blowing them a kiss she moved quickly out the door and into her red sports car. She accelerated it up the steep little drive and on to the road.

The main road out of Queenstown scooted the shores of Lake Wakatipu but she scarcely noticed its beauty through the tears trickling down her cheeks. Drawing a deep breath she told herself, 'Take a grip, girl. You've always believed you were not afraid of dying. Remember when you weren't supposed to survive the surgery you had five years ago. You weren't scared then. It's just that you've had a bit more time to think about this. You've had a great time with Sandy and Jake. Now concentrate on the road ahead and head north.'

She sped through the open countryside. The glorious autumn foliage still had a beauty, even though subdued by the rain. She passed through the village of Arrowtown with its picturesque main street, its various boutique shops and cafés, then entered the avenue of delightful colonial cottages. Colourful leafy trees dripped large drops of rain onto her car as she travelled the length of the avenue. A short while further on, and a left hand turn, and she was on the road leading up and over the Crown Range. This road had previously been notorious for its steepness, its shingle surface and many sharp bends. She stopped briefly at the lookout at the top of the hill, peering back at the road snaking its way up, and the extensive view back to Arrowtown and the Queenstown area. She climbed back into the car then sat for a while reviewing what she had just seen. 'If I had been feeling suicidal that road would have been great to have an accident on, and I wouldn't have to worry about waiting for cancer to finish me off. I'm so pleased to have been able to share this time with Sandy and Jake. Even though it upset them they were so supportive. We had such fun, played awful golf, we all sang out of tune on the boat trip around the lake, we all drank too much wine. Mm, I'm not ready for the high jump yet. Might be later on, but for now, let's carry on and remember the good bits.' She settled herself and then drove on down the road winding towards Wanaka and its beautiful lake. Driving on the sealed surface was a joy, it was much easier to negotiate the once hazardous corners, and she got a thrill of pleasure from swinging swiftly around them.

Once she reached the bottom of the hill she slowed down until she saw a low wooden building sited at the road's edge, with capital letters CARDRONA HOTEL emblazoned across the front. This was a well-known historic landmark in the area where Sandy had suggested she stop for a coffee. Anna pushed open the narrow front door, had walked through a small bar area, into a dimly lit room with dark stained furniture, and memorabilia of the area. Through the rear windows, a well-designed accommodation block built of schist, and a delightful back garden planted with a profusion of roses and hollyhocks, were visible. She sat on a couch beside a blazing log fire which was very appealing on the bleak wet day, and ordered coffee. While she waited she observed the other occupants of the pub. The family group of mum, dad and three children, having a noisy discussion, two women exchanging photographs, laughing loudly whilst enjoying their coffee, and a scruffy dark haired man, wearing faded, dirty blue jeans, leaning against the outer bar, who met her eyes then quickly averted his gaze, but not before she noticed he had a very pale eyes, a shifty look, and several days growth of dark stubble. A truly revolting creature.

The warmth of the fire lulled her into a further reverie of her final few days with Sadie and Jake. She and Sandy had been enjoying a cognac with their coffee when Sandy surprised her by saying that she thought Anna seemed quiet, was rather pale and was she all right? Initially Anna said "No", then realised she wanted to share her distress and told Sandy she had terminal cancer, and only three months to live. Sandy's face tightened with shock, and they hugged each other then burst into tears. Once they took control of themselves they had another cognac and discussed her situation.

"You poor little love," Sandy had said pushing her hands through her short blonde hair. "A mistake surely? Tell me, you're joking?"

"That's what I hoped, but no such luck. It's definite and I've pretty well come to terms with it but every now and again I have a bad moment. But I knew what I wanted to do and that was to catch up with you and Jake, buy a red sports car, drive home via the West Coast, then home to mum for a while and get my affairs in order. Being here with you both has been marvellous."

"Stay a bit longer," Sandy urged.

"Thanks, but no thanks. We've had a great time and I've done what I wanted, we all played terrible golf, all as bad as each other, a ride on the Kingston Flyer – I've always wanted to go on a steam train and now I've accomplished that, lots of walks and drives. The trip to Glenorchy and Paradise, were just that – visiting paradise. That is such a wonderful spot in the mountains. The reflections in the lake are beautiful, wonderful scenery, touches of snow in the mountains, it's all been fabulous, and nothing could match it. I need to leave now, while I'm so full of it, and so happy at being with you. Don't let's spoil it by my being here too long. Please tell Jake for me, and don't worry. I've faced death before when I wasn't expected to survive a couple of lots of surgery, and I felt so calm then and I am now. You and Jake are wonderful people. Pray that it won't be too drawn out or too painful a process for me. Sandy, I'm going to bed now. I want to reach Fox Glacier tomorrow and that's a long drive. Thanks for everything goodnight and God bless."

Sandy hugged her again, and said "Break your trip at the Cardrona pub. It's a great place to stop for a coffee and also time to have a break after coping with the worst of the Crown Range."

Anna came back to the present and looked around her. Yes, it had been a great place for a coffee. She'd enjoyed the warmth of the fire, the coffee was good, she'd relived some wonderful memories, and she was ready to get back on the road. She exchanged a few pleasantries with a waitress, identified by her name badge as Sarah, before moving through the bar area toward the front door.

As she approached the door and assessed her chances of reaching her car without getting wet, the scruffy man straightened up and walked after her.

Sarah commented to the staff at large "That man at the bar is going, thank goodness! He gave me the creeps." She promptly forgot about him, then chanced to glance out a front window to the road. As Anna unlocked her car the man ran to the passenger door and wrenched it open.

"Hey," cried Anna. "What do you think you're doing? Get out of my car at once."

"Lady, if you know what's good for you, just get in and drive," he said pointing a pistol at her.

Anna went to protest again, then looked at his eyes and recoiled. He looked malevolent with the hardest, coldest eyes she had ever seen. Should she run?

"Don't even think of it," he said, reading her thoughts. "I can drop you before you turn around."

Anna climbed into the driver's seat, fastened her seat belt, and inserted the ignition key, the whole time keeping a wary eye on the intruder. She noted that his knuckles and neck were ingrained with dirt, and wrinkled her nose at the unfortunate body odour emanating from him. He waved the pistol threateningly and Anna, noting his expression, quickly slipped the car into gear and pulled out onto the highway.

"That dreadful man got into that girl's car," cried Sarah as she looked out the window. "Should we do something, phoned the police or what?"

"Nah," said the chef. "Nothing to do with us."

Sarah gave him a look of disgust and ran to the telephone.

Anna put her foot down hard on the accelerator. The heavy rain made visibility difficult. Maybe she would be picked up for speeding by the police, perhaps she could attract attention, but she'd have to take an opportunity as and when it arose. Internally she was quaking, but determined to conceal her fear from this monster. She swung defiantly around corners, sent several pukeko squawking indignantly out of her way, their indigo plumage, the distinctive dash of white under their tails and their red peaks and feet, making a brief splash of movement in the murk, and then came to a sudden stop as she rounded a corner and was confronted by a herd of cows crossing the road from one paddock to another.

"Careful there," snarled her passenger. "Slow your speed or I'll shoot you in the knee and drive myself."

"And while you're shooting me what do you think I'll be doing?" said Anna bravely.

"Smart mouth aren't you. You should be scared stupid."

"Why?" asked Anna. "You don't scare me," she lied. She was terrified but an idea was starting to germinate. She recalled her reverie at the top of the Crown Range when she had thought that an easy way to cope with her situation would be to drive off the road into the valley below. Then she had dismissed it as a coward's way out but in this current situation it could be a solution. If she took them both off the road they might or might not be killed, he had a life to lose but she had limited time, so nothing to lose, and why not sooner rather than later. This guy was obviously a criminal, running from something. He'd not be a loss to anyone, probably not even his mother. Although this was still a chilling option it was feasible and she saw a lot of sense in it.

"Since we are obviously going to be together for a while," she said quietly, "why not tell me your name and what you're doing here."

He gawped at her. "You're a cool one alright," he said. "Okay what's your name or what are you doing here?"

"I'm Anna, and I'm on my way to stay with friends further up the coast. I've just come from Queenstown."

"I'm Max. I escaped from prison two weeks ago and I've been on the run ever since. I'm heading for the Fox, have a place to hide, and I'm going to take you for company. We'll have fun together, kiddo. You've got a great body, it'll be even better in the nick. I'll do things to you you've never even thought about."

Anna felt ill at the thought of him touching her, and now her idea seemed a far better one than what Max was proposing, and she resolved to carry hers through. She gripped the steering wheel even tighter. They had long ago driven through Wanaka township, and the road was now winding round the shores of Lake Hawea. The landscape was primaeval which under normal conditions would have fascinated her, but with the overcast sky, heavy rain cover and her unfortunate companion, it had limited appeal.

"What were you in for?" she asked.

"Murder," he snarled, looking sideways to see her reaction.

"Really" she drawled. "So you're not a nice type of fellow at all."

He laughed hoarsely. "You'll find out soon enough."

Anna picked up speed and kept their foot down hard as they wound round the lakeside. Max assumed an unpleasant palette and finally couldn't tolerate the speed any longer.

"You'll have to stop," he cried. "I'm going to spew."

"Ugh," said Anna, "not in my car you're not." And she slammed the brakes on. Max's head crashed into the windscreen. Anna thought he had blacked out but next moment he grabbed a handful of her hair and tugged it sharply.

"No more funny tricks or I will really do you a damage," he growled.

'You already have,' thought Anna as her eyes watered and she pulled her hair free from his hand. He put his arm across in front of her and pulled the keys from the ignition. "Out you get, over to the side of the road." Anna obliged reluctantly and averted her eyes as he retched noisily. What a horror. If Sandy and Jake could see her now.

"Back into the car, bitch," he called. "I'm driving."

'Not too long you're not,' thought Anna. 'This could put paid to my plan, damn it. No I won't let it.' She climbed slowly into the passenger seat and fastened her seat belt, then watched as Max climbed into the driver's seat, adjusted it, then took off down the road. She noticed he had not fastened his seat belt but refrained from mentioning it.

"Now, no funny business," he warned. "Or I'll do you." Anna sat back, admitted to herself she was scared, horribly scared. Her legs felt like jelly. She really was not quite ready to die but it was the better option of what was available. She needed to take action though before Max was able to harm her. What could he do, rape her, beat her, cut her throat, torture her? Forget it, just concentrate on her plan. Max drove expertly, if somewhat conservatively, and the kilometres fled behind them. Finally they reached the sea, which the road followed for some time. It was when they were travelling down a steep incline with a drop to the sea on the left, that she saw her chance. She grasped the steering wheel and pulled it hard to the left, at the same time attempting, unsuccessfully, to unclip her seat belt, open the door and leap out of the car, but Max managed to grab her arm before she could do so.

"What the hell are you doing?" he screamed. "Stupid bitch, you'll have us both over the edge."

"That's the plan," she cried, and laughed hysterically as the car plunged down the bank, hit several large, jagged rocks, and landed on a strip of beach, the passenger door hanging drunkenly on its hinges. Max's grip on Anna's arm loosened as they landed on the beach. Once again Max hit his head on the windscreen, but this time he was knocked out and flung back onto his seat. As the car shuddered to a halt the side windows shattered, and Anna was cut about the face and neck with flying glass. She lapsed into unconsciousness so was unaware of a police car pulling up near where they crashed over. William O'Rourke, a solidly built, swarthy skinned constable from Whataroa, despatched by Police Communications to check on a small red sports car proceeding north from Wanaka area, where the female driver could be in danger from a Caucasian male in his late 20's, looked down at the scene then summoned fire brigade and ambulance to attend as soon as possible. Two bodies visible but extent of injuries not known. The message completed he made his way quickly down to the beach to assess the damage.

One female, badly cut about the face, appeared to be knocked about by the fall, and unconscious, and one male, who had obviously been thrown against the windscreen, also unconscious, appeared to have a broken neck but this was over to the professionals to ascertain when the ambulance arrived. He checked the woman's pulse, there was a faint beat. He took a cotton pad from his first aid kit applied pressure to a major cut on her neck. Shortly after the fire engine and ambulance arrived and the occupants made their way cautiously down the bank. "Did a great job of this didn't they," said one of them.

"Can I leave this to you?" William said, indicating the pressure pad on Anna's neck, and as the man assented, wandered away and picked up a handbag which had obviously been thrown from the car at the impact of the crash, and went carefully through it. It held a soft leather wallet containing money, several credit cards, drivers' licence, small diary, and a folded sheet of paper which William took out and read. 'Poor girl' he thought, reading the note advising Anna of her terminal illness. 'But what a way to go, save her months of pain and worry. But I'm getting ahead of myself, she may be perfectly alright.' He moved to the other side of the car studying Max's face. 'Mean looking bastard' he thought. 'Guess he would have done her damage if this hadn't happened. Hey that face looks familiar. Who is it now? I've seen it recently. Ah ha, I know. I've seen his photograph in the paper. It's Max Bissett, he murdered a service station attendant, a long gaol term, and escaped a few weeks back. Well, one less for the taxpayer to be responsible for.'

The St John's ambulance staff member walked over to him and said "The driver's had it. Broken neck, obviously fell hard against the windscreen."

William responded "No loss to anyone. An escaped murderer, if my memory serves me right. I'm sure his photograph was in the news. Been on the loose for several weeks. Someone from Cardrona pub telephoned saying a man had got into a red sports car and they thought the driver could be in danger. How was the girl anyway?" he asked.

"Opened her eyes and closed them again. Pulse weak, no bones broken, badly cut, bleeding from the cut on her neck, and fairly battered. Lost a lot of blood."

As if on cue and Anna opened her eyes and looked at William O'Rourke. She smiled up at him, an exquisitely beautiful smile, and gazed directly into William's eyes.

"I know I'm dying. Please, there's an address book in my bag, contact my mother, Adrian Ludbrook, and my friends Sandy and Jake Turbott, tell them that I love them, and say that I said 'What a Way To Go.'"

William's blood ran cold. That was exactly what he had said. He looked at the lovely girl lying on the stretcher, and a tear slid down his cheek. "Of course, girl," he said. "I'll tell them that. Now you just take it quietly and you'll be fine."

She smiled at him again, reached for his hand, and was still clutching it with her eyes closed when she breathed her last.

Constable Murray Saunders nosed his police car into the driveway of the Turbott's residence in Queenstown, and made his way to the main entrance. He hated this kind of assignment but knocked on the door, and as it opened braced himself for his task. "Mrs. Sandy Turbott?"

"I am," replied Sandy. "What can I do for you?"

"I'm Constable Murray Saunders. I have some bad news for you," he said quietly. "Is your husband at home?"

"He is, one moment and I'll call him." Sandy's voice shook as she called. "Jake, please come."

"Sure honey, be right there." Jake went up the stairs.

"What's the problem?" His step faltered as he spotted the constable.

"Not bad news I hope?"

"Sorry Sir, unfortunately it is. Anna Ludbrook is a friend of yours?"

"That's correct," said Sandy, a chill running down her spine. "Jake, this is Constable Saunders. Constable, my husband Jake. Now please tell us quickly what happened."

"Anna Ludbrook has been killed in a car accident. The man who was driving was killed immediately. Miss Ludbrook survived the crash but suffered severe injuries, and died soon after the police and ambulance arrived."

"What man driving? There shouldn't have been a man in the car."

"He was an escaped prisoner ma'am, and he forced his way into Miss Ludbrook's car at the Cardrona Hotel. Now, I was asked to break the news to you in person, but Constable William O'Rourke of Whataroa will be telephoning you shortly. He arrived at the scene of the crash just after it happened, he was with Miss Ludbrook, and she spoke to him just before she died. Asked him to contact you, and give you a message, so he'll be in touch shortly."

Tears welled in Sandy's eyes, and she turned to Jake who took her in his arms. "Oh God, poor baby, what a rough spin. I wonder if her mother knows?"

"I believe so ma'am. Constable O'Rourke was going to contact her also. Now if you will excuse me. Sorry I had to break such terrible news to you."

"So am I," said Sandy. "But thank you for coming. I hope Constable O'Rourke telephones soon."

"He will. Don't worry about that. Now good day to you. Call me at the Queenstown Police Station if you wish."

He turned and walked out to his car, and had hardly disappeared from their driveway when the telephone shrilled and a gruff voice introduced himself as Constable O'Rourke from Whataroa speaking. "I've just been speaking with Constable Saunders from Queenstown and he tells me you are aware of the death of your friend, Anna Ludbrook."

"Unfortunately yes. Could you please wait a moment and my husband will pick up another phone and we can both hear what you have to say. Jake this is Constable O'Rourke. All set now thank you Constable. We can both hear what you have to say."

"I'm sorry we have had such bad news to impart, but now you are aware of the situation I will tell you a little more. A young woman from the Cardrona pub telephoned 111 to advise that your friend had stopped for coffee that morning, and when she was leaving a suspicious looking man left the hotel and climbed into the car. She thought he had a pistol, and there was one found in the car. The accident occurred late afternoon yesterday, when the car went off the road and landed on a beach. The man, who was an escaped murderer, was apparently killed on impact, but the young lady lived long enough to ask me to give you both a message."

Sandy and Jake looked at each other in astonishment, and simultaneously both had tears welling in their eyes.

"Anna left us a message?" Jake asked.

"Yes, sir, she did. The man had not had his seat belt done up and he, as I said, was killed immediately. Miss Ludbrook was wearing her belt, her face had been cut by flying glass from the side windows, and she suffered severe loss of blood. Her pulse was very faint but she regained consciousness long enough to smile at me, to hold my hand, and ask me to tell you both 'What a Way To Go'. That gave me quite a start as I had just read the note in her bag regarding her illness, and had thought those exact words. But she gripped my hand firmly, smiled a beautiful smile, said those words, closed her eyes and that was the end. It was quite something. But she looked so peaceful as she died. You can feel happy for her. She was ready to die."

"Thank you Constable," whispered Jake, "we appreciate your call. We're upset of course but we'll appreciate your words even more when we've had time for all this to sink in. Goodbye, and thank you."

Sandy wiped her eyes, said a muffled "Thank you and Goodbye." Then threw herself at Jake amidst a storm of tears, and they held each other closely until the sun had gone down, and the room was dark.

They both stirred when the phone shrilled, and Jake picked it up. "Hello, Jake Turbott. Yes, Adrian, we have just spoken with Constable O'Rourke this afternoon. We can't believe it, we're just getting used to the idea of Anna having terminal cancer, then hearing of her death has really thrown us both. Yes, of course, we'll will come up. When will the service be? No problem, we can come up at any time. Thanks for calling. How are you coping? Great. Anna would be pleased. She didn't want any of us to mourn, but easier said than done. We're going to toast her now. By chance we have a couple of bottles of Moet in the fridge and we'll crack one tonight and bring one with us to share with you. Yes, Sandy's fine, upset of course, but don't worry, we'll be okay, and we'll see you in a couple of days. Thank you for your call."

Sandy said "I heard all that. How is Adrian?"

"Upset of course, but sort of relieved that Anna won't have to go through all the trauma of being ill. I think that is giving her courage, and helping her cope. We've got to think of it that way too, love. Anna was so positive here, and such fun. She was brave, we must be brave too. And Constable O'Rourke certainly seemed sure that she died peacefully. Now, you get the flutes, I'll open the Moet."

They smiled tearfully at each other as they raised their glasses to a special friend, and in the days to follow both divulged they felt Anna was there with them.

"Safe journey Anna," they both murmured quietly. "Rest in peace."

ZPAGHETTI BROTHERS INCORPORATED

Leigh Leslie

The only physical attribute that connected Damien and Frank as brothers was their hair. Their blonde dreadlocks set them apart from everyone in a time and place where such a style was the antithesis of acceptability. Their crowning glory was not so much the result of intention as the outstanding consequence of sibling rivalry coupled with their familial obstinance.

Years—even decades—ago, they had been school rivals and the targets of a class dare. As a result, they let their hair grow beyond an accepted conservative mullet, and it wasn't such a big leap from there for rat tails to develop. Nor did it take their classmates long to call the two boys The Spaghetti Brothers. And the name stuck.

Now their dreads reached their waists and neither brother could be convinced to shed their trademark look. They waged a constant battle of 'I'll cut my hair when you ...' whatever was the contest at the time, be it a girl, a job or the latest trend. It was a challenge which neither brother was prepared to participate in. If the truth be told, neither wanted to be the one to back down. Besides, rather than taking exception to being known as The Spaghetti Brothers, they felt pride in the nomenclature.

Everyone in town knew, or at least had heard of, The Spaghetti Brothers. While they had been at school it was as much for their prowess on the sports field as it was for their hair. However, since entering the workforce their renown usually came with bad connotations, thanks to Frank.

Frank, who as a child—and later, growing up—had been Damien's shadow, replicating his every action, resented that it was always Damien who received the accolades for their shared successes. Little wonder then that Frank was convinced that he was never as good as his brother. As a child that hadn't stopped him from trying. His adult mind took a different approach and he forged a name for himself in other areas where he was not in competition, but still gained notoriety.

Damien, the older brother, by a mere 5 minutes, and totally unaware of Frank's feelings of inadequacy, was tired of being the responsible brother forever bailing Frank out of whatever misdemeanour he had strategically fallen into. No matter how much time and energy Damien had taken to steer his younger brother away from yet another get-rich-quick scheme or dodgy scam, Frank was always convinced that his way was the only way to prove that he was as good, if not better, than his brother.

Frank's latest nefarious venture had convinced Damien that to save his brother from yet another possible stint with the police he would have to come up with an idea. And if he hoped to remain solvent—it would be wise to formalise their partnership as an incorporated entity. Especially if they were serious about launching a tattoo business together. On paper, the idea made sense. Frank, Damien had to admit—however reluctantly—was a gifted artist. His graffiti and tag work testified to that, and his sketches were both striking and easily adaptable to skin. Damien, though lacking any artistic flair, had strengths of his own: he excelled at administration and had a solid head for business.

Frank had been blindsided when Damien had first broached the idea of The Spaghetti Brothers combining their respective talents and opening a tattoo studio. In his wildest dreams he had never anticipated that his brother would ever want to be buisnessly associated with him. He'd always thought, sometimes with secret delight, that Damien had considered him to be his own personal albatross necklace. But now, if they were to be going to open a tattoo studio together then he'd better get some training.

But, at the same time he was chuffed to realise that Damien acknowledged his skill with a drawing implement. And he warmed to the idea, even offering assistance in the setting up of the studio. An offer which, typically, was rejected. Damien had it all under control. He even knew what equipment would be required. Unlike Frank, whose only knowledge of tattooing was what he had seen firsthand when he had first been inked, Damien had fully researched all aspects of the industry.

That was when Damien realised the potential liabilities that could occur due to negligent maintenance of tools, poor ink quality or physical harm. He'd gone to his solicitor for guidance. Knowing Frank's track record of disasters, Mr. Humphries had advised Incorporation as a safety net. So, Spaghetti Brothers Inc, came into existence.

It had taken several months of looking, but now the two brothers stood on the pavement, hands in their pockets, and looked across the street at what was to soon to be their tattoo studio. Nestled between a barber's and a café, it offered opportunities aplenty for the patrons of these establishments to become their customers.

"We'll need to spruce the place up. Make the front attractive. Don't want the locals to think that we are going to be ruining the town," Damien said, shuddering to think what Frank might have in mind for attracting clients.

"I could put up a display of tatts in the window," Frank said as he pulled his hands out of his pockets and squared them in front of his face as would a painter or photographer framing a potential masterpiece.

Damien stared at his brother, and shook his head as, remembering the walls of Frank's bedroom when he was a teenager, he imagined a menagerie of A4 pages taped haphazardly across the glass.

"I was thinking more along the lines of a nice sheer curtain and framing the window in gold paint, with a large gold circle in the centre where our name would be professionally signwritten."

"What about the awning? I thought that would be where the signage would be."

"Too high. No one would see it up there. Don't you think?"

Frank's mouth dropped open as he looked at his brother. Damien was asking *him* what he thought? He looked back at the shop that was to be *his* studio. Where, in a week or so he hoped, he would be working. Working legitimately. He felt a wave of pride spread through him. To think that his brother was so in awe of him that he was setting him up in his own business. Well, not really *his*, it was *their* business. But Damien had recognised his talent and it was he who would be inhabiting the studio. Only him. Damien would not be there. Not that Damien was a silent partner, but he would be relegated to the back room, or the reception. No, this studio was going to be all his. And now here was Damien asking him where the signage should go. He felt good.

Frank looked back at the building opposite them. He conceded that his brother had a point, but rather than admit it, he chose to take exception to the mention of a professionally painted sign. He had a friend, well, more of an acquaintance, who was a great graffiti artist – his tags, with their inconsistencies, were known across the country – and he owed Col big time. This could be a terrific opportunity to rid himself of that debt. And it would save them money.

"Yeah, but why employ a professional? I know someone who owes me." Frank stuck his hands back in his pockets and crossed his fingers. "I could ask him to do the signwriting for us. At mates' rates, of course."

"Right. Spaghetti Brothers Inc. Tattoo Studio across the window. What do you think?" Damien took a step off the curb and walked across the street.

Frank, grinning, followed.

"Um, would you like me to get that sorted then?" Frank asked as he joined his brother at the shop door.

Damien, the shop key in his hand, stopped and turned to look at his brother. Frank reminded him of an eager puppy, shimmering with excitement. It would save him the hassle of looking for a signwriter so why not?

"Will this guy do a good job?"

"Col? Sure." The fact that Col and his masterpieces could sometimes be considered to be 'dodgy' he would conveniently neglect to share with Damien.

There was something in the tone of his brother's reply that set Damien's 'Frank Radar' twitching. Choosing to ignore the warning, Damien opened the door to the shop and took a step into the cavernous interior. The previous occupant had removed all the trappings of their trade, leaving bare walls and floor and piles of rubbish. Damien gave one pile a kick, sending dust particles scurrying. There was a lot to accomplish before they could open. He stepped out where he imagined the needed partitions would go, along with shelves, chairs, tables and other furnishments.

At the sound of Frank entering the shop Damien turned around and walked to stand in front of the window. He ran his finger across the pane, leaving a clear trail. He then moved his arm in an arc, creating an improvised circle. Yes, a large circle encompassing their name and trade would look good. If this friend of Frank's could be trusted to do a good job. His immediate inclination was to distrust anyone that Frank had dealings with, but this whole enterprise was to build fraternal bridges. He would just have to take that gamble. He stepped back, imagining the enticing curtain, There to provide privacy for their clients. Yes, he could see that, with his guidance this venture could prove to be a profitable and stable career path for Frank.

"Right then. You'd best get going. We have a lot to do before opening," Damien said brushing his hands together as he made his way to the front door.

Frank looked around the room, and felt his heart swell with anticipation. He already had a file of designs which he was itching to transfer onto skin. Then he looked at the window and his heart thudded to his stomach. Was Col the right person? For a moment guilt fought for a place in him.

"Um, there's one thing that maybe you ought to know ..."

But Damien had already walked away and didn't hear. Frank shrugged his shoulders and the short-lived guilt was quelled. He smiled. Maybe it didn't matter. This might be his opportunity for Damien to get his come-uppance.

A month and week later the brothers sat in Damien's car in the car park space reserved for staff at the back of the tattoo studio.

"Ready?" Damien asked, his hand on the door handle. The inside revamp had been completed to both their satisfaction, but neither had seen the face that the public would see – Col had not completed the painting until late the previous night. While both brothers were anxious to see how it had turned out, Damien had decided to drive directly to the back of the studio rather than be seen by the pubic rubber-necking their own premises.

Frank looked across at his brother and grinned.

"You bet." He was anxious to be in *his* studio. But he was also anxious to see Col's work. He and Col had only managed a quick catch-up, and, according to the 'under the table' protocol, there was nothing in writing. He just hoped that what he had verbally shared with Col had been transferred accurately.

"Then let's go." Damien opened the car door and stepped out. He reached into the back of the car and retrieved his jacket which he slung over one shoulder. While it was only a tattoo shop, he still wanted to look at least half-way presentable and professional. He'd tried to impose a formal dress code on Frank, but acquiesced to his proclamation that as a tattooist he had an image to maintain, and that included his free-flowing dreads, unlike Damien's which had been tidily wound into a huge bun.

Frank, still in the car and wearing black jeans with a black t-shirt which exposed his own dragon tattoo, took a deep breath. Yes, here it was. The first day. His first day as a tattoo artist. He'd completed a concentrated training programme with a mate in a neighbouring town, but he was still nervous, and excited to be working on his own.

Damien, tired of waiting, walked around and opened the passenger door for Frank.

"Come on, we need to open up."

"Do you think we'll have any clients waiting out the front?" Frank asked. His hands twisting around the strap of the seat belt across his chest belied the confidence in his voice.

Damien shrugged. He'd never known his brother to be nervous, and wasn't sure if he should warn him that he'd arranged for the local paper to meet them when they opened up.

"Well, you won't know if you're sitting out here, will you?"

Frank's confidence visibly shrank, and Damien silently cursed himself as he shoved his arms into his jacket. Today of all days he wanted his brother to be the confident sassy person he knew.

The two Spaghetti Brothers, now Inc., walked to the back door of the studio. They both stood there and took a deep breath before entering.

The back room had been set up as a dual purpose room – a retreat room for the brothers as well as a place for the sterilization equipment and the store cupboards for the needles, inks and pigments.

Damien and Frank walked through this room and opened a door to a corridor. In the small space the fresh paint could still be smelt. Off the corridor was a bathroom on one side and a small room on the other where clients could change if needed. At the end of the corridor was a bead curtain which rattled while the brothers walked through and into the studio itself.

Frank stood, breathed in deeply and slowly turned around. This was his kingdom. His domain. It had been divided into three areas – a reception desk, a consultation area with a low table and easy chairs, and two screened workstations, complete with comfortable-looking reclining chairs for the client and stool for Frank, with easy-reach equipment stands.

Damien, anxious to get outside—where, through the sheer curtain, he could make out the silhouettes of the journalist and photographer waiting—placed his hands on Frank's shoulders to gently move past him, then opened the front door and stepped out.

The photographer was trying to keep his camera—aimed at the front of the shop—steady, while the journalist, one hand on the photographer's arm, laughed and waved at the window with his other.

Damien rushed over to join them. "What's funny?"

"That!" the journalist said, wagging his arm up and down in front of him, before bending over at the waist and guffawing again. "I thought you were the Spaghetti Brothers. But that is clever."

Damien turned and looked at the shop. He couldn't believe his eyes. He gritted his teeth together as he felt his ire simmer up his body. This was all Frank's fault. He should have known better. Obviously his brother was like the leopard who didn't change his spots. "Frank! Get your sorry arse out here," he yelled, his cheeks puffing out and fingers clenching in and out. "Now!"

Frank, heard the familiar frustrated tone in his brother's voice. A tone which usually heralded an unwelcome bollocking. He sighed, and wondered what was new. He should have known that the affable camaraderie of the past few months wouldn't last. It was typical that his brother would upset the euphoria of the day by yelling at him.

Wracking his brain, and speculating what it was this time, he made his way outside, surprised to see that a small crowd had gathered. His immediate thought was that Damien was upset that those around him were not likely contenders for clients. Then of course, it was a school day so it was only to be expected that students would be on the prowl at this time of day.

Damien rushed forward, grabbed hold of Frank's arm and dragged him away from the door and into the middle of the road. He waved his other arm in the air, encompassing the front of the studio.

Frank followed his brother's gesticulating arm and burst out laughing.

"Why are you laughing?" Damien almost screamed. He wanted to shake his brother till his teeth fell out, but the gathering spectators kept his intentions in check. How could his brother laugh? This was meant to be a new start for him. Or both of them. And now, because of Frank and his mate, they were going to be the laugh of the week, or month or year. Who was going to take them, or their tattoo studio seriously?

"I think it's brilliant," Frank said between breaths.

"Brilliant? How on earth can you say that?" Damien screeched. "It will be the death of the business before we have even opened. Have you no sense? Or did you do this on purpose?" He looked at Frank, and squinted. "Or was it that mate of yours? You said that he was in your debt, or something. Is this his way of getting at you? At *my* expense?"

"*Your* expense? Is that what this funk is all about? I thought this was *our* tattoo studio. And I think Col did a great job. I like it. It'll work."

Damien took a deep breath. "How the hell can it work? We are the *Spaghetti Brothers*, everyone *knows* that, and we are *Incorporated*."

Frank, still laughing, shook his head. "I still say it'll work. 'Ink' makes sense as we are a tattoo studio, and as for the Zpaghetti, well, Col couldn't help that, could he? Look how he spells his name," he said, pointing at the signature in the corner of the window.

Damien stepped forward and peered at the corner where Col had painted his name 'Kolyn'. Damien shook his head in disbelief. Zpaghetti Brothers Ink made sense after all. "I like it. Yes, I do like it," Damien said with a smile tugging at his lips as he drew Frank into a bear hug.

Did you love *ALLSORTS*? Then you should read *Monty*[1] by Leigh Leslie!

[2]

Life is comfortable for Monty—until his past unexpectedly resurfaces, shattering fifteen years of suppressed guilt.

A letter was all it took for his structured life to crumble.

Charles Montgomery Chinthurst III is expected to take his place in the echelon of society that he was born into, but one indiscretion when he is at university sends him halfway across the world to Outback Australia where Teddy Delany exposes him to a world not constrained by the demands and expectations of his family.

Just as he begins to embrace this newfound freedom, an unexpected tragedy pulls him back into the privileged world he was

1. https://books2read.com/u/bzxWB9

2. https://books2read.com/u/bzxWB9

born into. That is, until Teddy reappears, upending the status quo once more.

Now he has to decide where his heart really lies. Is he happier being a stuffed shirt, or embracing the freedom that he tasted long ago?

www.ingramcontent.com/pod-product-compliance
Lightning Source LLC
Chambersburg PA
CBHW032204190626
46810CB00018B/388